THE TRUTH
BENEATH
THE LIES

THE TRUTH

BENEATH

THE LIES

AMANDA SEARCY

Delacorte Press

Text copyright © 2017 by Amanda Searcy
Jacket art: front cover photograph © 2017 by Henry Arden/
Getty Images; back cover figure © 2017 by Halfdark/Getty
Images

All rights reserved. Published in the United States by
Delacorte Press, an imprint of Random House Children's Books,
a division of Penguin Random House LLC, New York.

Delacorte Press is a registered trademark and the colophon is
a trademark of Penguin Random House LLC.

randomhouseteens.com

Educators and librarians, for a variety of teaching tools, visit us at
RHTeachersLibrarians.com

Library of Congress Cataloging-in-Publication Data is available
upon request.
ISBN 978-1-5247-0089-8 (hc) — ISBN 978-1-5247-0091-1 (ebook)

The text of this book is set in 11.8-point Adobe Caslon.
Interior design by Jaclyn Whalen

Printed in the United States of America
10 9 8 7 6 5 4 3 2
First Edition

To my parents,
for all the library trips

CHAPTER 1
BETSY

I can't see it, but I know it's there.

Always.

Beat. Beat. Flash.

Beat. Beat. Flash.

One persistent pulse of the red message light for every two beats of my heart.

Beat. Beat. Flash.

Under the bed, in the arms of a stuffed bear, wrapped in a sweatshirt, zipped in a duffel bag, the flash cuts through my brain. *You self-centered little bitch,* it screams. *It's all your fault.*

The heavy curtains printed with unicorns and rainbows block out some of the sun, but not enough to keep me from suffocating in this oven.

Above my head, a stream of tepid air spills out of the ceiling vent and deposits a thin layer of sand over everything. Whenever I blow it off, it comes back.

It's a sick joke.

All of it. The sand, the sun, the unicorns. This place I'm supposed to call home.

Five months ago, the shuttle driver from the El Paso airport deserted us here. Somewhere near the Mexican border. Nowhere near anywhere else.

It was spring, and it was already hot.

Beat. Beat. Flash.

I've left it for twenty-three and a half hours this time. If I don't call back before it hits twenty-four, the black burner phone will stop blinking. Then he'll send someone to kill me.

It's my choice.

Whatever that means.

There's a timid knock on my door. "Betsy?" the voice asks, hopeful, as if somehow after entering the room, Betsy has turned into someone else. A happy girl with long, shiny hair and a big, bright smile. Not a sad, pale girl with a dark and crooked cropped mop, wearing only a grungy white bra and too-big shorts that sag around the waist.

No such luck, Mom.

She tries again. "Betsy, I don't want you to be late for your first day of school."

I pull the corner of the sheet over my exposed chest. I'm the mouse. The cat has my tail. My legs spin and slide and scrabble, but there's no getting away.

Your debt will be paid in blood.

"Betsy?"

I grunt at the door. It's enough to send her away. I can't go to school. I don't remember how to act in the company of other human beings.

At twenty-three hours and fifty-eight minutes, Mom comes back.

"Betsy? Teddy's going to take you to school. Isn't that nice?"

Teddy. I've avoided him all summer. Every time he drove down from El Paso, I stayed in my room. He and Mom talked and laughed in the living room, but I didn't come out.

I've been a good girl.

I grab a shirt off the floor and stumble to the door. My fingers rattle the lock until it pops open. Mom shrinks back when she sees me.

"No," I say. Her forehead wrinkles. My mouth twitches and jerks as it tries to remember what a smile feels like. "I can walk to school."

"Don't be silly," she says. "Teddy will take you. He wants to." Her face lights up every time she says his name. He's not her boyfriend. But you would never guess that from the way she acts.

I look at her hard. She's happy. She has a good job. Her cheeks have color. Her clothes fit, like she tried them on before she bought them.

I am a selfish little bitch.

I slam the door and fall to my knees. I have to make the call before it's too late. I have to make it for her.

The carpet burns, but I dig my nails in and pull myself inch by inch to the bed. I rip open the bag and shake the phone onto the floor.

He picks up after two rings. "Good morning, sweetheart," he sings. "Cutting it a little close today, aren't we?" Hearing his voice brings it all back. The reason Mom and I left. The reason I'm far away in the middle of nowhere. The reason I'm alive. For now.

"You aren't going to be late for school, are you?"

"No." My voice sounds as dry and crusty as the desert outside.

"Well, I hope you have a lovely day." It's a lie. The happy tone, everything he says. All lies. "Just remember that there are lots of eyes out there. Lots of eyes that would love to get a look at you." He laughs. "After all that time in your room, do you need a reminder of what can happen in the big, bad world?" It's a rhetorical question. I don't answer.

I will never, ever forget.

The pain that constantly gnaws at my stomach, floats tears behind my eyes, and makes my teeth bite into my lip won't let me.

"I'll talk to you later." He chuckles and then hangs up. I want to throw the phone against the wall and watch it smash into a thousand pieces. But I can't. He'll call again. Whenever he feels like it.

I wrap the phone in the sweatshirt, place it in the arms of the bear, and shove the bag back under my bed.

Mom laid out clothes for me, like I'm a small child incapable of dressing myself. A white button-up blouse and a flowered skirt that comes to just above the knee flop over my desk chair. I hold the skirt up. A different person would probably like it. Think it was cute.

The blouse is too see-through. I can make out the hint of my bra through it. I pull on a tight, opaque tank top and button the blouse up to my neck over it. Better.

The trip down the hallway makes me sweat.

"Don't you look pretty," Mom says when I turn the corner into the kitchen. She's a liar. The hack job that is my hair sticks out at odd angles. I'm not wearing any makeup. The double shirts make me feel bulky. My knobby, pasty knees haven't seen the sun in months. She should just say it. I look like walking death. *I am walking death.*

Teddy sits at the table and shovels a forkful of pancakes into his mouth. The pool of syrup on his plate assaults my nose and makes me want to throw up. Teddy's tall, thin figure is all cowboy boots and Wranglers. Perched over his mouth of yellow teeth and stuck to his leathery skin is a neatly trimmed thick brown mustache. It twitches as he chews.

"Teddy came over for breakfast," Mom says, as if the man sitting at our table isn't enough proof of that. She rushes a plate of pancakes to me. My stomach won't acknowledge it. It's focused on the other thing on the table. Halfway between my plate and Teddy's is a cell phone.

It's girly. Pink. Sparkly case with a cartoon character. Nothing like the black monster that lives under my bed.

Looks can be deceiving.

Teddy nudges it toward me. "For you."

"Teddy says every teenager should have a phone." Mom fluffs flowers in a vase on the counter. She's been practicing for her job at the flower shop. She just had her three-month anniversary. They gave her a raise.

Teddy nudges the phone again until it touches the edge of my plate. He laughs, showing that mouth of yellow teeth and sending microscopic drops of spit and pancake into his mustache.

"How else are we going to keep track of you?"

CHAPTER 2
KAYLA

"Get the cops. My baby's missing!" the woman screams into a borrowed phone.

I step back from my register. My checkout line in No Limit Foods is frozen, their eyes locked on her. They won't remember I'm here until the spectacle is over.

My manager, Albert, rushes over and tries to soothe the woman. Natalie on register three rolls her eyes.

This is our fifth missing child.

Like every other time this summer, Albert will get the woman on her feet, walk her back to the stupid "castle" he made from six-packs of cherry cream soda, point to the child-sized doorway, and magically produce her missing little one.

Paper crinkles in my ear. I turn around.

A guy a couple of years older than me holds a bag of peanut M&M's. He wears a gray hoodie—and a smug grin.

I look away.

"The mom's totally a tweaker," he whispers, and pops an

M&M in his mouth. He moves forward until he's so close behind me that I feel the heat radiating off his body. He smells like sugar and the slightest hint of masculine soap.

"She does meth," he clarifies.

"Ah," I say. He probably thinks he has enlightened me with his retro-grunge-boy knowledge of the seedy. I know the carefully created illusion he sees when he looks at me. Dark blond hair pulled back in a ponytail with the curled ends flowing out over my shoulder blades. Bright brown eyes surrounded by the perfect amount of liner and shadow to make them pop. Jeans that hug a toned body. In other words, someone who doesn't belong in this part of town.

Albert can't get the woman up on her feet. She's too hysterical to follow his instructions. The automatic doors swish, and two cops enter.

They approach the woman and peer down at her dirty, stringy hair; rotting teeth; and stained clothes. One pulls out a notebook and asks a question I can't hear. An anguished howl leaves the woman's mouth. The second cop mumbles codes into her shoulder radio.

A customer walks from the back of the store holding the hand of a tiny crying girl. Albert rushes forward.

"Found her!" he announces, and straightens his manager's vest.

Albert's a dick.

The hysterical woman leaps up and pushes past the cops to reach her child. Her cheeks redden, and her eyes dart from face to face as she grabs the girl by the shoulders. "Where were you? You're going to get me in trouble."

M&M's guy's breath tickles the back of my neck. "No way are the cops going to let her take the girl home." He chomps down on more candies.

The social worker is already waiting outside. The cops wave her in, and she enters holding a gently used teddy bear.

"No!" the woman yells. "You can't take her. You can't . . ." She dissolves into a heap on the floor again.

The girl accepts the bear but doesn't cuddle it close to her chest. She reaches out for the social worker's hand.

This isn't her first time.

"Poor thing." The candy wrapper crinkles in my ear as he shakes out the last of the M&M's. "I bet she cries all night."

I nod. But it's a lie. She won't cry. She'll sleep soundly in a strange house in a strange bed, the teddy bear cast off onto the floor. I know because the second time I was taken away, I didn't feel sad. I felt relieved.

"My name's Jordan," M&M's guy says. I take two steps forward so that I can turn around without running my face into his. He's medium height, with brown hair that curls and frizzes in the cold summer humidity. Muddy-brown eyes. He's kind of good-looking, I guess, in a boy-next-door way. But that arrogance is enough to turn anyone off.

The cops haul the woman to her feet and move the whole scene outside. My customers rise up onto their toes to watch.

"Do you want to get coffee or something on your break?" He crumples the empty wrapper in his hand.

"Sorry, I don't have any more breaks." Lie. I've just started my shift. He doesn't move. "I have to get back to work." I point to the line of scowling people who are coming down from their misery contact high.

As I ring up the next customer, I glance over my shoulder. He's gone. Like he melted into the walls.

Home is a fifteen-minute walk from No Limit Foods. In the daylight, you can see who lurks behind the trees. You can see the trash and syringes discarded in the wild grass along the sidewalk. In the dark, only broken glass glitters under the weak streetlights.

My shift ends at ten p.m. I wear a long, oversized black raincoat with the hood up to disguise my hair and figure. A cold, wet breeze carrying the heavy scent of rotting vegetation brushes over my exposed face. I keep my head down, eyes locked on the cement. Out here, I'm just another junkie looking for a score. I get left alone. Mostly.

Ahead of me, a black sports car tears around the corner. Its headlights bounce over my face as it hits potholes and debris in the road. I look away as it passes.

At the end of the street sits Bluebird Estates, a prison-like, three-story chunk of battered brick and cement, where the government sticks those of us it takes pity on. Tonight, its dim, buzzing lighting is joined by flashes of red and blue. Masses of them. I break into a run.

Fire trucks, ambulances, and cop cars pack the cramped parking lot. The door to the side staircase is open and surrounded by flapping, yellow police tape. I sprint for the front entrance.

Before I make it, a pair of meaty arms grabs me around the shoulders and forces my head into a powdered, pillowy bosom.

"Kayla, honey, thank God. I thought that was you in there."

Mrs. Lacey releases me.

"What happened?"

She raises one hand to the top of her head. The other rests on her hip. "I was going out the side"—she motions at Tippy, her little rat dog—"and, honey, I saw the blood. That girl's clothes were torn right off her. Left her lying there on the stairs." She peers up and shakes her head at the heavens.

At hearing the news, my breathing doesn't speed up. My heart doesn't race. My stomach doesn't roll over. I should feel shocked. I should feel grateful that I'm standing in the parking lot with Mrs. Lacey and Tippy, yipping at my feet. I should feel something.

A team of paramedics crashes out the side door with a stretcher. She's strapped down. Most of her body is covered with a blanket. An oxygen mask obscures her face. Mrs. Lacey cries out. Tippy barks.

A lock of her dark hair falls over the side. On impulse, I step forward to tuck it up neatly under her head, but Mrs. Lacey pulls me back.

I recognize the girl. We've waited at the bus stop together before school. She wore a navy-blue Northside High School sweatshirt. A silent understanding had passed between us. We weren't meant to be friends. Her bus went one way. Mine, the other.

I know what happened to her. Dark stairwell, drunk guy, throwaway girl. I don't feel anything because I've always known this would happen. I just expected it to happen to me.

The ambulance pulls away. Mrs. Lacey grabs me again

and squeezes hard before leading Tippy off for his nightly potty break. In her eyes, I'm a nice girl. Quick with a smile. Keeps my nose clean. Helps an old lady with her groceries. Pets her horrible little dog. The other girl, the one who may or may not live, had to be broken and bloody on the stairs to get noticed.

I turn my key in the door to the lobby. It doesn't unlatch. As usual, the lock's been jammed to keep it from clicking shut. That pisses me off. I stomp up the stairs and along the mildewed, dirt-colored carpet to apartment 26. It flies open as I get there.

"Kayla!" I dodge her arms before she can touch me. "I tried. When I heard the sirens, I went to look for you. I got all the way to the stairs, then . . ." Her voice drifts off. I dump the raincoat onto the floor. "I knew it wasn't you. If something had happened to you, I would know."

The trash smells. I rip the bag out of the cracked plastic bin and tie the top.

"I have three years sober, Kayla. Three years." Her normal refrain. Because she has those years, she can't come to my dance team performances, pick me up from work, or take out the trash.

The trash chute is next to apartment 21.

I charge out the door with the trash bag flapping against my leg. Apartment 21 opens. "Hey. Hey, Tracey's girl."

I dump the trash down the chute.

"Hey, Tracey's girl."

I spin around. He's a walking skeleton now. Clumps of his hair are gone. Open sores dot his inflamed face. "What do you want, Finn?"

"It's lonely in here, Tracey's girl. Come in, have a taste with me." He opens the door wider. Inside, it reeks of pot, alcohol, and vomit.

I cross my arms. "A girl just got attacked in the building, and you want me to come inside?"

He steps out and jabs a finger at me. "I don't touch little girls. You know that. When you and your ma were staying with me, I never touched you."

Back when he had hair and clear skin, he used to bring me presents like gum and suckers. Then he'd pass out in the middle of the living room floor.

His eyes travel up my body. "How old are you now, Tracey's girl?"

I know what he sees. Young, pretty girl. Good for running errands. Good for paying back old debts.

"Sorry, Finn. Still sixteen, like the last time you asked."

"Come have a taste with me. It's in your blood. You know it is."

I walk away. "Send your ma over," he calls, laughing.

Mom has been watching through the peephole. She wrings her hands and paces back and forth. Her clothes hang unflattering on her slight figure. Her hair sticks out in all directions from a messy bun that slipped to the side of her head. "I can't lose you again. I can't. One time, Kayla. That's all it takes. One time."

"I know, Mom." I take her hands to quiet them. The familiar guilt knocks on my heart. She holds it together for *me*. She doesn't leave the apartment for *me*.

"You've been sober for three years." I hug her.

She holds me tight. "I love you," she whispers.

My mother never sees *me*. She sees her sixteen-year-old self. Bright girl with a bright future. Waist-length brown hair. Fell in love with a boy named Finn. Nice boy, nice family. She and Finn went to a party at the rotting flophouse of a friend of a friend. And never came out again.

"I love you, too, Mom."

And I do. Still, she terrifies me.

Finn's right. It's in my blood. It always has been. One slip, one mess-up, one very bad day. One needle in one vein, and I will be her.

I take a shower to wash the grit of No Limit Foods and bloody stairwells off me. The steam on the cracked mirror evaporates to expose my eyes, my nose, my hair dripping puddles onto the floor. Just me. No makeup, no clothes, no curls.

Truth is, when I look at myself, I'm not sure who I see staring back.

CHAPTER 3
BETSY

Teddy's truck rumbles past a football stadium filled with splintered bleachers and patches of brown grass to the drop-off lane of San Justo High. It's a sprawling, flat-roofed, one-story compound in the center of town. Like everything else, it's sunbaked, dust-covered, and falling apart. We're early. The first ones in line.

Teddy puts the truck in park and turns it off. He gives me the once-over, steps out, and slams the heavy door behind him. Through the windshield, he shoots me a warning glance. I get out and follow him like a baby duck to the main office.

The secretary is startled by our sudden appearance. Teddy smiles at her. Redness passes over her cheeks. He throws an arm across my shoulder.

"This is Betsy Hopewood. She's a brand-new junior."

The secretary shuffles papers around on her desk. And again. And again. "I'm sorry I don't have her paperwork."

"Not a problem. I can fill out anything you need. I'm her uncle."

"He's not my uncle," I mutter.

"I practically am. I've known Betsy since she came into this world." He smiles at me, but his fingers press hard into the bones of my shoulder.

The secretary doesn't seem to care who we are. She hands over the paperwork. Teddy whistles as he fills out my pertinent details.

A woman walks in the door behind us. She's tall, fit, and blond. Her sleek, tailored clothes didn't come from Walmart or the mall in El Paso like everyone else's I've seen in my brief encounters with life around here.

Teddy tries his magic smile on her. No such luck, Teddy. She's too young to be dazzled by you.

The secretary points to the woman. "This is Miss Jones." Her eyes run up and down Miss Jones's body. "I've got a new one for you, and I don't have any paperwork," she says *with a tone.*

Miss Jones smirks. "Come on back."

Teddy tips his hand in a wave. "See you after school, buttercup."

Buttercup. That's new. I don't like it.

I follow Miss Jones. She unlocks a door and motions for me to go inside. Even though the walls are decorated with bright posters and snappy sayings, I can tell it used to be a closet.

I sit in a hard plastic chair. The air conditioner blows directly in my face. The skin on my arms goose-bumps. I don't make eye contact.

The secretary flaps the papers with Teddy's scrawl at Miss Jones. She takes them and nods as she reads about my educational history. Skinny girl from North Dakota. Has all her shots. Passed all her classes so far.

"My cousin lives in North Dakota." A bead of sweat runs down the back of my neck. "He says it snows a lot." She laughs. "Not something you're going to have to worry about here."

My face grins in downward-looking agreement. I think.

"It's going to take a while to get the records from your last school. Until then"—she picks up the keyboard resting on top of her computer and puts it in her lap—"we'll have to give you the standard junior schedule." She starts typing. "Are you good at math?"

I want to scream, *Yes! Let me have something. Something that is a part of me. Something from before.* Sweat coats my skin under the tank top. I shake my head.

"Okay, we'll put you in Algebra Two."

I don't cry. I try to smile. I try to act like I'm a normal girl from North Dakota, where it snows a lot. Where I was bad at math. Where no one died.

Where it wasn't my fault.

She makes one more definitive tap on the keyboard. "Welcome to San Justo High, home of the Juggernauts." A printer activates in the hall.

She leans in close. "I know, right? Why pick juggernauts when it's pronounced San WHOSE-toe?" She winks, as if we're both in on it now. Two pale girls from *somewhere else.*

———

My first class is something called Life Skills. Miss Jones examined me and decided that I need help with living. She is so right.

The hallway is filling up. I go directly to the classroom and sit in the middle seat in the middle row.

A short, chubby girl bounces in. She's surrounded by an entourage of thin, perfumed, made-up girls. One carries her book, another her backpack. They walk her to the seat catty-corner to mine, circling her like a pod of dolphins protecting its young.

They glare at me. I'm a shark.

The girl slides into the seat. From the way the others are focused on her stomach, I can guess what they're fawning over. She's knocked up, expecting, *with child*.

"I'm starving," she announces. "I didn't have time for breakfast."

Chastising clucks come from the circle. They riffle around in their bags and purses but don't produce anything. They look relieved when the bell rings.

I don't have control over my hands. They unzip my backpack and feel around for the lunch Mom packed in the misplaced hope that I would eat it.

I watch myself balance an apple at the end of the girl's desk.

"Thanks," she says with a big smile. "I'm Happy."

My eyes glide over to her. My face feels blank. I don't know how to respond to this strange greeting. *Hi! I'm a ticking time bomb.*

When she giggles, her eyes squish together. She's so young and innocent. In need of protection.

"That probably sounded funny, huh? My name's Mirasol Alegría, but everyone calls me Happy."

I can't help but glance down at her stomach.

When the final bell rings, I bolt. I throw open the door to the outside, but the heat knocks me back like an explosion. The pregnant girl catches up.

"You wanna hang out?" she asks.

Teddy's truck is parked in the pick-up lane. I can go with the pregnant girl or I can go with Teddy.

"Okay," I say to her. She giggles. Her world seems to be a joyful, funny place.

A boy runs up carrying her purple backpack.

"Happy, you can't keep leaving your stuff everywhere." He freezes when he sees me. Our eyes meet. His are a deep, soul-searching brown. I have to look away before he sees the blackness inside of mine.

The pregnant girl talks constantly as we walk off campus. I take out my toxic pink, sparkly phone and text Teddy.

Going out with friends :)

I delete the :). I don't want him to come chasing after me, guns blazing, thinking I'm being held against my will.

Seconds later, his truck pulls out of the pick-up lane and drives slowly past us. I turn away.

"Hey, what's your name?"

Happy asks me twice before I realize she's talking to me.

"Betsy. It's a family name."

"Betsy's a nice name."

No. It's not.

She juts a thumb over her shoulder. "That's Adrian Morales." I don't turn around to acknowledge the boy with her backpack.

We cross the street against the light to the strip mall where Mom works. Next to the florist is C&J's Mexican Restaurant. Mom's talked about eating lunch at this place. She's made friends with the owners.

Adrian hands Happy her bag as we go inside and then disappears into the kitchen.

Paper flowers in faded bright colors collect dust on the tops of booths. Chipped, wobbly looking tables are scattered haphazardly through the remaining space. It smells like ancient cigarette smoke, bleach, and yesterday's cooked onions.

I slide into a booth across from Happy. The seat is torn. I have to scooch against the wall to keep from sinking into its fuzzy white insides. I put my elbows down, and they stick to the table.

"My boyfriend, Tomás, always picks me up here." Happy looks around the restaurant. We're the only people in it.

The door doesn't jingle when it opens. A waitress in her early twenties wearing a name tag that says ANGIE slips in, catching the door behind her to let a kid through.

The kid sees me. She moves at hyperspeed to our booth, stops, and locks her fingers behind her back. "Hi," she says.

I glance at Happy. She points to the kid. "That's Rosie."

The kid laughs at my name when Happy introduces me. "How old are you?" Rosie asks.

"Sixteen," I mumble. I force myself to look at her shiny, smiling face. "How old are you?"

"Four," she announces. "But my birthday is October sixth." An awkward moment of silence passes between us. I'm afraid she's going to ask about my birthday. Then she throws her arms open. "Can I give you a hug?" That's worse. Much worse.

I shake my head. She scrambles onto the red vinyl seat anyway. Angie dives forward and grabs her wrist. "She said no." Rosie's little face crumbles.

"You can give me a hug, Rosie." The kid grudgingly crawls off the booth and into the open arms of Happy the pregnant girl.

"Sorry about that. The preschool wants us to work on boundaries with her," Angie says, like this is something I need to know.

Two red plastic cups of soda appear in front of us, followed by two straws. I feel Adrian's stare on the side of my face.

"Where'd you move here from?" he asks. This is a small town. Everyone who sees me knows I'm not from around here.

"North Dakota," I say.

"What's it like there?"

I shrug. "It's okay." I raise my eyes and look at him. A mistake. He regards me with suspicion, like I'm a trespasser in his territory. I don't like the way he searches my face with his stare. Like he's trying to read it. Read me. Figure out who I am. I can't let him figure me out. I can't let anyone do that.

He smiles. A quick bounce of the lips. "North Dakota. That's like Mount Rushmore, right?"

I bite my lip. *Shit. Where's Mount Rushmore?*

I nod. I smile pretty and show him all my teeth. He picks up the straw wrappers from the table. "Welcome to San Justo," he says, and walks away.

Happy sticks her straw into her soda. Angie whooshes past our table. "Uh-uh." She rips the cup from Happy's hand.

A couple of minutes later, the cup, filled to the top with orange juice, is returned by an older woman. Her face is lined and sags. Her black hair, threaded with gray, is pinned up in a messy mass of curls. She's short but strong. She looks like she hasn't slept in decades.

Her eyes glance at Happy and then land on me. Disapproval washes over her face. She knows. She can sense it. I'm here to rain plague and ruin upon her household.

She turns toward the kitchen and yells something in Spanish. A hairy arm reaches through the window and gives her a thumbs-up.

Happy giggles.

The woman turns defiantly and marches away.

"Mrs. Morales thinks you're too skinny. She's going to feed you."

I lean over the table. At any moment my eyes could fill up and send my head ducking for cover. "I don't have any money," I whisper.

Happy snorts. "Even if you did, she wouldn't take it."

I rub my eyes.

Happy unzips her backpack and takes out an object about the size of a quarter. She puts it on the table inches from her belly.

"What's that?" I ask.

"It's my good-luck charm." She holds it up in front of my face. It's a figurine of an orange fish.

My heart stops.

I tug up on the neck of my shirt and cross my arms high on my chest.

"Where did you get that?" I try to make it sound like a casual question, but she has to hear the shake in my voice, see the sweat forming on my forehead.

"From Adrian. He got it for me in Seattle. He was picked to go to a school conference there freshman year." She beams. "It was a conference for really smart people. He came back with his chest all puffed out. That didn't last long around here." She laughs.

Black spots appear in my vision. I try to appear calm. "You got that from Adrian?"

Happy tips her head and narrows her eyes. She studies me. I drop my hands down to the table and try to smile. It's a weak effort, more like baring my teeth than pleasantness.

It's a coincidence. It has to be. This can't happen twice in one lifetime. Unless . . . unless that was the plan all along. Something to keep me in line. Under control.

"Yeah. Adrian has one too. He usually carries it in his pocket. . . . Hey, Adrian," she calls into the back of the restaurant.

"No," I whimper, but in three large strides, Adrian is

standing in front of us. I will my hands to stay in plain sight. I don't touch my shirt. I look straight ahead.

"Show Betsy your fish," Happy says. Adrian digs around in his pocket. He flashes it in front of my nose.

"Nice." My voice cracks, and my eyes meet Adrian's. And I see it. The smug upturn of his mouth and a little spark. A glimmer of something. Of curiosity. Why do I want to see his fish?

I look down. I can't speak. I can't cry. The pain in my stomach shoots up to eleven. I feel Adrian step away from the table. Happy makes her fish swim through the air between us. Then she places it on her belly.

I have to get out of here.

The hairy arm comes out of nowhere and puts a plate in front of me. Bright yellow cheese melted between two tortillas and cut into perfect triangles. The owner of the arm winks. "No chile."

Adrian, pretending to sort silverware, watches me from the bussing station. I have to eat. I have to act normal. I can't let him see what's happening inside of me.

I pick up one cheesy triangle. This is something you would feed a child. My lips clamp themselves closed.

Happy talks with her mouth full. She has no problem raising the fork, chewing. Adrian's still watching.

I take a deep breath. I'm in control. I force my mouth open and shove the entire triangle in. My throat closes. I cough and choke. But I swallow.

Mom walks out of the flower shop and appears in the window outside. She sees me force another triangle into my mouth. She clasps her hands together and holds them under her chin in delight. She comes inside and approaches the booth.

"Hi, I'm Happy."

Mom smiles at the giggling pregnant girl sitting across from me. "Everyone calls me Happy."

"I can see why," Mom says.

"Can I give you a hug?" Rosie pulls on Mom's pant leg.

"Sure, sweetie." Mom kneels down and wraps her long arms around the kid's little body.

Adrian stands behind them. Eyes on me.

My stomach rejects the food.

I slap my hand over my mouth and push past them out the door that doesn't jingle. A mush of cheesy triangle floating in bile splatters to the hot asphalt.

I sit back on the curb. My skin sizzles. Mom comes up behind me. Mrs. Morales joins her. Mom says I have a stomach bug. I'm grabbed hard around the upper arms and hoisted to my feet and shuffled down the sidewalk into refrigerated, carnation-scented air.

I am sat down on a stool. The whisper of a voice blows through my ears. "You have to try, Betsy. You have to try."

Mom settles herself among the vases of flowers. I do have to try. She smiles sadly at me. It's not only my life that depends on it.

CHAPTER 4
KAYLA

I'm way too old for this, but still my heart dips down to my knees at the thought that she might not come. I hang my toes over the edge of the curb in front of Clairmont High School and rock back and forth. The bell is going to ring soon. Paige and the rest of the girls from the dance team stand a respectable distance away. They glance over, but Paige distracts them by holding up her freshly manicured nails with tiny paintings of moons and stars on them. We're the Clairmont Explorers, and this year's Explorer theme is space.

Relief sloshes up through my body when Marie races around the corner, stumbling over cracks in her sensible heels. Her hair bounces out to the sides and strains against the clips that hold it to her head. Her green jacket flaps open over its matching green skirt. A wild patterned silk scarf hangs around her neck. I have to suck in a deep breath to stop from crying.

She pulls me into her arms and squeezes tight. When she

lets go, her eyes are glassy. "I heard about that poor girl," she says. "I was terrified something had happened to you."

"I'm fine," I say. I've said it about three hundred times since they found the girl in the stairwell.

"How's your mom? Is she going to her meetings?"

I nod. Lying to Marie makes me feel like I belong in Bluebird Estates.

"Good," she says, and reaches up to sweep the hair out of my face. She places a hand on my cheek. I'm taller than she is now.

The dance team is getting restless. Marie drops her hand.

She slides her giant purse from her shoulder to her wrist, digs inside, and pulls out what I have been waiting for all summer.

A metallic pink pencil with a sparkly unicorn eraser on top.

"Happy first day of school, Little Mouse."

I wore waterproof mascara because I knew this was going to make me cry. Marie's runs in black streams down her face. On my very first day of school, I had only been living with Marie for a few weeks. I was so scared. I didn't know anybody. Nothing was familiar. When I woke up that day, a special pencil was perched on my pillow next to my head. It's been our tradition ever since.

Marie produces a tissue and dabs her face. She's going to have to fix her makeup before she goes to her job at the bank. "Come over for dinner sometime soon. I have mail for you that I forgot to bring." Marie lives two blocks from school. Getting mail to me wouldn't be hard. But I appreciate that she's giving me an excuse to see her.

I nod. If I speak, I'll start crying again. She hugs me, turns quickly, and walks away.

I grip the pencil next to my heart and take two breaths to compose myself before sealing it inside the front pocket of my backpack. I turn and smile at Paige. That's her cue to release the dance team. They race over to me.

I'm smothered in arms as they all try to hug me at the same time. No one says anything. They've elected a spokesperson to broach the delicate subject of my home life. They know where I live now, and most of them knew me when I lived with Marie, but otherwise, they, except for Paige, know nothing more.

Sierra steps forward, and the others back up. She looks down at her hands. "We saw about that girl on the news. We're so thankful that you're okay." She pauses. This is probably harder for her than asking James McEllis to the winter formal last year. "*Are* you okay?"

I smile my big Clairmont Explorers Dance Team smile at them. "I'm fine. Really. That girl is already out of the hospital." And long, long gone.

Sierra's shoulders relax. The others have probably been coaching her on what not to say to me since it happened. I hate that they pity me. I have to be extra nice, extra helpful to everyone so that they will see me as a team member, a friend, and not a girl who was released from foster care to her messed-up mother in public housing on the other side of town.

The first bell rings. With more hugs, the dance team scatters. I walk with Paige.

I can't keep it inside anymore.

"That girl has friends too, you know. Right now at North-side, they aren't hugging her and saying they're glad it wasn't her. Because it *was* her. How would everybody here feel if it had been me and that girl's friends were celebrating?"

Paige doesn't say anything. We don't talk about things like this. We talk about nail polish and lipstick and boys. And that's good. I would rather talk about those things than how Finn has started showing me off like a new car to his junkie pals whenever I pass apartment 21.

"Do you want to come over after school? Mom can drop you off at work later, if you want." Paige's voice is soft, meek. She's trying her hardest.

"Okay." I won't see her again until the end of the day. I'm in AP everything. She's not. I squeeze her arm. "Have a good first day."

Carol Alexander is a perfect, grown-up version of Paige. They both have sleek brown hair that falls in layers around their faces. Small, slightly pointed, upper-class noses. Big blue eyes without the slightest hint of redness. Both wear clothes my minimum-wage checkout girl job could never afford.

Carol doesn't work. Paige's brothers are in middle school now, but Carol is still a stay-at-home mom. That's something Paige and I have in common. I have a stay-at-home mom too.

We pull up in front of No Limit Foods. In my lap, I have the dinner Carol packed for me in neat little containers inside a shopping bag from another grocery store. A nice store. One with a serve-yourself olive bar and samples on the weekends.

I may be dirt poor and live where the water doesn't get hot three days a week, but the nice people from the government give Mom and me food stamps. I'm not starving. No one would look at me and think that.

"It was so nice to see you, Kayla." Perfect smile showing perfectly white teeth. I don't know if the kid-glove treatment Carol's been giving me today is the normal one or an extra-special one because of the attacked girl.

She watches a scruffy customer exit No Limit. She turns back to me with the perfect smile still emblazoned on her face. "One of my friends mentioned the other day that her husband's office was looking for someone to do general office work after school. I'm sure they would love to have you. Paige could drive you home in the evenings." She leaves the next part unspoken: *It pays more.*

"Thanks, but I really love No Limit. I've been here almost two years now. On my anniversary day, they're going to throw me a party."

Carol nods, but there's no way she believes my super-chipper lie.

No one actually likes working at No Limit. But I got this job on my own. I'm proud of that.

I open the car door. Before I can get out, Carol catches my arm. "You can come over anytime. Anytime, day or night. Just ring the doorbell. Or call. Someone will come get you."

I imagine her wrapped in her pink satin robe, sitting in her white BMW in front of Bluebird Estates in the middle of the night. I know she means well. And I'm grateful that people care about me, really, I am.

"Thanks." I smile my big Clairmont Explorers Dance Team smile at her.

On my way to the break room, I pass Elton. He's a regular. He appeared out of nowhere a couple of months ago and has been coming in every day since. I think he lives in his car—an old station wagon filled to the brim with odds and ends—that found its way to the corner of the parking lot. Albert grumbles about having it towed, but until someone complains, it's not really his problem.

Fingers splayed and wiggling, Elton's short arms stretch to reach for a box of cereal on the top shelf.

"Let me get that," I say, and reach up easily for it. A tuft of his wild hair blows in the stream of my breath. He's small for a full-grown man. His shirt is untucked. He uses a plain black cane when he walks, but I don't think he's old. He could be thirty-five or sixty. There's an agelessness about his disheveled appearance and his hyperaware eyes.

He takes the cereal box. For a second, I think I see emotion flash across his face. Something big, something dark. But then it's gone. Blank. He nods.

I spread the containers of Carol's dinner out on the break room table. Some of the checkers and baggers aren't as lucky as I am. The food will be gone before my first break.

I switch registers at eight p.m. Albert likes the night crew to work squished together at registers one, two, and three. He says it's safer that way. Sure. Whatever helps you sleep at night, Albert.

At register two, the closed sign is up and the light is off, but still someone waits in line.

He rips the corner off a bag of M&M's.

"I'm not quite open yet," I say, and fumble the money tray into the register.

"That's okay. I don't want to buy anything."

I raise an eyebrow at the M&M's in his hand. He salutes me with them. "Like I said before, my name's Jordan."

I don't say anything. His watching me makes my hands shake. I can't get the money tray to latch into the back of the drawer.

"And I'm Kayla," he says in a falsetto voice.

I snap my head around. He laughs and points to the plastic name tag pinned above the giant abdomen pocket of my red No Limit Foods apron.

Finally, the tray catches. I close the drawer and enter my code. He's still watching me.

"Can I help you with something?"

A woman with a cranky toddler rolls her overflowing basket into line behind him. He leans over the belt. "You see that McDonald's?" He points to the one and only McDonald's in the parking lot. "I'm going to have a cup of coffee over there. Maybe during your break you'd like to join me?"

"I—I can't." He's starting to creep me out.

"Let me guess, cream and two packets of sugar? Probably decaf because it's late and you'll need your beauty sleep?" That smug smile is back.

"I have to help this customer." I motion behind him. The toddler gnaws on a frozen dinner box. The mother's eyes skip between us, like she's pondering whom to murder first—the checkout girl or the guy flirting with her.

M&M's guy—Jordan—slaps his hand down. "For the candy," he says.

Not that I care, but I think I've made him mad. I cringe and wait until he's all the way out in the parking lot before I glance down.

A crisp hundred-dollar bill glitters on the worn conveyor belt.

The smell of French fries slams into my nose when I rip open the door of McDonald's. I have $98.71 wadded up in my hand. I'm not his charity case. And I'm certainly not some kind of pay-in-advance hooker. He can keep his money.

He sits at a table in the corner, reading a newspaper. A cup of coffee steams across from him. He sees me and folds the paper in half.

I stomp over, open my hand, and let the sweaty money fall all over the table. "Your change."

He points to the coffee. "Decaf. Cream. Two packets of sugar. I took the lid off so it wouldn't be too hot when you got here."

I'm going to turn on my heels and walk out of here. I'm going to show this jerk I'm not whoever he thinks I am.

He smiles. Now it's all pure and happy, like he's a different person from before. He nudges the coffee toward me. Before I can think about it, I pull out the chair, and I sit.

It's exactly how I would have ordered my coffee.

He places his hands on the table where I can see them.

"Let's start over again. I'm not an asshole. I just wanted to get your attention. I'm Jordan." He reaches his right hand out professionally. I tentatively shake it. It's warm, soft with the right amount of grip to show that he doesn't have to prove anything to anyone.

"Kayla," I say without his confidence.

He laughs. "How nice to hear it in your own voice."

I eye the coffee. I don't know a thing about this guy.

He must see it on my face. "You're probably wondering if I'm a serial killer or something. I'm not. I'm Jordan Bloom. I'm nineteen. I take community college classes online. I moved here from Florida a few months ago." I still don't touch the coffee. "And apparently, I'm not good at making friends." An honest, awkward grin floats over his lips. "But you seem like someone I would like to be friends with."

I'm still on guard, but part of me relaxes. I've had guys at the store hit on me before. But this feels different. There's something electric in the way he looks at me. I feel charged like static making my hair stand on end.

He reaches into his pocket and places something on the table. "I saw this and thought of you."

"Um, thanks," I say, and lean forward to examine the stubby brown acorn on the table. It still has a hint of dirt on it, like he just picked it up off the ground.

He smiles sheepishly, and a piece of hair falls over his eyes. "I saw your oak leaf."

"My oak leaf?"

"The one you have taped to the side of the register. It seemed like it was important to you."

My oak leaf. It's been there so long I'd forgotten about it.

It's a leaf from the huge tree on the side of Marie's house. We collected it and carefully ironed it between two pieces of wax paper for a project in second grade. I found it again when I was packing for Bluebird Estates. It became something else to me then. A piece of home, my real home.

I can't believe he noticed that. Maybe he is different from the other creeps who hang around No Limit Foods. He waits for my reaction. "Thanks," I say again, and rub the acorn between my fingers.

"Acorns are also symbols of potential. There's a giant tree inside there. I guess I was kind of hoping"—he looks down and blushes—"that maybe when you looked at the acorn you would think about that—about the potential of the person who gave it to you."

I don't mean to, but I laugh. Not at him exactly. More at how cute his red face and downturned eyes are.

He glances up at me. The smile is still there. "That sounded stupid, didn't it? This whole night went better in my head."

I don't realize that I've picked up the cup and taken a sip of coffee until it's running hot down my throat. I set the cup down and roll the acorn around my palm. Jordan's eyes shine. Potential.

A soft sizzle fills the space between us. I maintain eye contact until I feel the blush rise on my checks too.

The screech of a chair on the floor brings me back to reality. Back to my No Limit Foods apron. My heart sinks. I can't do this. This isn't me. There's too much at stake for me to get distracted by this guy.

I stand up. "I have to go. My break's almost over, and my

boss *is* an asshole." I attempt a good-natured chuckle, but it comes out sounding high pitched and fake.

"It was nice meeting you, Kayla."

I nod in acknowledgment and walk casually outside. Then I run until I swoosh through the doors of No Limit.

The acorn's still in my hand. I put it in my pocket and feel it brushing against my leg for the rest of my shift.

It's late. Too late for a good girl to be walking home alone in the dark.

There's a man standing on the edge of the No Limit parking lot. He has a scraggly, patchy beard; long matted hair; and dirty sagging jeans. Maybe he's homeless or maybe he's too strung out to remember where he lives. When I pass by, the stench of alcohol and urine wafts off him. I don't flinch. It's nothing I haven't smelled before. He does a one, two, three shuffle with his feet, like he's dancing the cha-cha with an imaginary partner.

I pull the hood of my raincoat farther down over my forehead. Before I step onto the sidewalk, I look over my shoulder to see if he's following me. He isn't. That's good. I'm too poor to afford a luxury like fear.

My paranoia doesn't subside as I walk down Bluebird Lane. Jordan freaked me out with how he made me feel. One moment I was hating his obnoxious behavior, and the next I was drinking coffee, like I was on a date.

I can't do that. Too much is riding on me always doing exactly the right thing. I have to get good grades. I have to participate in extracurricular activities. I have to work. I have to get a scholarship, go to college, and get out of here. I can't risk everything because a guy made me feel special for a brief moment. That's what happened to Mom.

I turn around. No one is there. Still, I feel like I'm being followed.

Up the street in front of me, two cars facing opposite directions stop in the middle of the road. One is a beat-up black Camaro with a Florida license plate. Its driver hangs his arm out the window. Tattoos that I can't make out dance and swirl up it.

Busted. The other driver's a narc. His car is old and beat-up too, but there's something about it that tries too hard to appear inconspicuous. Most of us around here could spot him a mile away.

The drivers slap hands over the asphalt. The narc pulls away and rolls toward me. I feel the disapproving, clinical examination of his gaze as he passes.

I make the rest of the walk with my eyes glued to the cement. Tonight, Bluebird Estates is quiet. The front lobby door is locked. Finn is inside apartment 21 sleeping it off. I make it to apartment 26 safe and sound.

The next girl isn't so lucky. It happens at Sandhill Manor, the pretentious name for the dump a couple miles away. The news says she was alone, asleep in her apartment. He broke in, dragged her out, and left her crumpled in a back staircase. She didn't make it.

I'm just grateful it wasn't me.

CHAPTER 5
BETSY

"You need to come. Rosie adores you. You'll break her heart if you don't show up." Mom wraps a bunch of blue hydrangeas in decorative green paper. My head lies on the kitchen table. The wood cools my cheek.

I've been going to the restaurant with Happy on the days when Mom has to work late. It's either that or hang out with Teddy. He doesn't think I should have to come home to an empty house. At C&J's, Rosie won't leave me alone. Every time she asks for hug. Every time I refuse.

"No," I whisper. I already have a heart. I have to keep it alive, and beating, and safely inside my body. The kid's heart isn't my responsibility.

Mom holds up the flowers. "What do you think?"

My head lifts up, but my neck isn't strong enough to keep it there. It flops back to the table. "Five-year-olds don't want flowers for their birthdays."

"I got Rosie a doll. These are for Connie."

"Who's Connie?" I can't handle any more peripheral people in my life.

"Connie. Connie and Juan Morales. C&J's?"

Right. Connie. Mrs. Morales. Rosie's grandmother.

Mom points the flowers at me. "I'm not making another excuse for you. Get dressed in something nice and let's go." I don't move. "Come on. Everyone will be there. Angie and Happy and Adrian."

I pick my head up. "Adrian will be there?"

"Of course. He's Rosie's uncle. The whole family will be there." Mom turns her head and tries to hide a smile. "He's a nice boy. Connie says he doesn't have a girlfriend."

I place my head back on the table. "Great," I mumble.

At least it's not as hot now. It's starting to be fall, sort of. Later, I come out of my room wearing khaki pants and a black turtleneck that I ordered online. Mom turns me right back around and makes me change into one of the frilly blouses she bought me for school. I put a camisole on underneath it, but still the neck slips too far. I'm going to have to be careful.

Mom gathers up the flowers and the doll for Rosie wrapped in sparkly pink-and-yellow paper. "Teddy should be here any minute." She moves to the front door.

I take a slow step behind her. "Is there a reason why Teddy is coming?" I can't hide the ire in my voice.

She raises an eyebrow, but lets it go. "He didn't have anything else going on today. And I told him there would be cake."

On cue, Teddy's truck rumbles around the corner. "Can you lock the door?" Mom asks, using her head to motion to her full arms.

I pull my house key out of my pocket. It's suspended from a cheap, made-in-China rubber key chain of a distorted Mount Rushmore. The presidents don't have faces. Just dots of black paint where eyes should be.

It came from a gas station near the highway. They had something from each of the fifty states. A peach for Georgia. A chile pepper for New Mexico. The Space Needle for Washington. You could pretend to have gone anywhere and have a key chain to prove it.

Teddy gives me a big grin. I don't return it. Mom steps out of the way so that I can slide into the middle seat. When she gets in, I huddle against her so that no part of me touches Teddy. He hums a song instead of turning on the radio. Mom smiles.

There's so much noise coming from the Morales house—loud voices, shrieking, running footsteps—that we can hear it from the street. No one answers the door when we ring the bell. Teddy puts his hand on the knob and tests it. The door pops open. He sticks his head in, shrugs, and opens the door for us to pass through.

I don't make it all the way inside before I'm sideswiped by a blur in a blue party dress. Rosie throws her arms around my legs. "Hi, Betsy!" she yells.

I peel her off me.

"Don't you look pretty," Mom coos. Rosie lifts the sides of her dress and curtsies. Mom claps.

Mrs. Morales bustles around the corner, wiping her hands on a dish towel. "Come in, come in," she says. Mom presents her with the flowers, and Mrs. Morales leans in to give Mom a one-armed hug and a kiss on the cheek.

I don't realize my back is pressed into the door until Mrs. Morales focuses on me. She waves me toward her. "Come, Betsy. Everyone is outside." I take a step forward, and she places her arm over my shoulder. I'm taller than she is, so it's awkward, but it's also nice, warm.

She walks me out to the backyard. Mr. Morales has the grill fired up. Smoke rising from it fills the air with the mouthwatering smell of cooking meat and partially obscures his face. He raises his spatula and hairy arm at me in greeting.

Another man, not too much older than me, hovers next to the grill with an empty plate. I've seen him before at C&J's. I recognize the tattoo of a cross surrounded by roses on the inside of his forearm. He looks like he wants to say something to me. I keep walking.

Adults holding beer bottles or red plastic cups of punch mill around a table covered with food. Happy stands alone at the far end and plucks one potato chip at a time out of a giant bowl. She looks hopefully at a passing couple, but they either don't see her or don't want to see her.

When she sees me, a smile explodes across her face. "You came."

I shrug and then remember to stand up straight to keep my blouse in its proper place. Happy stuffs a handful of chips into her mouth, like she just ran out of willpower. She points at Mom and Teddy. "Who's that man that's always around?" Potato chip flecks rain from her mouth. "Is he your mom's boyfriend?"

"No," I say forcefully. "He's some old friend of Mom's who pretends he's my uncle and tells me what to do." I can't stop the bitterness from leaking out in my voice.

"I've had some of those," Happy says. Mom laughs and slaps Teddy playfully on the shoulder. "At least he's nice to your mom, right?"

I nod. Happy looks off into the distance, watching an old memory. I recognize that face. I've seen it in the mirror. I want to hug her, ask her to tell me her story. Share my story with her.

My arms stay by my sides. I can't get attached. I've learned my lesson about what can happen when you get attached.

Happy waves at a boy who's sitting in the corner of the yard playing with his cell phone. "That's my boyfriend, Tomás. He's Rosie's other uncle." She rubs her thickening belly. "My baby will be Rosie's cousin."

I narrow my eyes. I can't keep track of all these people. Happy laughs. "It's confusing, huh?" She slides the chip bowl to the side and uses her finger to draw an imaginary family tree.

"Adrian and Angie are brother and sister. Angie and Lawrence"—she points to the guy with the tattoo—"are Rosie's parents. Tomás is Lawrence's brother. So Tomás is Rosie's uncle, and our baby will be her cousin. See?"

No. But I nod anyway. Happy giggles. "It doesn't matter. We're all family."

Tomás walks over to us, his thumbs still texting. He puts the phone into his pocket.

"This is Betsy," Happy says, and wraps her arm around

his. He wears dark sunglasses that obscure his eyes. It's unnerving.

"Nice to meet you," I say. He gives me a chin raise. Then we stand there in silence, his dark glasses focused squarely on me. He doesn't move. I can tell he's sizing me up. But he has the advantage. He can see every move my eyes make.

His phone buzzes in his pocket. Happy's smile fades as she lets go of his arm. He moves back to his spot in the corner.

"Tomás thinks you're a narc," Happy says.

I snap my head over to her. "What?"

"You know, like when the cops recruit people who are, like, twenty-five but look young, to go into high schools and make friends. Then they bust everyone with pot in their lockers."

"What?" I ask again. "Why?"

Happy shrugs. "I don't remember anyone ever moving to San Justo out of the blue. And you don't say much. No one knows what your deal is."

"I'm not a narc." I laugh, but it's too forced, too unbelievable.

Happy smiles. "I know. I think that's only on TV anyway. Ever since this"—she points at her belly—"Tomás's been super paranoid. Besides, I like that you're mysterious," she adds, and then sweeps her arm around the yard. "Everyone here knows every single thing that has happened to me since the day I was born. I don't get to have secrets." She sighs. "Eventually, they will know everything about you, too." She gives me the same smile Mom did earlier. "Adrian's been asking about you."

I try to keep my face neutral, but the pain in my stomach forces bile into my throat. "I have to go to the bathroom," I say, and stumble back into a man who has to hold his beer way out in front of him to keep from spilling it. "Sorry," I mumble. "Sorry," I say again as I rush past Mr. Morales and into the house.

I duck into the bathroom and dry heave twice into the toilet. I sit on the floor with my back against the counter. Tomás thinks I'm an undercover cop. A spurt of maniacal laughter leaves my mouth, but then I'm hanging over the toilet again. This time I throw the bile up. It burns my throat and sears my tongue. I wipe my mouth with a piece of toilet paper and lie down on the fuzzy green bath mat.

The only thing I know about narcs is that girls like me get them killed.

I hear Adrian's low voice in a back bedroom. If I'm going to stay alive, Adrian has to think I'm a weird, shy girl who occasionally visits his parents' restaurant. That's it. I can't draw attention to myself. I can't have him wondering about me, talking to people, making phone calls. Bringing the black monster to life under my bed.

The shrill giggle of little girls joins Adrian's deep ha-ha laugh.

Everyone on the other side of this door thinks he's perfect. Someone you would trust to watch your house while you're on vacation, someone who would sign up for your charity walk, someone you would leave your kids with. It's so, so easy to be misled. To not see the danger right in front of your nose.

The little girls laugh again.

I was misled too the first time. But now I know. You can't trust anyone.

I won't let Adrian do it. I won't let it happen again.

I propel myself to my feet and open the door a crack. The hallway is clear. I dash out into the living room. I need a plan. Then I see it. A crystal bowl filled with those pastel-colored, chalky mints that melt in your mouth. I grab it and tiptoe to the bedroom.

I peek around the open door. Adrian has his back to me, with five little girls gathered around him. They're playing a board game. Adrian rolls a three and moves his piece four spaces.

"That's too many," one of the girls squeals.

"No it's not. See: one . . . two . . . three." He moves it five spaces this time. All the girls giggle. But one girl's face isn't as bright as the others. She sits a little farther away. Her overalls clash with the frilly dresses. She watches the game but doesn't participate.

She's the one.

I can save her.

I wave. She looks up. I wave more frantically and point to the bowl of candies. She hesitantly stands up. The others don't notice her walk to the door. It's terrifyingly easy for me to lead her into the hallway.

I hand her a mint and kneel down to her level. "Do you want to go play outside with me?"

She shakes her head and looks back at the game. I give her another mint. "Come on, let's go outside." She steps back into the room. I can't let her do that. I take her hand and pull gently.

I've almost got her to safety when, in the living room, she yanks away from me. The force sends the mints flying and showers us in a pink and green rain. She bumps her head into the wall.

It isn't hard. She's more startled than hurt, but it's still enough for her to cry. I drop down to my knees. "It's okay," I say to her. "Don't cry." *Don't cry, or Adrian will come out and get us.*

The girl stumbles to the sliding glass door. A woman opens it and takes the girl into her arms. "What happened?" she asks the girl, but then raises her eyes to me on my knees in the scattering of mints.

Mom, Teddy, Mr. Morales, and several other people peer inside.

"She, uh . . ." I look up, and Adrian has come into the hall-way. He steps forward until he towers over me. "She wanted a mint and bumped her head." I wave a hand at the wall, like that explains everything.

I glance down, away from Adrian's scrutiny. In the ker-fuffle, the top of my blouse has dipped down. My exposed skin stares up at me. *Adrian can see down my shirt.* I slap my hands over my chest and leap to my feet. I have to get out of here. Now.

Adrian's between me and the front door. I push past him hard, careen outside, and take off blindly down the street.

Teddy's truck circles the block for a fifth time. The first time, he tried to convince me to get in. The second time, I gave him the finger. I don't know how long I've been walking, but it's getting dark.

On Teddy's twelfth circle, I flag him down. It's totally dark now. I crawl into the truck when it stops. He opens his mouth, but I put my hand up to stop him. I don't want to hear it.

When he deposits me at home, I give the same hand to Mom and slam the door to my room. I pull the black monster out. My evening routine. I expect it to be hot in my hands from all the missed calls after the party. But it isn't. It's cold.

It buzzes. The familiar number, the one with the fucking Washington area code, pops up on the screen. I send it to voice mail. I don't want to talk to him. I know what he's going to say. Not that it matters. I won't be alive twenty-four hours from now anyway. If Adrian didn't know who I was before, he knows now. I've signed my own death warrant.

CHAPTER 6
KAYLA

Lying to Mom is easy. I told her I had to work. It's my night off, but she doesn't pay attention to things like that.

Marie's house is painted blue. It has an honest-to-God white picket fence that separates its little front yard from the sidewalk. Masses of tall, white, sweet-smelling flowers hang over the pathway to the door and glow under the gray skies. The first time I saw the house's steeply pitched roof and trim that matched the flowers was when an anonymous social worker said soothing things and helped me out of the car with my gently used teddy bear. I thought I was going to be living in a fairy tale. That I would get to be a princess.

I still have a key. I could unlock the door and go inside, but this isn't my house anymore. I ring the doorbell.

Marie hugs me on the front porch. Without her heels she has to stand on her toes. "Dinner's almost ready," she says.

She motions to the side table next to the door where a stack of envelopes marked with the Clairmont High Explorers symbol—the Earth with satellites buzzing in electron-like tracks around it—sits. They're addressed to "the parent or guardian of Kayla Asher." Marie hasn't opened them.

Whereas Marie doesn't tolerate lying and makes that clear on the first day with her new charges, this is one lie she lets slip by. The reason I get to stay at Clairmont and don't have to transfer to Northside is because the school thinks I still live here.

I wish I still did.

Marie sticks her head out of the kitchen. "Come meet my new little bear."

Marie has had lots of little bears over the years. Their school pictures line the mantel over the fireplace in the living room.

I was her only little mouse.

A boy, whose chin barely clears it, sits at the table. His hair stands straight up off his head, like he's been electrocuted. His dark eyes are wide. He hasn't been here long.

"Hi, I'm Kayla," I say with a bright smile. He doesn't acknowledge me. His gaze is fixed on his plate and the solitary mound of broccoli in the middle of it.

Marie puts a plate down in front of me. I look at it and then at her. She nods. My eyes well up, and I have to sniffle hard. Next to my pile of broccoli is a big helping of macaroni and cheese.

I'm an adult now.

I have to set the example. I pierce a broccoli tree with my fork and pop it into my mouth. Marie does the same thing. When we foster kids showed up at Marie's, most of us had never seen a vegetable before. And all of us, for as long as we lived here, had a plate of vegetables placed in front of us while our favorite foods hovered nearby. No broccoli, then no mac and cheese, or pizza, or lasagna.

It worked. Without even thinking about it, I still eat my vegetables first.

The new boy sniffs at the broccoli. I know what's running through his head. He's been on his own from day one. He's developed a certain discipline. He can outlast Marie. We all thought that in the beginning.

Marie will wait forever.

Marie hands me a dripping plate, and I dry it and stack it in the cupboard. The new boy still stares at the cold green aliens in front of him. I turn my back, but out of the corner of my eye, I see him sneak one. Marie smiles knowingly at me.

Before I head back to Bluebird Estates, I slip into the guest room. This was my room. It's missing my clothes and stuffed animals, but otherwise, it's trapped in time, waiting for me.

It makes me swallow hard. I want to lie on the bed and refuse to get up again. I want to stay and never go back to Bluebird Estates. Never go back to Mom. I blink to clear my eyes and feel like a traitor.

In the back of the closet there's a loose piece of molding. I pry it open to reveal a place where the dry wall has been hollowed out. Marie doesn't know it's here. It was empty when I found it, but it became a place for my special things. Things I couldn't stand to take with me to Bluebird Estates.

I pull the wad of pictures and papers out of the hidden cubby. In the beginning it was just little things I found. A nice leaf, a perfume sample from one of Carol Alexander's magazines. Then it was A⁺ smiley-face spelling tests.

At the end of eighth grade, when I was returned to Bluebird Estates and my newly clean and sober mother, I realized Marie had saved my life. Because of her I was okay. I wasn't going to be one of those foster kids who ended up on the streets addicted, beaten, and used. Marie gave me a chance to live a real life. A good life.

I began to think that maybe I could do that for someone someday. I started collecting newspaper and magazine articles that would remind me. Horrible stories about children being abused and neglected. I don't know yet what I'm going to do about it, but I smooth out my stack and go through it every time I visit Marie.

I hear water running. The bedtime ritual has started. I roll up my papers and old treasures and replace them in the wall.

Jordan's acorn is still in my pocket. I can't get him out of my head. And I've realized something. The acorn and the stuff about potential were more than a pick-up line. It was like he saw a little piece of my soul in the oak leaf and responded in kind. That's never happened to me before.

I lay the acorn on top of my other things. This way I will always have it and the memory of how it felt when Jordan gave it to me.

I press the molding closed over the hole.

"Good night," I call to Marie, and slip out the front door before she can answer. Taking my leave quickly, like ripping off a Band-Aid, is the most humane way to go. For Marie and for me.

When I get to the sidewalk, I glance back over my shoulder. The oak tree still stands its strong, silent vigil over the house, just like I remember it.

"I'll get the carts." I intercept Tim the bagger at the front door of No Limit. He eyes me suspiciously and looks over his shoulder to see if this is a setup. Everyone hates doing the carts. "I need some fresh air, and besides, it's dead in here." I motion to the aisles empty of customers.

Tim steps aside and lets me pass. I dash out before Albert can question it. I hate doing the carts too, but not tonight.

Despite the fact that I know I should leave it alone and keep doing what I need to do to get out of Clairmont, I can't help it.

Jordan's outside.

He stands in front of McDonald's with a backpack thrown over his shoulder and a bag of M&M's in his hand. He waves when he sees me. "Kayla," he calls. I roll an errant cart over the choppy asphalt toward him.

"Hi." I try not to look too enthusiastic.

"Hi. I was hoping I would see you tonight." He smiles, and I get that spark again. I can't help my heart from dancing. "A buddy of mine texted me this joke, and it made me think of you." He awkwardly pulls his phone out of his pocket.

"Really? What was it?" I ask.

"Give me your number and I'll forward it to you." He looks down at his feet. I want to laugh. The slick, hundred-dollar-bill-waving Jordan is flustered asking me for my number.

There's only one problem. I don't have a cell phone.

Last year, Carol Alexander tried to add me to their family plan. She even picked out a fancy smartphone for me. Paige was thrilled that we would be able to chat, text, and Facebook at all hours. But I couldn't accept it. I have a job. I'm responsible for me. I didn't want to be beholden to the Alexanders any more than I already am.

A short time later, a Walmart bag appeared in my locker. Inside was a cheap, prepaid flip phone. The note on top said "For safety." It's still sealed in the box in the back of my closet.

"My phone's broken. I haven't had time to get it fixed." I try to look remorseful. I don't want Jordan to think I'm blowing him off.

He unzips his backpack and rips out a piece of notebook paper. He scribbles on it. "When your phone gets fixed, text me." He hands it to me and winks. I grip the cart to keep myself from melting into the pavement.

He points over my shoulder. "I think you have to go."

I glance behind me. Albert stands in the doorway of No Limit with his hands on his hips.

"I'll see you tomorrow?" Jordan's slick exterior cracks again. There's a hint of fear that I'm going to say no.

"I'll be here," I say. I'm always here.

My causal gait across the parking lot isn't fooling anyone. All day I've been jumpy and nervous. Since I started my shift, I've craned my neck a thousand times toward McDonald's. And every time, the setting sun turned the windows opaque and bounced the reflection of No Limit back at me.

I wrap my shaking fingers around the door handle and pull. Air whooshes out and sends my hair flying. The red hair tie I left at register two yesterday wasn't there today. I look wild. Out of control. Another reason to be nervous.

The restaurant is almost empty. It isn't the usual dinner hour. A girl with her hair constrained by a high, tight ponytail wipes down a table to my right. She glances up and smiles a weak smile of recognition at me in my apron—another minimum wage girl who would rather be doing something else.

I don't get much farther through the door before I see him. There. Sitting at the same table. A cup of coffee in front of the chair next to him.

Another guy—he's young, but he's a man, shaved head, the tattoo of a snake that curls up his well-toned biceps, a faint scar that runs from the back of his ear to under the neckline of his shirt—sits across from him. They both turn. I continue my not-so-subtle, casual walk across the restaurant.

Jordan stands up to greet me. "Kayla, meet my friend Drake."

The man has no expression on his face. He sticks out his hand. I take it. He squeezes hard like someone with something to prove.

Jordan motions for me to sit. I slide into the chair and grip the coffee, as if I'm freezing. Jordan smiles his happy smile that lights up his whole face. His friend's eyes bounce around the room. They stop and focus on me. His face is blank, but his look intensifies. I feel myself turn red under his scrutiny. Maybe coming here was a bad idea.

His phone rings. It takes two more rings before he moves. He tips his chin up at Jordan, and an unspoken moment passes between them. He leaves. I watch him walk through the door into the twilight.

"He didn't have to go," I say, but only to be polite. I'm glad he's gone, and not just because he seemed creepy. I want Jordan to myself.

"He's got stuff to do. Tell me about your day."

I raise the coffee cup to my lips. I already know that the coffee has cream and two packets of sugar. Jordan smiles again. Elation blossoms in my stomach. I push my hair behind my ear.

I don't know what's going on here. This isn't me. I don't do things like this. I don't *feel* things like this.

I play with the coffee lid on the table. He leans forward on his elbows. "Are you hungry? Do you want something to eat?" He reaches for his wallet in his back pocket.

Before I can stop myself, I wince at this offer. He doesn't seem to notice. "No thanks. I'm fine." He doesn't protest. I like that. Usually, I have to decline two or three times before people leave me alone.

I cast my eyes back down to the lid and roll it along the edge of the table.

"So, tell me about yourself, Kayla. All I know is that you work in the supermarket, you have a broken phone, and you're really pretty."

The blush brushes against my cheeks again. *I'm only sixteen, and you're nineteen,* I want to say. I should say it. I should stop this stupid fantasy here and now. Instead, I shrug.

"Where do you go to school?" His head bobs as he tries to make eye contact with me.

I force myself to look up. Marie taught me to always look someone in the eye when speaking to them. "Clairmont High School." There. It's done. We should not be having coffee together.

"That's pretty far from here, isn't it?" He pauses, but I don't answer. "It seems nice. Got all that space stuff going on."

"I'm on the dance team." The words erupt out of my mouth.

He smiles. "I thought you might be a dancer." He doesn't run his gaze over my chest or down to my leg half sticking out from under the table. He focuses on my eyes.

I stare back into his.

Warmth spreads up my whole body. My gaze drops down to his lips. And I want to kiss him. He's a perfect stranger, and I want to kiss him. So much it terrifies me.

I stand up fast. The chair tips on its hind legs. "My break's over." I turn and charge out to the parking lot. No Limit Foods glows white and red in the falling darkness. Even after the oak leaf, the acorn, and all the electric static zinging through my body, I can't do this. I can't like this guy. He's too old, too mysterious, too nice. There's got to be a catch. There's always a catch.

For the rest of my shift, every door swish, every throat cleared in my line, every shadow I see in my peripheral vision makes me jump. I was super rude. I don't think he will come in here or wait at the McDonald's again. I have killed it. Whatever it was starting to be.

And it hurts.

When ten o'clock rolls around and the fluorescent lights go dark, I'm exhausted. Every day, I catch the early bus across town, kick ass in my classes, go to dance team practice and to work, then do my homework by the light of the bare bulb in my bedroom. This is my life. It's only October and already my energy reserves are flatlining. I drag my raincoat on.

In the parking lot, Elton leans against his junk-filled station wagon. He watches me. I tip my hand up in a good night wave. He nods in response.

My feet feel extra heavy clomping on the wet sidewalk. I focus on putting one in front of the other. It stops me from thinking about Jordan and what I wanted to do.

I turn the corner onto Bluebird Lane, where thick trees create dark curtains on either side of the road to shield the good citizens of Clairmont from having to see Bluebird Estates. The streetlights are out on this stretch. I dig my hands into my pockets and try to will up the energy to move faster.

A car approaches. Its lights hit me square in the eyes and leave spots in my vision. It slows and pulls to the wrong side of the street. My side of the street. It's a dark-colored Camaro. I walk faster. The driver reverses, keeping pace with me. His window goes down.

"You wanna ride?"

I don't acknowledge him. He pulls even with me and sticks his elbow out. A snake curls up his biceps.

"Kayla, right? Let me give you a ride. It's not safe out here."

I turn toward Jordan's friend. His face is softer than in

McDonald's. He gives me a half, nonchalant smile, like he doesn't care what my answer is. It reminds me of Finn. Not the Finn I know now, but the Finn I remember from when I was about four years old. The one who produced a teddy bear one day, held it out, and half smiled, as if it didn't matter to him whether I liked it or not. But it did. A lot.

I can't accept a ride from Drake. I don't know who he is. Getting in that car could be much more dangerous than anything in the woods.

"No thank you." I keep walking.

The Camaro comes to a stop. "Suit yourself," he calls. The car moves forward.

"Wait," I yell. It's a rash, split-second decision—the kind I don't make. Maybe it's because I live in Bluebird Estates, or maybe it's because of Mom, or maybe it's because he reminds me of Finn. I run to his open window.

"The narcs are on to you." Surprise and confusion cross over his chiseled face. "I saw your deal go down with them the other night. They're probably building a case to have you picked up."

He gives me a salute before peeling out and disappearing into the darkness.

CHAPTER 7
BETSY

I stare at the tuna sandwich Mom made me before she left for the florist. I'm still alive. It's been almost a whole day since the party, and I'm still here. I don't know what that means.

It could mean I'm wrong about Adrian. That he really is the guy everyone thinks he is. Or it could mean he's messing with me. Dragging out the suspense.

The doorbell rings.

My heart beats in my ears like a freight train. I've thought about my death every day for seven months, but now that it's here, all I can think is *I don't want to die.*

Tears flood out of my eyes, and snot fills my nose. I drop down to the carpet and crawl. I won't let him see me.

The door handle jiggles.

The chain isn't attached. It's the only hope I have of living a few more seconds.

I leap through the air and slide the chain across. I land on my hands and knees and curl myself into a ball on the dusty mat where Mom meticulously wipes her shoes.

Knocking. My palms slam against my ears to block it out.

"Betsy?" A soft, distorted, feminine voice. "Betsy? I know you're home. Your mom told me to come get you."

I creep up to the peephole. She sees my eye and waves. Now she won't go away.

I wipe my face with the bottom of my shirt and open the door. Happy's always smiling face greets me on the other side. A shined-to-perfection, low-riding red truck idles in the street behind her.

"Are you okay?" she asks.

I nod, but I don't think she believes me. "About what happened yesterday at the party—"

She waves a hand through the air. "Don't worry. Adrian explained to everyone what happened."

"He did?"

"Yeah, he told us how that little girl bumped her head and started to cry, and you were taking her to her mom."

"Right," I say. Adrian knows what happened. Who I really am. But he has as much to hide as I do.

He wants to get me alone. Not leave any witnesses.

"Your mom said I should ask you if you wanted to come over and hang out." Happy tips her head in a thinking gesture, as if this, even in her childlike mind, is an odd assignment.

I lock the door behind me and follow her to the shiny red truck. Happy slides up against Tomás. I perch on the edge of the seat. Tomás raises his chin at me. He's still wearing the sunglasses.

No one puts a seat belt on. The radio is loud. Something deep and booming. Happy fiddles with it. Tomás turns his head. Happy changes it back and cuddles next to him.

We drive up and down streets I've never seen. I stop looking out the window and focus on my hands in my lap until we come to a mobile home sunken into the sand and surrounded by a chain-link fence. Other fenced-in houses line the makeshift dirt road. A conflagration of structures that put down roots together.

Tomás glances down at his phone and then at Happy. I step out of the truck. Across the road a snarling, snapping dog jumps up. Saliva flies out of its mouth, and the fence leans precariously under its weight. Happy doesn't seem to notice.

I follow her up the rickety wooden steps to the front door. The truck pulls away. For the first time, I see Happy's smile break.

Inside, it smells like old cooked food. Something spicy.

Lawrence has a video game controller. The tattoo on his forearm pulses as he mashes the buttons. Adrian has the other controller and stands a few feet away. Their backs are against the living room wall. When I step over the threshold, I see why. A flat-screen as tall as a person dances with explosions and thrashing animated characters.

Happy points at it. "Lawrence fixed some guy's car, and the guy paid him with the TV. Angie was so pissed."

We stand in a pile of boy detritus. A couple of beer bottles, a discarded shirt, food wrappers. Lawrence glances at me before his eyes snap back to the game. "What's up, Mount Rushmore?"

Adrian treats me like I'm invisible.

Happy opens the fridge and pulls out a bottle of beer.

"You can have one of these if you want." I shake my head. She puts it back and pops open a Coke—she doesn't offer me one—before plopping down on a threadbare couch.

I sit in a metal chair at a retro kitchen table with a Formica top. A math book is splayed open in front of me, resting next to a notebook erased to within an inch of its life.

"Angie won't marry Lawrence until he gets his GED," Happy says. "He just needs to pass the math section."

Happy's attention drifts back to the TV. She lies down and lets her feet hang over the armrest.

I stare at the notebook. My fingers pick up the pencil and twirl it around. The gamers cheer. I need something. Something to stop my heart from beating out of my chest. Something to make me forget for even a second that I'm in a room with Adrian. I flip the pencil around and start writing.

I'm on the third page of problems, showing every step in clear detail, when I realize Tomás has returned. Happy sits on his lap. Her shirt rides up. Her face is turned to meet his lips. His hand rubs her bare, fuzzy belly while they kiss deeply. It's beautiful and horrible. I can't look away.

Adrian catches me staring. I drop the pencil.

The sun, low on the horizon, sends orangey light through a window and illuminates the sides of Adrian's and Lawrence's faces. The dog growls and barks outside.

Tomás's phone buzzes. He glances at it, detaches himself from Happy, and leaves without looking back at her.

The ceiling caves in on me. *My phone is flashing.* I've been too distracted worrying about Adrian coming after me. I never called back after the party. When it gets dark, my time will be up. Adrian may be planning some creative way to kill me, but I'm still alive. That gives me a chance. If I don't get to that phone before it stops flashing, my death will be a sure thing.

I leap out of the chair. "I have to go," I say to Happy.

"You wanna ride?" Adrian asks, and raises an eyebrow like a challenge.

Fear shoots through me. This could be it. I can't be alone with him. I shake my head.

"You sure? It's a long way."

I shake my head again.

Happy is flat on the couch with her eyes closed. "Thanks for inviting me over," I whisper, and let myself out into the cooling evening air.

Rocks catch between my skin and the flimsy rubber of my flip-flops. I walk down the middle of the dirt road. On either side of me dogs slam into fences and bark until my hands cover my ears to make it stop. My face is wet. When I reach the end of this road, I won't know which direction to go. I've glanced behind me a hundred times, but Adrian hasn't followed.

Tomás's truck idles in front of the first house on the right. As I approach, I see him standing passively at the back of the house while a thin, red-haired man gestures wildly. Red drops his arms in resignation and reaches into his pocket. He pulls out a wad of cash and palms it to Tomás in exchange for a tiny plastic sack.

Tomás knows I'm here. I feel his eyes watch me through those dark glasses. My arms wrap around me, my head points down, I turn left.

Insects chirp. My feet bleed. My throat aches. I've been wandering for an hour, maybe two. Emerging stars sparkle in the endless darkening sky. I don't know where I am. The dirt road is paved again. A few houses dot large expanses of weed-covered desert. I reach an intersection. The stop sign has been graffitied with illegible swirls of purple spray paint. A wooden cross carved with "Manuel" in crooked block letters pokes out of the ground next to it. At its base, a photo of a young boy in a cheap frame is propped up against three candles in glass holders and a wilted bundle of grocery store flowers. One of the candles still burns.

I drop to my knees and lift the photo. The boy had beautiful, big brown eyes. Full of life and potential. I know what the cross means. It means he's dead.

I hear the car pull up behind me, but I don't turn. The driver gets out, and his feet crunch over the gravel. I'm too tired to be afraid.

"Put it down." Adrian rips the photo from my hands. He places it back against the cross, closes his eyes briefly, and mumbles something under his breath.

When his eyes snap open, they are full of fury directed at me. I sit back in the dirt and rest my chin on my hands. So now we're alone. What Adrian's been waiting for.

I point to the picture. "Who was he?"

"Lawrence and Tomás had another brother. Manuel. He was only eight when a guy in a truck ran the stop sign." Adrian points an accusing finger at me, as if I am the one who killed the child. I look away from him to a colony of ants disturbed by the commotion and scattering around the candles.

"Lawrence and Tomás were twelve and six. They were riding their bikes behind Manuel. They saw it happen. Their mother comes here every day to light the candles." I feel him still pointing, still accusing.

"I'm sorry," I say.

Adrian's heavy footsteps crunch back to his idling vehicle. "Get in."

He holds open the heavy door of an old, faded, red and rusting Ford Bronco. I turn my eyes back to the cross and shake my head. I'm not ready to go yet. I don't want to leave the smiling, happy child.

Adrian's fingers close tight around my upper arm. He pulls. I don't have a choice but to stand.

"Let go." My voice comes out calm, strong. He's almost as surprised at hearing it as I am. He lets go.

"Get in," he demands again.

I take a step toward the desert behind the altar. He bounces in front of me and blocks my path. When I move around him, he grabs my wrist.

"Stop," I snarl. I still have a little fight left in me, and I'm going to use it.

He releases me. I collect myself and try to think of what to do next. To find a way out of this.

I've got nothing.

"I know you aren't who you say." Adrian's voice is solid, controlled, terrifying. I have to stay calm. Not let him see the fear in my eyes. He steps forward, like he's trying to intimidate me with his size, which isn't too much bigger than my frame, but it works anyway. I shrink back.

"Don't mess with my family. They're good people. They would feed you if you had nothing to eat. Give you a bed to sleep in. Treat you like you belonged to us, no questions asked. I don't know what kind of game you're playing, but you"—he steps forward again—"do not get to take advantage of them."

I look into his eyes. He's angry for the wrong reason. This isn't why we should be alone at a dead end in the dark desert.

I clear my throat. "What do you think you know about me?" It's too late to deny it now.

"Come on, Betsy. Mount Rushmore isn't in North Dakota."

"North Dakota?" I repeat. *North Dakota?* That's what he thinks he knows about me?

I straighten up to my full height and try not to smile. "Please take me home," I say, and step around him to the passenger side door of the Bronco. The front seat is filled with debris—papers, schoolbooks, fast-food bags. I close the door and crawl into the backseat.

He slams the driver's-side door and throws the Bronco into gear.

"Why were you out here?" I ask. I should leave it alone; I shouldn't give away that I know who he is.

"I don't trust you." That's not an answer. His eyes watch

me in the rearview mirror. I tug up on the neck of my shirt, then drop my hand and silently curse myself.

"You were lost. Going in the wrong direction," he says.

"Thanks for picking me up." My voice is overly cheerful. I know he's lying. It's in the slight quaver in his voice. The nervous way he taps the steering wheel with his thumb. I might have been going in the wrong direction, but that isn't why he was out in the desert.

He slams on the brakes at a yellow light. I'm not wearing a seat belt, and I'm propelled forward. I put my hand on the floor to catch myself. Something rolls out from under the seat and taps my outstretched fingers. I peer down at it. Duct tape.

Adrian watches me. I sit up, leaving the duct tape on the floor. I glance over my shoulder into the back. A case of water and a box of granola bars were unseated by the sudden stop, and they sit askew on top of something. A length of rope.

Gotcha.

When Adrian stops in front of my house, I jump out. Neither of us says goodbye.

I get a drink of water. Change out of my sandy clothes. Wash my cut-up feet. My time ran out when I was still in the desert. The monster under my bed won't be flashing anymore. I survived once tonight, and it felt great. But it was only temporary. I know that.

Maybe it's time for this to be over. This isn't a life for me. Maybe no life would be better. Or maybe I don't mean that.

The jury's still out.

I kneel by the bed, unzip the duffel bag, and shake the

phone out. I press the call button. He waits until the fourth ring to pick up.

Silence. A heavy sigh. "Someone's been a naughty, naughty girl."

"I didn't know what time it was. I got lost." I won't beg him for my life.

Another sigh, overly dramatic. "Since I'm feeling charitable tonight, I'm going to let it slide."

My body flops to the floor.

"Really?" I ask like a little girl. I hate myself for it.

Paper crinkles. "Hmm, while you were out fooling around, a federal warrant was issued for your arrest."

I scooch my head under the bed. I'm surrounded by darkness.

He whistles through his teeth. "Murder. Wow, that's a tough one."

"But I didn't—"

"You know, the feds have the death penalty."

"I'm a minor," I whimper.

"I heard they've got some pretty good prosecutors." He laughs. "I'm sure if they want to fry you, they'll find a way."

"I'll be good. I promise. I'll be better about the phone. I won't leave it anymore. Please." *Please leave me alone.*

"I don't know that I trust you. The phone is obviously too big of a responsibility." His voice drips with condescension. "Two hours."

"What?"

"Your deadline is now two hours. You have two hours to call me back."

That means I'll have to take the phone everywhere—to school, even. "I can't—"

His breathing is rough and deep. "If they find out about you, they find out about me. And I will personally kill you with my own two hands before I let you fuck things up again," he growls.

"Two hours," I whimper. "I'll be good."

"You better be. One more slip and *pop*, that's the end of Betsy. So I suggest you get yourself a goddamn watch and a map and don't let it happen again."

The line goes dead.

CHAPTER 8
KAYLA

Marie, with her little bear next to her, waves to me from the bleachers. The boy looks lost. He closes in on himself and rests his head against Marie's upper arm. He's thinking it's too loud, too bright.

I love it.

Paige, beside me in line, smiles and waves at Marie. For tonight's performance, we wear black bodysuits and long, pink off-the-shoulder tops with sequins that shimmer around the gym and over the faces of the spectators. It's our third costume change this season. My hours at No Limit Foods aren't going to be enough to keep paying my share. At this rate, I'll be flat broke by Christmas.

The music kicks on, and I'm lost in the beat and the swirls and the turns. Nothing else matters. I'm surrounded by my friends; the energy is electric and the crowd, pumped. This is what I live for. This is why I keep going.

When we hit the final pose, the stands erupt. The giant

smiles we wear are true. Loose pieces of hair stick to the sweat on the back of my neck. Marie jumps to her feet, clapping furiously. She pulls the little boy up next to her. He half-heartedly slaps his hands together.

My eyes scan the bleachers. It's the usual crowd. The football team in their letter jackets whistling and catcalling, the parents dragging along younger siblings, the wannabes who refuse to clap and send glares like knives our way.

My gaze stumbles. In the upper corner on the right, a blank patch. No, not a blank patch. A person, a man, blending in. Arms spread out on the bleacher behind him. Legs apart.

Jordan gives me a thumbs-up.

He came. Even after I was so rude last week, he looked up our performance dates and came. To see *me*.

My heart sprints. I feel flush and faint, like the smile will never come off my face.

"What?" Paige asks. She looks up at the bleachers, but she doesn't see who I do.

"Nothing," I say, breathless. I don't want to tell her. Jordan is from the dirt and broken glass parts of my life. Paige belongs with the shiny sequins and bubble gum lip gloss. When they mix, you end up with bleeding feet and grit between your teeth.

Marie blows me a kiss. She leaves right away to get her little bear home for bed. The wannabes follow her out, critiquing our outfits, our hair, and who's put on a few pounds. The football players stand and shake out their numb butts.

"Pizza?" Sierra peers at each of our faces for agreement.

She doesn't have to ask. We always go to Zaparelli's after a performance. I glance back over my shoulder. The blank spot is empty.

Carol Alexander's BMW smells like leather and expensive perfume. I toss my bag into the back. Paige slides into the driver's side, checks the mirrors, checks the gauges, and adjusts the seat. She's had her license longer than I have, but she still freaks out every time she gets in the car.

"Seat belt," she says.

I point to my chest. "Already fastened."

She nods with approval. "Let's go." She puts the car in reverse, and we inch our way out of the parking space.

I met Paige in the middle of sixth grade. I knew who she was before that, of course. But I was the free-lunch foster kid, and she was someone magical. Girls followed her around, doing favors for her and complimenting her sweaters, just to get her attention. Paige could have been mean, she could have gotten away with whatever she wanted, but she didn't. She was nice to all of them.

Even so, I didn't dare try to be her friend. Not all the girls were like her.

She sat next to me in math class, and one morning she forgot her book. I slid my desk over and shared mine. Later at lunch, she waved me over to her table. I assumed right away that she felt sorry for me, but I was entranced. I nestled my free-lunch tray in between the colorful sacks and tiny Tupperwares filled with baby carrots and triangle-cut sandwiches.

A couple weeks later, I opened my locker and an envelope

fell out. Inside was a glitter-covered invitation to her birthday party. A lot of girls in our grade got one, but in that moment, I felt something I never did before. I felt special. Paige picked *me*.

The Alexanders' house is five times the size of Marie's. Paige has her own bathroom and a big bed with a pink satin comforter. I was sitting on that bed admiring a poster of ballerinas when I first met Carol Alexander.

Paige was opening presents with the rest of the girls downstairs. I had brought a present, but it was nothing like what the other girls were able to give her. I wandered upstairs before she could get to mine. Carol dashed in for something and stopped dead in her tracks when she saw me. Someone must have told her who I was, because I recognized her overly big smile coupled with pitying eyes. It was the look all the parents gave me.

She saw me staring at the poster and asked what I did after school. I shrugged. That night she called Marie, and on Monday, I was riding next to Paige in the back of Carol's car with a brand-new pair of dance shoes and a purple duffel bag containing a leotard and tights.

I've been Carol Alexander's charity case ever since.

Paige pulls into the parking lot of Zaparelli's at a crawl. By the time she peels her fingers off the steering wheel and we get inside, the dance team is already seated around a giant pizza. Two places set with empty plates, sodas, and straws wait for us.

Sometimes I wonder if Paige's driving is an act. She drives so slow that no matter where the dance team goes, by the time we get there, the money has already changed hands and my meal, movie ticket, or ice cream is already paid for. I know they have the best intentions. But it leaves a bad taste in my mouth. Grit between my teeth.

The front window reflects Sierra's laughing face and Paige's attempt to sneak another slice. Then it shows me Jordan. He's wearing an unbuttoned brown plaid flannel shirt over a white T-shirt and khaki pants. Neutral. He beckons for me to come outside.

I sit up ramrod straight. Paige starts a quick explanation about why she needs another piece. Sierra pauses midsentence. I force my shoulders to relax and put the girls back at ease.

I wait until Paige has her mouth stuffed full with the purloined pizza. "I'll be right back," I whisper.

The bells on the front door clang against the glass. The team turns as one to witness my exit. I bound to the edge of the building, away from the window, with Jordan on my heels. When I stop and spin around, I don't smile. He followed us here from school. There's no other explanation.

I'm equal parts freaked out and thrilled. Oil and water separating inside me. I'm so happy to see him again, and it scares me.

"What are you doing here? You're creeping me out."

"No I'm not." He takes a step forward. My back brushes up again the brick wall.

"Yes you are. All I have to do is scream, and the whole team and Mr. Zaparelli will come running."

He presses farther forward and places a hand on the bricks next to my head.

"You're biting your lower lip, your fingers are rubbing your collarbone, and you keep moving that piece of hair away from your eye."

I drop my hands. I didn't even know I was doing that.

He laughs. "People's bodies give away what's hiding in the dark recesses of their minds. Things they don't even know they're thinking."

He steps back. I'm finding it hard to take much air into my lungs. My adrenaline spikes. I try to convince myself that it's because this guy I hardly know is following me around. But that's a lie. I feel the current course between us. I lean in to it.

He laughs. "Your hand is back on your collarbone."

Dammit.

His lips move to my ear. "I loved watching you dance." The little hairs on my neck prickle from his breath as he whispers, "McDonald's tomorrow. I'll buy you a coffee."

He turns and walks into the darkness to a Jeep parked on the street. I stay frozen, my back against the damp bricks, knees shaking. My brain duels with my heart. Jordan's wrecking my concentration. He's getting me in trouble at work. He keeps questionable company. But I like him. *Really* like him.

When I regain my composure, I stumble back inside Zaparelli's. The bells on the door clang again, and the whole restaurant turns to look. I'm still hot and flustered. My eyes flit to the dance team.

Paige's face has concern written all over it. Sierra raises her eyebrows, waiting for me to dish the secret. I pull out my chair, and I sit on my hands.

I have to say something to break the silence, but I can't look at him. I can't do anything but grip the coffee cup with both hands. I'm wearing my apron with a giant HELLO MY NAME IS sticker because my name tag is missing today. My cheeks burn. "So you moved here from Florida?" I ask.

Jordan takes a slug from his coffee. Black, lid on.

A single flower, a wildflower from the woods, sits on the table between us.

"You don't have to be nervous," he says.

I'm about to protest, but then I realize it wouldn't do me any good. I am nervous. Butterflies dancing the tango in my stomach.

He reaches across the table to touch my hand. "Most human communication is nonverbal. Everybody does it all the time. I'm good at picking up on it. It's sort of a hobby of mine."

I freeze every muscle in my body. I won't even let my eyes blink. I can't let him see how I feel. I have to stop whatever this is now before I fall any deeper.

He pulls back. "Florida, yes. A few months ago. My mom came out here first, after my dad passed away."

"I'm sorry," I say. His hand is still on the table. I tap it limply. It is the least comforting gesture on the planet, but it is all the physical contact I can handle.

"Thanks," he says. "It happened years ago. I lived with my uncle in Florida until I finished high school. Then I had nothing else to do. So here I am." He shrugs and picks at his coffee lid.

"I live with my mom at Bluebird Estates." It feels better to get it out in the open.

"I know," he says. I shift in my chair. He picks up on my discomfort. "Drake's seen you walking at night," he adds quickly. He looks up. "You shouldn't do that. It isn't safe."

The girl with the high ponytail picks up a discarded tray from the table next to us. I didn't realize how young she was before. I bet she barely makes the fourteen-year-old work cutoff. She could still be in middle school. She's pretty. Flawless dark skin, big eyes, a defiant diamond stuck to the side of her nose.

Jordan watches her wipe down the table with a smelly rag. Something is going through his mind, but I don't have his superpowers to determine what it is. He nods slightly, like he's come to a decision and turns back to me.

"You should let me give you a ride home after your shift."

The duel inside my body is back. I want to scream *yes!*, but the reasonable side of me knows that I can't do that. Jordan is like a drug. I've taken a hit. Now I've got to stop before he becomes an addiction.

"I have a ride home tonight." Lie. I glance at my watch. Time has moved with superspeed. Even if I run across the parking lot, I'll be back late. "Thanks for the coffee and the flower."

He tips his cup at me.

Albert stands just inside the door of No Limit. He taps his wrist. "Someone's been a naughty girl. That's your first strike, Kayla." He shakes his head. It doesn't take a superpower to see his disappointment in me.

———

My tired feet feel like lead weights stuffed into my shoes. I have too much on my mind to pay attention to the cracked sidewalk and the discarded beer cans. I need to stay away from Jordan. My plan to get out of Bluebird Estates is working. I only have to hang in there for another year and a half.

Jordan makes me want to skip school, skip dance team, skip work just to sit with him and sip lukewarm coffee. I feel buzzed and on edge and fuzzy and twitchy, all at the same time.

I like that. And I want more.

A soft rustle comes from the trees along my path. Some brave animals stubbornly make their homes in the strips of wild between the even wilder streets and housing blocks.

It comes again. The streetlight above me blinks on and off, not giving my eyes time to adjust to the dark. I walk faster. The rustling increases. It's following me.

It's probably a drunk lost in the trees, or a Halloween prank. But with what happened to the two girls on the news, I don't want to take a chance. I run. The hood of my raincoat flops down over my shoulders. My heavy backpack slaps me, forcing extra air out of my lungs with each stride.

At the corner of Bluebird Lane, whatever is after me isn't trying to disguise itself anymore. It's between me and Bluebird Estates, driving me back the way I came. I turn left and dash across the street. My right shoe is untied. The laces drag through puddles and threaten to trip me. This end of Bluebird Lane is pitch-dark and even more overgrown. I feel like I'm entering a fairy-tale woods with the big bad wolf hot on my heels.

I risk a glance over my shoulder. A man dressed in solid

black, his face covered by a ski mask, charges out onto the sidewalk.

He crosses the street.

Terror ricochets through my body. I run without seeing what's in front of me. This is my night. I'm going to be Girl Number Three.

Bluebird Lane is a dead end. An abandoned house with rotting wood and broken steps sits nestled in the tall weeds and baby trees. I leap onto the porch. Something sticks into my left ankle and almost brings me down to my knees. I don't feel any pain, just my foot twisting and throwing me off balance. I shove it back underneath me and keep moving.

The front door of the house is long gone. I dive into the blackness.

I land on a mass of smelly, drooling, writhing bodies. I crawl to a corner and curl myself into a ball. A woman, eyes rolling around in her head, pats my arm. In her drug trip, I must look like a small child. Maybe even her small child.

A tweaker with no front teeth, patchy hair on his chest, and wearing only dirty underwear, staggers over to me. The man in black is on the porch. Wood cracks under his weight.

The tweaker flops down in front of me and blocks the door. His reeking breath blows over a split, scabby lip onto my face. His hands paw at my raincoat. All I can think about is hiding. Even here, even this way. Black boots step into the doorway. The moonlight is behind him. I can't make out any details. I sink farther down. The man in black doesn't come inside. He makes a sound of disgust.

The wood on the porch cracks again, and the sound of

heavy footsteps tromping over muddy earth fade into the distance. I pull my knee up tighter to my chest and kick the junkie hard in the stomach. He rolls to the floor, taking my pink-striped tennis shoe with him. I jump up. Tears run down my face. Blood seeps through my jeans above my ankle.

I hobble to the door in one shoe and one sock, not caring about the exclamations coming from the bodies I step on. I slowly emerge. The air is cool and sweet. I suck in a lungful through my nose to try to erase the smell of rotting flesh.

It's too blurry to see where I'm going. I feel the pain now. My ankle burns. My sock is soaked. Sobs crash out of my mouth. I stumble down the center of Bluebird Lane. He's waiting for me in the darkness, blocking my way home. I feel his eyes, patient, in between the trees.

I head toward the light.

The parking lot of No Limit is empty. Not even Elton is parked in his usual corner. It glows like daytime. I sit on the curb by the front entrance. An ancient pay phone hangs on the bricks behind me. It doesn't work. The change box was busted out years ago. Besides, who would I call? The police? Carol Alexander?

I put my head down on the cool cement next to a round of smashed, blackened gum. At least I will see him coming. When he comes back to make me Girl Number Three, I'll get a good look at him.

Car tires roll over the asphalt. I'm too spent. I can barely lift my head. Somehow, I still have my backpack. Its weight presses me down farther. The driver jumps out of the car and walks with a steady gait toward me. If it's the man in black, then I'm Girl Number Three. I don't have any fight left.

A large hand rests on my shoulder. I blink to clear my vision and follow the hand up. A snake lined in green ink with a glowing red eye hisses at me.

Drake doesn't make eye contact. He doesn't say anything as he helps me up and into his Camaro. He buckles me in. When we get to Bluebird Estates, he walks me to the main entrance.

"Why are you helping me?" I ask in a dried-out, cracking whisper.

"Jordan seems to like you."

I push open the lobby door. It clicks locked behind me. Through the scratched glass, I watch Drake walk away.

My eyes move down toward his shoes. On his feet are heavy black boots caked with mud.

CHAPTER 9
BETSY

Angie walks purposefully over to me. "Are you sure you don't want anything? Not a piece of toast or a tortilla or something?" I shake my head. She scowls. I'm taking up a table where she could be getting tips.

It's Saturday. Mom has to work, so I rode with her to the strip mall. The door that doesn't jingle let me in. I sit at a corner table and sip a glass of water. I'm trying. Trying to make them see me as normal girl and not like a narc, an escaped convict, an alien, or any of the other rumors I've heard swirling around me. Trying to keep an eye on Adrian.

Now that I know for sure who he is, I have to do something to stop him, even though all I want to do is be at home, curled up under the covers of my bed.

C&J's has a weekend breakfast special. On the table next to me is a finished plate smeared with drying yellow egg yolk. It sits on top of a twenty-dollar bill.

I watch Adrian out of the corner of my eye. He makes

small talk with customers as he refills their coffee or brings out extra toast. When his glance flits in my direction, his face tightens, his eyes narrow, his lips purse.

He whips the eggy plate off the table and stuffs the twenty into the pocket of his apron. His clenched fists and tense biceps dare me to say something. I take a gulp of water.

He leaves to deposit the dish in the kitchen. When the door flaps open, the sound of singing briefly fills the restaurant. A deep, rich voice carrying a melodic Spanish tune. Angie rolls her eyes and refills a glass.

She spins toward me with the orange juice carafe and eyes the check with the ghostly impression of the eggy plate. Her glare lasers in on my face. She grabs the check and storms back to the kitchen.

Angie thinks I'm weird. Maybe, like Adrian, she thinks I'm here to wreck her family. But her mom likes my mom, so there's really nothing Angie can do about me.

When Lawrence and Rosie show up, I stand to leave, but I'm too late. Rosie rips her hand out of her father's and races toward me. She waves a piece of paper at my stomach. "I made you a picture."

I look down at the colorful swirls on the page. I take it gingerly between two fingers. Her little face peers up at me. It's sparkly, gleaming, brand-new. It doesn't have lines from worrying, a down-turned mouth, or pinched brows. For her, the world is still beautiful, still exciting. Still worth living in.

I can't look at her. I can't smile sweetly back at her like everyone else. She reminds me of too much. Too much of what happened. Too much of what I did.

"Thanks," I whisper, and hold the page away from my body. Rosie giggles and bounces up and down, as if she's in one of those bouncy fun houses.

Lawrence catches her by the ponytail. "Let's go. Giddyap." She makes a loud, high-pitched neigh and gallops to the kitchen.

I don't look at the drawing again. It brushes my leg as I walk out of the strip mall. I glance behind me. C&J's Mexican Restaurant is out of sight. I suppress the sob wanting to leave my chest, crumple up the page, and toss it in the dark hole of a trash can.

The black monster is in my pocket. It doesn't fit well, and I'm wearing a long shirt to keep it hidden. I keep checking for messages. If the buzzing doesn't alert me, I'll miss the new deadline. Then he'll come and kill me with his own two hands.

I wander down the sidewalk, past the school, through one dust-covered traffic light after another. Even though it's November, the sun still shines fiercely. It's never stopped shining in the almost eight months I've been here. I push the sleeves of my shirt up.

As I wait at a red light for the Walk man to glow, a vehicle rolls to a stop in my peripheral vision. A wave of paranoia washes over me. There are others out there who would like to make me suffer before they killed me with their own two hands. The hairs on the back of my neck stand up. My lungs involuntarily constrict. I am out in the sunlight on a street corner. Exposed. There's too much cross traffic to run.

The vehicle pulls up next to me. I keep my eyes straight

ahead. My hair is short and dark. I'm super skinny. I'm covered up to my neck. I have to stay calm. Panic will destroy the illusion.

The window rolls down.

"Hi, Betsy!" the occupant screams. Happy hangs halfway out the window. Her growing belly throws her balance off, and she pitches forward. Tomás grabs her shoulder to keep her from falling out.

I wave.

"We're going to my dad's house. You wanna come?" Her mouth smiles like usual, but her face isn't a happy one. It's a manic mask of a smile. Her eyes want to cry.

"Sorry, I can't," I say. The light has turned. The glowing Walk man is blinking.

"Okay," Happy says, and maneuvers herself back into the seat. "See you later?"

I nod. They pull away as the light turns yellow. I mash the Walk button again and cross my arms.

A black sedan with dark tinted windows was waiting patiently behind Tomás's truck. It never honked. It pulls even with me now. I can't see the driver. But I feel eyes on me. My skin crawls again. It's not my usual, constant, surface-level panic like before. This feels real. Really bad. I clutch the top of my shirt against my neck and slap a hand over the pocket containing the black monster.

A flash of light from inside the car. It has to be the sun reflecting off something. It can't be anything else. Yeah, right. Thinking the best of people is what got me sent to this dot of a desert town in the first place.

Across the street there's nothing but empty lots and a few scattered houses. I glance over my shoulder. There's a drugstore with a couple of cars in the parking lot.

I throw my hands up, like I can't wait for the light a second longer, and turn on my heels. I march through the rocks separating the drugstore from the sidewalk with purpose, as if there's someone in there waiting for me. Someone big and tough. Possibly armed.

I have to turn back and look. The light is green. The sedan doesn't move. I'm overreacting. It's probably someone texting and not paying attention.

When I reach the doors of the drugstore, the sedan pulls away slowly. Not the quick jump-start of a surprised texter. I make sure the monster is still covered and then go inside.

The drugstore is tiny. Not a chain. A locally owned place, where the pharmacist and the guy working the front know everyone who comes through the door. When I cross the threshold, the guy's taken aback. "Can I help you?"

"Tampons," I mumble. He blushes and points to the rear of the store. I disappear into the aisles and position myself in front of the feminine hygiene products and condoms. No one will bother me here.

My imagination goes into overdrive, and I can't catch it. It comes up with fifty unique and interesting ways I could die. I take a breath and try to get ahold of myself. I can't afford to have a complete breakdown in the tampon aisle. What kind of rumors would be started about me then? Pregnancy? Abortion? I will casually, nonsuspiciously browse the store until I'm sure the car is good and gone.

Then I will go back to the flower shop and pretend it never happened.

I wander to the end of the aisle, where there's a rack of tabloid newspapers. I pick one up. Over a photo of a thick forest with police tape superimposed onto it, the headline reads "Serial Killer on the Loose?" I suck in a breath and turn the page.

The story takes up the center spread. "Clairmont's Lady Killer." On the left is a picture of a rundown apartment complex. An officer holds out his hand to block the reporters from going farther.

On the right, grainy pictures of young women sit above columns of text describing what happened to them. I don't read it. I don't want to know. The scariest thing on the page, the thing that makes me close the paper and hang it back on the rack, is the photo at the bottom. A tennis shoe with a pink stripe lying in the grass by the side of the road.

A violent chill runs through my body. I retake my spot in front of the tampons. The door to the pharmacy jingles like a good door should.

"Adrian, what's up, man?" the guy at the front says. I hear the slapping of hands. I crouch. Make myself small so I can't be seen from the door. I feel Adrian move around the store, but he never comes down my aisle.

He must be in a hurry, because it's only a couple of minutes before I hear him thud one of the red plastic shopping baskets on the counter.

"Is Rosie sick?" the guy asks. He beeps the contents of the basket over the scanner.

I peek up over the panty liners. Adrian has several different kinds of children's medicine splayed out on the counter.

"Yeah, she must have picked something up from pre-school. Poor little thing." His voice is steady, practiced. He's a good liar.

"Give her a hug for me," the guy says, and hands Adrian the change from the crumpled twenty he used to pay.

"I will. Thanks." Adrian glances behind him. I duck.

The guy has forgotten about me. He jumps when I emerge. "Did you find what you were looking for?" I shrug and place a pack of gum on the counter. I have to buy something. I don't want him getting suspicious and calling the cops.

Teddy gave me ten bucks. Like an allowance. Like I'm supposed to be able to buy anything with ten bucks. I lay the bill down on the counter and collect my change.

I turn to go, but Adrian hasn't left. His Bronco still sits in the parking lot. "I forgot something," I say to the counter guy, and dive into the first aisle. I walk to the end and peer out the window at Adrian. The guy is still watching me, so I finger a pair of big socks for people with diabetes.

A dusty silver hybrid pulls up next to Adrian. A woman steps out. She is probably in her midtwenties. No makeup. Glossy black hair pulled back in a messy ponytail. Standard T-shirt and jeans. She's gorgeous without even trying. I feel a prick of envy in the middle of my gut.

Adrian unloads things from her car into his. I can't see what they are from my vantage point, but the woman twitches, like she's nervous to be out in the open. When Adrian slams the door, the woman takes another look around. She presses something into his hand. The sun catches it before it disappears into his pocket. It's round and glows amber. Like a prescription bottle.

The woman doesn't look like a dealer. Her face is set in fierce determination, as if she's going to fix the world and doesn't care who gets in her way. She pats Adrian on the shoulder. He lights up like a little boy being promised a puppy.

That thing pricks in my stomach again.

Counter Guy is still watching. Adrian pulls away. I take the diabetes socks up to the front and put them and the rest of my allowance down.

"You should be careful," he says.

My heart that I thought had exhausted all its beats for the day revs up again. I look up at his face. Does he know? Does he know who I am?

He hands me the socks and my receipt—no bag. "There's some pervert driving around taking pictures of kids. I bet he'd want to get a picture of a pretty girl like you."

I don't think he's flirting. It's more like he wants to protect me from the big bad world.

No such luck, dude. It's way too late for that.

Happy is sitting alone in Tomás's truck in front of C&J's. She doesn't notice me coming up behind her. In the side mirror, I see her swipe a finger under her eye.

When I appear in her vision, her face cracks open into her Happy whole-face smile. She rolls the window down. "Hi," she says. "Cute socks." She points to the industrial black knee-highs in my hand.

She turns away and wipes her eyes again. "Do you want to see what my stepmother gave me for the baby?" She turns back around with a white onesie—the kind that come three to a pack at Walmart.

"Wasn't that nice of her?" There's no snark in her voice. She's actually asking. Seeking confirmation. I nod.

"We couldn't stay long. They had to take the girls to their soccer game. My stepmom has two daughters. They are five and seven. They're cute. The house only has two bedrooms, so they have to share." Happy is talking more frantically than usual. I don't think she even realizes that the words keep leaking faster and faster out of her mouth. "That's why I can't live with my dad. They don't have any room." She pauses and bites her still smiling lip. "Plus, my stepmom hates me."

Watching Happy crumble is like watching rainbows and kittens and birthday cake rot and turn black.

Adrian has resumed his busboy duties inside C&J's. Through the window, his eyes shoot daggers at me, like I made Happy cry.

"Do you want to come inside the flower shop?" I ask her. She nods and opens the truck's door. My eyes can't help but slide to her lower half as she maneuvers herself down to the pavement. She sees me looking and wraps her arms around her stomach. She blinks hard. For the first time, I see it in her face. Shame.

My cheeks burn. "I didn't mean to . . ." I really didn't. The last thing on earth I want to do is to make Happy feel bad. Tears well up in my eyes.

"It's okay." Happy's smiley mask is back on again. "It's kind of there. You can't not look at it."

"Do you know what it is?" I whisper. "A boy or a girl?"

Happy shakes her head. "I hope it's a boy. Things would be easier for him." She points back at her stomach. "He won't end up like this."

CHAPTER 10
KAYLA

Lots of men wear boots. And this is Clairmont. It's muddy. If I didn't walk through a bunch of puddles on the way home, my shoes would always be covered in mud. It's totally plausible—barely even a coincidence—that Drake would be wearing muddy boots.

The school nurse is holding the wad of tissues and masking tape I used to cover the slash on my ankle. She stares at me.

"Sorry? What?" I ask.

She narrows her eyes. "How'd this happen?"

I shrug. "I'm a klutz. I tripped." She knows I'm lying. I force a smile. I'm worn to the bone. I couldn't tell Mom what happened, couldn't sleep, couldn't stand at the bus stop without glancing over my shoulder every ten seconds.

She clicks her tongue and shakes her head but rinses my ankle with saline and places a sterile bandage over it.

She presses extra bandages into my hand. "Keep it clean.

If it starts to look infected, come back right away. And no dance team for a couple of days."

I nod. I couldn't dance right now even if my ankle were fine.

Jordan jumps up from the table when he sees my gray-tinged, hollowed-out face and limping body. I grab the coffee and chug it. "Will you give me a ride home?" I don't wait for him to answer before turning and walking back to the door. The girl with the diamond in her nose stares at me. Our eyes meet. She gets it. My warning to her.

Jordan leans against the side of his blue soft-top Jeep in the drizzle. He opens the door for me. I climb inside and wince as my ankle taps the seat. He gets in, and I wait for him to ask me what happened. He doesn't. Maybe Drake told him something. Or maybe he's just giving me space. I like that.

He drives to Bluebird Estates without prompting me for directions. "Do you live around here?" I ask.

He shakes his head. "No, on one of the islands." He waves a hand dismissively.

"Oh." I sink down into the seat. We're inland. There's no water nearby. I feel my adrenaline rise. Why would he hang around No Limit in the bad part of Clairmont when he had to have passed a hundred nicer stores to get here?

After last night in the woods, I don't feel like I can trust anyone. I glance down at his feet. He's wearing canvas tennis shoes. They're perfectly clean.

When we pull into the parking lot of Bluebird Estates, a cleansing relief washes over me. I need to get out of this Jeep.

He reaches for my arm. "Please, Kayla. I want to talk to you." His fingers wrap around my wrist gently. He's letting me know I can pull away. He'll let me leave.

I open the door a crack as a compromise. The dome light goes on. Shadows create black holes where his eyes should be. I take my arm back, but I stay in the car.

"I used to live in a place like this in Florida. When I was little we lived in a house. Then my mom got sick. My dad worked in a factory, but he didn't make enough to cover the medical bills. We lost the house and pretty much everything else." He doesn't look at me as he speaks, but I can see the pain on his face twisting his profile.

"We ended up living off the government. Mom got better. She was able to go back to work. Her first week back, Dad's accident happened." His voice cracks. It's raining hard outside. I close the door all the way.

He's quiet for a long time. I want to ask, but I don't. I understand some things are too hard to talk about. When anyone has asked me about the night I was five and got taken away for the second time, I shake my head and change the subject.

He takes a deep breath. "The police came looking for Mom. I was twelve. I'll never forget that moment before I opened the door. I was eating ice cream and watching some stupid cartoon. The cops wouldn't tell me what they wanted. They asked me over and over again where Mom was. She worked as a nurse in the hospital. By the time they found her, she already knew."

"I'm sorry," I whisper. During his story, I couldn't help but lean toward him. Our shoulders are almost touching.

"A million lawyers came out of the woodwork trying to convince Mom to sue. They said the factory's safety record was abysmal. It was our chance to teach them a lesson. But Mom couldn't see through her grief. She gave up. I had to make our meals, wash the clothes, and go to the store.

"When the factory offered her a big check, she took it. But the ghost of Dad was everywhere. Mom couldn't cope. She sent me to my uncle's house, and she left. Months later, she called and said she was living in a big house on an island. I was just starting high school then, and I didn't want to leave my friends.

"My uncle's a good guy, but he doesn't know anything about kids. He made sure I was fed and had what I needed, but other than that, I was on my own."

He points at Bluebird Estates. "This is more my home than the island. Mom thought moving far away and buying a huge house would make things better. But she works six shifts a week, and I can't stay in that blood money house. Places like this remind me of a time when we were all together. We didn't have much, but we were a family."

He rubs his eyes. Overwhelming sadness and sympathy fill me. My story is different, but I understand in my core what he's feeling. I reach for his hand and cover it with mine. He flips his palm over, and our fingers intertwine.

"Sorry," he says. "I didn't mean to lay all that on you."

"I'm glad you did." And I am. I feel like we're equals now. In this world facing our demons together. It's too late for me to let go of him now.

But there is something I have to ask after what happened last night. "Who's Drake?"

He's alarmed by the question. Maybe even jealous. My heart lifts in my chest.

"We were friends in high school. Right after I moved here, his mom kicked him out. He had nowhere to go, so he made his way to Clairmont. He's staying with me until he can get his life sorted out."

"Oh," I say, and focus on our hands. Drake saved me from spending the night weeping on the sidewalk of No Limit. If Jordan doesn't already know, I'm not going to out Drake as a dealer.

"I should go." I don't want to, but the last twenty-four hours weigh on me. I need to sleep. I need to figure out how to do all the things I have to while still keeping Jordan in my life.

Jordan grips my hand and gazes out his window. "I'm going back to Florida for a few days to help my uncle with something."

He turns to me. In the darkness of the Jeep and the dim glow of Bluebird Estates, his eyes have character. They sparkle with flecks of otherwise-hidden gold. "I'll be back on Saturday. Will you be okay?"

Panic surges through me. I glance over my shoulder into the dark woods surrounding Bluebird Estates. I don't want him to worry, so I give him my bright Clairmont Explorers Dance Team smile. "Yeah, I have a ride for the rest of the week."

I open the door, reilluminating the dome light. The gold in his eyes disappears. They're plain muddy brown again. He pulls my arm into him before letting go. "I'm glad we met."

"Me too."

I use Paige's phone to call in sick to No Limit. I don't know what else to do. I've watched the news every day. They haven't caught him. The man in black is still out there. The thought of passing through those woods again by myself makes my vision go blurry and my breath quicken.

My ankle hurts. I skip dance team and ride the bus home. And I sit in my tiny room in Bluebird Estates and listen to toilets flush and bass pound and the neighbors fight.

I tell Mom I have a cold. She comes in and out looking concerned, offering me things, like I'm an invited guest. At dinnertime, she brings me a bologna sandwich on white bread with mayonnaise. The food stamper special. We don't pay rent on this dump, the utilities are taken care of, and the government covers the cost of the generic food I bring home from No Limit.

We're parasites.

I choke down the sandwich, only because Mom is watching, proud of herself for doing something motherly. She wishes she were the kind of mother who bustled around in an apron making pancakes and cherry pies.

I would rather she take out the trash.

A woman comes out of Finn's as I'm opening the trash chute. Her hair's frizzed up and sprayed. Her tight top isn't able to contain her sagging boobs. Her miniskirt's still pushed up in the back. She pulls it down. Her eyes travel from the top of my head down to my feet and back up again. She sneers. "This the girl, Finny?" she calls into the apartment behind her.

Finn steps out wearing only boxers. "Yeah, that's her."

I'm trapped between them and the stairs. The only place to go is down.

"She's kind of fat," I hear the woman say as I turn the corner.

Calling it a lobby makes it sound like it should have squishy chairs, a front desk, and a doorman. It's actually a small entrance that smells like pee. The open mouths of broken mailboxes yawn against the wall. The first-floor hallway shoots off from both sides. Some of the lighting is out; some of it blinks uncontrollably. This place is a death trap. Someday, it will either collapse or catch fire and take us all down with it.

I flatten myself into a dark corner until I hear the woman's spiked heels on the stairs. Her pupils are dilated. She sways back and forth, like she's fighting a heavy wind. Tomorrow, this whole night will have been erased from her memory.

She walks with a pseudoseductive swing of the hips to a car parked on the street. I step out of my hiding place and up to the glass. It's a black Camaro. Of course it is. Does Drake think he's smarter than the narcs? The hooker leans into the front window. Her skirt rides up to reveal a red thong underneath. Drake palms her something. She steps back, satisfied, and stumbles toward the woods.

I march out the front door. Drake shouldn't treat Jordan like this. Jordan took him in. He shouldn't repay that kindness by dealing drugs.

Drake is watching the hooker disappear into the trees when I knock hard on the window. He jumps.

As the window lowers, I place my hands in clear sight on top of the car. If the narcs are watching, I don't want them trying to bust me.

"Kayla," Drake says curtly. I examine his eyes to see if he's high. I don't find any signs. I've never seen any signs that he takes the drugs he sells.

"Are you trying to get caught?" I snap.

"Caught doing what?"

"Seriously? I just watched you palm something to that hooker. All of Bluebird Estates saw it."

He sighs. "Don't worry about it, Kayla."

"Yeah, right," I scoff. "What if Jordan finds out? You live in his house. What if you get him busted too?" I'm so mad I could burst into tears.

Drake turns his head and examines me. "You really care about him, don't you?"

I nod. My cheeks tighten. I blink rapidly. I'm not going to cry in front of Drake.

He sighs again. "Okay, Kayla. If it will make you feel more comfortable. No more drugs."

"Really?" I ask.

"Really," he says, and flashes me a little boy grin that sends my memory right back to the old Finn again.

It almost makes me believe him.

"Kayla, Kayla, Kayla." Albert shakes his head. I sit in a hard plastic chair in his immaculate office. He stands over me with crossed arms. "You called in sick three days in a row. I'm gonna need a doctor's note."

"I don't have one." I look down at the cheap throw rug covering a stain in the even cheaper carpet.

He sighs. "That's strike two."

A jogger finds the rapidly decomposing body of Finn's hooker a week later. The story's buried in the second half of the news. Another lost soul dying alone in the woods. The cops think it's an overdose. With all their resources tied up looking for the attacker of those two girls, the hooker is not worthy of an investigation.

CHAPTER 11
BETSY

My fingers pluck a chip from Happy's plate. My teeth chew. Salt coats my tongue.

It's one tiny thing. No one will ever know. I've been a model citizen. I check the black monster a hundred times a day. When it blinks, I take care of it. I don't wait. I don't play chicken.

It's not even a thing, really.

I take another chip.

It won't be much of a risk. I will be in public. I will be doing what people do. It will be normal. Everyone goes on Facebook, and I have to know. I have to know what has happened without me. What I've missed.

I realize it's quiet. Happy's fork dangles in midair in front of her mouth. Tomás watches me from over his phone. Adrian stands frozen by the table, holding a water pitcher.

The chip shreds my throat.

———

The San Justo public library smells funny. Like too many bodies and books with dirt glued to their plastic wrappers by decades of children's snot. I hunt through my wallet for the library card I don't remember getting. But it's there. Shiny and brand-new.

I glance around. It's after school, so the library is full of people. Mothers with huge bags of books browse Thanksgiving displays while their uncooperative kids flop around behind them. A few people I recognize from school flirt at tables while they pretend to do their homework. Middle schoolers sock one another in the arms until a librarian scolds them.

Most of the computers are full, but I find an empty one at the end of a row. The guy behind me is playing solitaire. The guy to my right—acne-scarred face, bad teeth—is pursuing smiling, fake women on a dating site. He looks over at me. I snap my eyes down.

I turn my screen ever so slightly away from him. A librarian organizing books on a cart gives me a dirty look. I turn the screen back. I wait for her to say something. To stomp over, hit the power button on the computer, and demand I leave. She stops paying attention to me. Soon, no one is paying attention. I'm invisible.

I log in with my library card number and open the browser. To spite my face, a smile creeps across my lips.

For twenty minutes, I fill my head with everything I want to know. My insides feel glee and despair in equal parts, mixed together to form a paste that coats my internal organs.

Thirty minutes. I go deeper and deeper. The man on the

dating site leaves, frustration evident in his gait. The chair next to me pulls out. I'm too wrapped up in getting away with it to notice who sits down next to me.

"Whatcha doing, Sport?"

I calmly, despite the way my heart thrums, click the browser closed.

I turn and look Teddy in the eye. Thirty minutes of freedom has made me cocky. "Homework."

"Sure, homework," he says, nodding. "For what class?"

"Life Skills." My voice is steady. It gives me a thrill.

He shakes his head. "They consider Facebook a life skill? Well, that makes me feel old." He laughs and shoots the librarian, whose attention is now focused squarely on us, an *aw shucks* grin.

"What are you doing here?" My gaze goes down. My shoulders slump.

He taps a gardening book on the table next to the keyboard. "Your mother was saying she thought some flowers in front would be nice. I told her I'd find something that would be pretty."

He stands up. "You want a ride home?"

My head shakes even though my legs yearn for any escape from having to walk the two miles over unfamiliar terrain.

"See you later." He points the gardening book at me like it's a threat.

My house glows like a beacon in a wasteland. Sickly, sticky bushes still in their nursery pots stand guard by the front door.

I go inside. Mom is flushed and humming softly in the kitchen. I stop in the doorway and drop my backpack.

On a rickety, secondhand desk, sits a computer. An old colossus tethered to the wall. The chunky monitor points toward the kitchen, allowing for free viewing from everywhere in the room.

Mom hurries over and places her hand on the contraption, like it's a prizewinning steer—hesitantly, but beaming with pride.

"Teddy had an old one lying around. Now you won't have to go to the library to do your homework."

She waits for me to share her enthusiasm. I don't. "And did you see the bushes out front? Teddy's going to plant them this weekend. This is what they will look like in the spring." She flips open the library's gardening book and shoves it in front of my nose. Her finger points to a spindly plant with dusty green leaves and cone-like magenta flowers.

Her eyes search my face. "Nice," I say. Every muscle in her body relaxes.

"I'm making dinner." She dances back into the kitchen.

"Okay." I wander to my room to deal with the black monster. It's flashing. It has been from the second I walked out of the library.

I press the call button. It rings twice. There's a party on the other end. Staticky chatter, silver clanking, crystal ringing, a woman's high-pitched laugh. It fades away.

"I thought we had a deal, Betsy."

"We do," I say. "It has only been like forty-five minutes since you called."

He clucks at me. I know he's shaking his head in disappointment. "You logged into Facebook? What are people going to think when they see a dead girl logged into Facebook?"

"I was careful. No one saw, no one knows I was on there." I have that pleading whine I hate so much in my voice.

"Speaking of getting caught, your ID," he says, referring to the piece of untouched plastic in my wallet that declares me to be Betsy Hopewell, sixteen, resident of San Justo, Texas, and qualified driver, "has been deleted from the system." He lets it roll off his tongue, as if he's licking an ice cream spoon.

"You don't exist." He laughs. "If the cops run it, they'll come back with nothing. They'll have to use fingerprints to identify you. They have this big database." In my mind, I see him waving his hand through the air to demonstrate how big. "And you are entered there as a fugitive."

I inhale sharply.

"My advice to you? Don't get caught. Ever. Or else, say it with me . . ." I don't say anything. "Come on, this is the best part. Say it with me."

I open my mouth and whisper along with him. "*Pop.* The end of Betsy."

"Oh, and one more thing—" His tone is conversational again. I brace myself for whatever will come next. "No more messages."

"What?"

"You heard me. No more messages. When the phone rings, you answer. Period. Understand?"

I wipe the tears that have started streaming down my cheeks. "I understand."

CHAPTER 12
KAYLA

The graphs in my AP calc book dance. They turn into stick figures that sway together to the songs in their heads. A jab in my side. They step apart and unfold themselves back into graphs.

"Are you okay?" Sierra leans across the aisle and pokes me in the ribs with her pencil a second time. I nod.

Other than hallucinating in math class, I'm great. Every night, when Jordan takes me home after work, we sit in the parking lot for hours talking, holding hands, moving closer and closer. I've told him things about my life—about Mom— that I've never told anyone. The more time I spend with him, the harder it is to keep doing everything else. Being with him is so easy. The rest is so hard.

I'm running on coffee, energy drinks, and chocolate. The dance team has noticed. I'm slow. I miss steps. The beat eludes me. No one says anything—to my face. I've overheard them speculate on what my problem is. It ranges from pregnancy to cancer to drugs.

I change into my new warm-ups—a "just because" present from Carol Alexander. She also gave me another box filled with the next three dance outfits, a nice pair of jeans, and a couple of expensive sweaters. This time she didn't send the box with Paige. She gave it to me herself. I had no choice but to accept it.

Paige is waiting by the locker-room door when I come out. Sierra and the other girls pretend to stretch, but they can't disguise the eerie silence or their furtive glances in our direction.

"Hi," Paige says, and concentrates on her feet.

"Hi?"

"Um, we're worried about you." She looks to the other girls for support. They focus on touching their toes.

"Paige, is this an intervention?" I laugh. She has no idea. Yes, I'm having trouble keeping up. But I wouldn't trade Jordan for anything. I've never had someone who gets me and where I come from. These girls mean well. They try. But at the end of the day, they go home to their plush carpets, cable TV shows, and nutritionally balanced meals. I can only pretend to belong with them.

"I'm fine, Paige. Really." I say it loud enough for the whole gym to hear. "I've just picked up a few more hours at No Limit."

She grabs my arm and pulls me into the corner. "You don't have to do that." She takes a steadying breath. "If you need something, I can help you. It's no big deal."

I have known ever since I showed Paige's glittery birthday invitation to Marie and saw the reaction that she tried to hide from me, that this day would come. Even without Jordan to make me feel wanted and important and *seen,* it still would have happened eventually. I can't be the person Paige wants me to be anymore. From day one, our friendship has been about her having more than me.

"Paige." My tone is harsher than I intend. She jerks back. "It is a big deal. It's the biggest deal. I'm a human being, not a doll for your mom to dress up or a pet for you to buy treats for."

Tears form in her eyes, and I instantly feel bad. It isn't her fault. This is the only life she's ever known.

I try to soften my tone. "I know that you care and you want to help. But there are things I need to do on my own. Okay?"

She nods, but the tears are already spilling down her cheeks. She runs to the locker room, followed by the rest of the girls sending confused glances my way.

I stare out the window at McDonald's. I would rather be anywhere but here at register two. What I said to Paige was too harsh. In less than five seconds, I destroyed six years of friendship. I have to fix this.

The pretty girl who works at McDonald's walks out onto the sidewalk. She's laughing at something the person coming out the door behind her says.

A customer clears his throat to get my attention back where it belongs. He thunks his basket onto the conveyer belt. I smile and try to look attentive, but when he turns to pick out a pack of gum, I glance back out the front window. The McDonald's girl is sliding into Drake's Camaro.

Dance team practice is miserable. Paige won't look at me. The other girls keep their eyes down. I feel like I'm back to being the free-lunch foster kid of sixth grade.

When Paige comes out of the gym, I reach for her elbow. "Please," I say before she can protest. "I need to tell you something." She lets me lead her to a bench.

We sit in silence while the other girls file out. Once we're alone, I turn to her. "I'm sorry. I shouldn't have said what I said yesterday. I was tired, and I just kind of snapped."

Paige's eyes well up, but she stays in control. "I didn't know you felt that way. Mom and I were just trying to help because we love you."

"I know. And I love you too. You've made a huge difference in my life." I suck in a breath to keep my own tears contained.

"There's something else." I don't know if confiding in her will matter now, but it's my last shot at saving this friendship. "I think I have a boyfriend."

Paige starts. "Who?" She glances around, as if the mysterious boy is hiding behind one of the bushes outside the gym.

"It's not someone from school."

"What do you mean you think you have a boyfriend?" she asks.

And I tell her. Everything that's happened since I met Jordan—all except for the man in black. I tell her how I'm afraid Jordan doesn't feel the same way about me that I feel about him. That I don't know if I'm his girlfriend or just some kid without a car he drives home at night.

"Wow," she says when I'm finished. "If he makes you happy, then I'm happy for you." She stops there. She doesn't call me naive for thinking Jordan is my boyfriend when we haven't even kissed. It makes my heart ache. I want to hug her and tell her I'm sorry again, put things back to the way they were before.

"Are we still friends?" I whisper. She nods, but sadness fills her eyes. I've done a lot of damage, and I don't know if our friendship will ever be totally okay again.

Paige looks at her hands. "Mom wants to know if you're coming for Thanksgiving."

"Sure." It will be horribly awkward, but I'll suck it up if it will fix things even a little.

"I have a coupon in here somewhere." Mrs. Lacey dumps the contents of her massive black handbag onto the conveyer belt. She's already given me her food stamp card, a couple crumpled dollar bills, pennies, and two Tic-Tacs. I haven't rung up her loaf of bread yet. We did her order item by item, carefully keeping track of the total. Her purchases aren't extravagant. Milk, peanut butter, a package of No Limit chocolate chip cookies, a tin of the cheapest dog food.

She fumbles through pieces of paper, a comb, plastic candy wrappers. The guy in line behind her crosses his arms. His face reddens.

"In here somewhere," she mutters.

I look over my shoulder. Albert's in his office. I put the bread in her sack and print out her receipt. Her head is still down, hands frantic in the pile. I hold the receipt under her nose.

"Have a nice evening."

She doesn't understand. "Have a nice evening," I say again, and hold the sack out to her, bread perched on top.

She gathers the contents of her purse into her arms and takes the sack. "Bless you, Kayla. Bless you."

I smile at Red Face behind her. "Can I help you?" I glance at his selections. Mixed in with his chips and soda is a bottle of whiskey.

"I'm sorry, sir. I can't ring up an alcohol purchase." I point to the NO ALCOHOL sign floating over my head.

"I think you can make an exception," he says.

"I'm sorry, sir. I can't. It's against the law."

The corners of his mouth push up. "Maybe it just goes in that sack right there."

"I'm sorry, I can't do that." My voice shakes.

He sucks in air and inflates in front of me. "I'd like to speak to the manager."

He's too confident not to have gotten away with this before. I bite my lip. I could make this go away. But a bottle of whiskey isn't a loaf of bread. He isn't an old woman who spends her entire day at Bluebird Estates with only her rat dog to talk to.

I pick up the phone and call Albert.

Albert makes soothing noises at Red Face. He takes him

to the customer service desk. They turn toward me. The man points. He pays for his alcohol and leaves. Albert calls for a backup cashier. He smiles at the customers in my line and leads them away to another register. My closed sign goes up.

His beady little eyes are resolute. "Strike three, Kayla."

Elton's savoring a burger at a corner table in the McDonald's. It's probably one of the few treats he gets with whatever little money he lives on. His eyes bounce up to me when I walk in. They follow me around the restaurant.

The girl with the diamond stud in her nose pushes her hair behind her ear and laughs. Jordan leans across our table, smiling with expectation, like he's just finished a joke. She wipes her rag across the same spot over and over again.

He sees me, and his whole countenance changes. The girl jumps. I know my eyes are puffy. I wipe my nose on my sleeve. My red apron has been replaced by my raincoat. My water bottle, the oak leaf, and the few things I had in my No Limit's locker are in a toilet bowl cleaner box.

"Can we go?" I ask before I start crying again.

Jordan takes my box and leads me out to his Jeep. Elton's watching through the window. He seems as sad as I feel.

"Do you want to go home?"

I shake my head. I had barely started my shift. The sky glows with the last remainder of fall sunlight as we drive through the streets of Clairmont. Past the school, past Marie's, past the street Paige lives on. Cute, quiet houses containing cute, quiet people.

Jordan doesn't ask, but I tell him anyway. He stops along the curb of a park. He turns the Jeep off.

"You're amazing, you know," he says softly.

"What?" My ears are stuffed up from sniffling. I'm not sure I heard him right.

When he looks at me, the gold flakes are back in his eyes. "You're amazing." I feel myself blush. "I don't know anyone who has been through what you've been through and is still a nice person."

I don't know what to say. Two boys climb up the jungle gym, laughing and shoving each other. Their mothers sit on a bench and gossip while the boys run off their predinner energy.

It was Marie. Marie made me a good person. She made me remember I was a human being, that I was worth something, that all people are worth something. I've never told Jordan about her. He knows I lived with a foster mother, but he doesn't know about *Marie*. I don't tell him now. I can't. Marie is mine and only mine.

We sit in silence and watch the boys play. I'm trying not to think about what getting fired means. It's bad enough that I got *fired* from my first job. But it also means the end of having a few extras we can't leech out of the government. I'm back to where I was the day I was delivered by the social worker to Bluebird Estates.

I don't know what Jordan is thinking about. His face is blank. He has good control over it. With the exception of a few brief, unguarded moments, he shows the world exactly what he wants it to see. I envy that.

The gearshift and the stubby central armrest are the only things keeping our entire bodies from touching. I lean into him. Our heads touch. His thumb makes gentle circles on the back of my hand.

My pulse is elevated. I swallow hard. My pupils let in every photon of available light. I want him to kiss me. And I want him to know it.

Jordan pulls back. For the last three nights, our lips have come centimeters from touching. Then Jordan bails. I try not to feel bad about it. I know he wants to kiss me, too. It radiates off him. But something keeps getting in the way.

"Is it because I'm sixteen?" I ask, breaking the breathy silence that fills the Jeep. He doesn't answer. Confirmation.

I sigh and lean back hard against the seat. I can't magically make myself older or more experienced.

"It's not that." He still has my hand. He examines it in the warm glow of the sunset. "It's hard for me to get close to people."

I watch his profile, his upper body, his arms and legs. I scan him for any hint of deception or manipulation. I don't see any.

He's telling the truth.

It's an awkward maneuver, but I twist and lean over the gear shift until I can wrap my arms around him. He lays his head on my shoulder.

When the mothers gather their still rambunctious children to head home, and darkness invades all the nooks and crannies in the Jeep, Jordan turns to me.

"Can I take you somewhere tomorrow?"

"Sure." I try to laugh, but it comes out creaky. "I don't have anything else to do."

I dash to the gym before the other girls can get there. I don't want them making a big thing about this. I leave the box from the fancy designer store containing the next three dance outfits on the bench in front of Paige's locker. Resting on top is a note officially resigning my place on the dance team.

Tears slide down my face. I almost can't remember a time when dance wasn't in my life, but where does it end with Carol Alexander? Since I got fired, I won't have the money to continue, and if I accept this box from Carol, what's to stop her from giving me another one. To stop me from accepting it?

Every time I step out on the gym floor, I'll be reminded. Reminded that to her, I'm still the free-lunch foster kid. That's not me anymore. I'm a different person now. Now that I've found Jordan.

Maybe when I find another job, I can save up and then reaudition for the dance team next year. But if I do, it will be on my terms. My money. My life.

CHAPTER 13
BETSY

I kneel down in the dirt. A freezing wind swirls sand around me. Blasting my face. Crunching between my teeth. I pull up the hood on my jacket and cover my ears.

Even though I already knew, I asked Happy about Tomás and Lawrence's other brother. She told me exactly where it happened. I Googled the streets and found my way back here.

The smiling child in the cheap frame stares beatifically at me. I have another child's picture in my head. This one wasn't as smiley, but she was beautiful and perfect and alive.

I can't get the match to light. The wind blows it out the second I get a spark. I've come with my own candle encased in red glass to add to the memorial.

I hold the match and the candle so close to my body that I risk lighting myself on fire. But I have to do this. I have to get this candle lit. She deserves it, someone lighting a candle for her.

The wick catches, and for a brief moment, the glass glows

bright and warm. Then the wind finds its way in and blows it out like the world's saddest birthday. I nestle the dark red glass between the others. Red, green, blue, white. A symphony of colors for dead children. I'll come back another night and light them all.

I'm still crumpled on the ground, bathed in shadows, when a vehicle shoots past me. It drives fast and throws up little rocks that pepper my body. It's Adrian's Bronco. In the weak, dust-filtered moonlight, his profile stares straight ahead.

The Bronco keeps going past where the pavement ends. He drives out into the desert. A cloud of dust makes him disappear like a magician into smoke. He's up to something. That's why he didn't want me here. Something that will prove he isn't the Goody-Two-Shoes everyone thinks he is. He's something dark. Something black. Something that comes out at night when no one is looking.

I'm looking.

I get up and leave the candles to stand their lonely watch. The Bronco turns behind a low hill in the distance. It's gone.

I should be a good girl and walk away. Go back to Mom's car, parked three blocks over. Pretend I didn't see anything. Pretend that Adrian is who everyone thinks he is. I glance back down at the candles.

No.

This time I have on boots that protect my feet from the desert grit. I run.

The distance to the hill is an illusion. Like an island floating on the sea, the closer I get, the farther it seems. My legs ache. They aren't used to this kind of exercise. But the fear in the pit of my stomach, the memories that flash through my brain—rain, gunshots, cold dead eyes—propel me forward.

The hill doesn't provide much cover. It slopes too gently into the desert floor to be much of a hiding place. I flatten myself along the upslope and peek over the top. The Bronco is parked in front of the ruins of an old shack. Three walls and half a roof of grayed, weathered wood lean and creak in the wind. Adrian pushes stuff around in the back of the Bronco. When he steps away, the moonlight catches what he holds in his hands: The duct tape. And a knife.

He takes them into the shack. I slide along the sand, trying to see what's inside. Who's inside. I can't make out much. I see Adrian kneeling, duct tape in hand, in front of two figures. Coughing fills the night air. The smaller of the figures convulses under a pile of ratty blankets.

I've got to do something to get them out of there and away from Adrian. But I have nothing—no knife, no gun. The car is parked far away.

I feel around the ground. The rocks are pebble-sized. Something pokes my hand. I whip it away and see a pinprick of blood forming on my palm.

Adrian glances up in my direction. I freeze. Maybe I can stay here until he leaves. Then I'll get the car and take them to a police station. They can expose Adrian, and no one will ever know I had anything to do with it.

I lie flat on the hill. I have to wait.

My pocket rings.

The world stops. Even the wind seems to cease its howl. I paw at the black monster that's lit up, buzzing and singing.

I silence it. I don't know what to do. I glance down at Adrian. He doesn't turn around.

I *have* to answer.

"What?" I whisper into the phone with my head down, like maybe that will block the sound.

"No 'hello'? No 'how ya doing'? No 'how's the weather'?"

"How's the weather?" If I don't humor him, he will never let me hang up.

He sighs. "Raining. Always raining."

A shadow passes over me. Hands clamp down on my shoulders.

CHAPTER 14
KAYLA

"Where are we going?" I ask for the tenth time. And for the tenth time, Jordan raises his eyebrows and smirks.

I watch the trees and the houses go by out the window. We cross a bridge and then another one. I try to draw a mental map of all we pass. I want to remember this—being with Jordan outside of Clairmont—forever.

The November gloom flops over the land like a wet wool blanket as we get closer to the water that stretches out past the horizon. We turn onto an unmarked dirt tract. Jordan gives me a huge, excited smile. He hits the gas and whoops.

The Jeep flies over ruts. The whole interior rattles. My seat belt tightens to keep me in place. I grab the armrest, but I can't help laughing. Jordan's excitement is contagious.

The road curves through thick trees that black out the sky and threaten to swallow us whole. With a sudden lurch, we hit payment, and the ride smooths out.

I peel my fingers off the armrest as we pull up to a house. Jordan stops on the circular drive in front. My jaw drops.

The scene outside my window is like a page from Marie's Frank Lloyd Wright calendar. The house is flat-roofed and boxy. All right angles and glass. Polished wood and geometric overhangs.

I snap my whole body around to face Jordan. He juts his chin at the structure. "Blood money house."

A snake of disappointment slithers around me when I notice the Camaro parked by the trees on the side of the house. Drake's home.

Jordan's already standing on the sliver of front porch before I manage to tear my eyes away from the house and get out of the Jeep. He holds the front door open for me, and my breath is taken away—again. The entire backside of the house is made of floor-to-ceiling windows. They look out on a vista of the ocean and a small, private inlet that washes against the cliff the house is perched on.

"You have your own ocean," I say before I realize how stupid it sounds. Jordan wraps his arms around me from behind and rests his chin on my shoulder.

"Yes," he whispers.

I hear laughter coming from a hallway. Jordan straightens up. He holds me, like he's prepared to throw me out of the way of an oncoming monster. The laughter gets closer. Two people—a man's deep laugh and a high-pitched giggle.

Drake comes around the corner. On his head, he wears a pink paper crown. Loops of green and purple Mardi Gras beads hang around his neck. Jordan squeezes my arms. Drake freezes. A little blond girl bumps into the back of his legs. Her crown teeters on her head and dips over her eyes.

The girl can't be more than five. She adjusts her crown

and surveys us, but she doesn't come out from behind Drake. I feel Jordan's body stiffen. He steps around me.

He kneels down so that he's at eye level with the girl. "Hi, sweetie," he says. He looks up at Drake. "What's she doing here?"

Drake's eyes are wide and focused on me. "Kayla."

"What's she doing here?" Jordan asks again.

"The babysitter is sick. She couldn't get ahold of anyone, so she called the house phone." Drake says this to me. He doesn't look at Jordan.

Jordan pulls a half-eaten package of M&M's from his pocket. He holds it out to the girl. She shyly steps out from behind Drake and takes them. "Can you go play in your room?" The girl holds the candy in front of her like a prize and disappears down the hallway.

"Since you're here," Jordan says to Drake, "we need to talk about your rent money." Jordan turns and faces me. "Sorry, we'll be right back." He motions to the immaculate white living room. "Make yourself at home."

After they leave, I try to sit, but I have too much energy. Who is the little girl, and what does she have to do with Jordan? I'm suddenly afraid that I've walked in on something I'm not supposed to know about. Like Jordan has a deep, dark secret. He'd have told me if he had a kid, right?

I have to know. Drake and Jordan are still ensconced in a back room. I walk down the hallway.

I find the girl sitting on the floor in a room that contains a little bed and a random assortment of toys. Dolls, trucks, finger paints, a blank sketchbook, a muscly action figure, a plastic tea set. It's like someone didn't know what to buy a child, so they grabbed something from each aisle of the toy store. The walls are blank and the closet empty but for a couple of dresses on child-sized hangers.

This can't be where she normally lives. It feels so cold, and she looks lost in the midst of all the nothing. Who is she?

I sit down across from her. "Hi, I'm Kayla. What's your name?"

"Grace," she whispers without looking up at me. She seems overwhelmed at having to talk to a stranger. I felt that same way many times when I was little. My heart goes out to her.

"Do you want to paint a picture?" I ask, and hold up the finger paints. I pull a page out of the sketchbook and open the blue paint. I dip my finger in and draw a line down the center. As I dip my finger in the red, I feel her eyes watching me. I place a piece of paper in front of her. She copies my blue line.

Soon our hands are covered in paint. I forget and rub my cheek. The girl giggles when I realize what I've done. I reach out and give her a matching paint smear.

When our papers will hold no more, we step back and admire them.

"What pretty pictures." I jump at Jordan's voice behind me. He laughs when I turn around and he sees the paint on my face.

"I got bored sitting in the living room. Grace was kind enough to play with me." I wink at the girl. She turns scarlet.

"Let's get you cleaned up, Gracie." The girl hesitates for a second, but then lets Jordan lead her into the bathroom across the hall. The shower curtain is covered in yellow rubber duckies. A matching ducky-shaped soap sits on the counter. Jordan lifts the girl up to the sink with one arm around her waist and picks up the soap.

"Quack, quack." He swims the soap in front of the girl. Then he dips it under the running water and makes a muffled quacking sound. The girl giggles. They're great together. I don't know who this girl is, but she looks at Jordan with big, admiring eyes. I've never had a father, but I imagine that's what it would be like.

When the paint has been scrubbed off, and the girl dried with a fluffy towel, she skips back to her room.

Jordan leans against the wall and gives me a dreamy smile. I move toward him. I have never wanted to kiss anyone as much in my entire life. But I have to know.

"Who is she?" I whisper.

Jordan rolls off the wall. "Come on."

I follow him across the house to a giant bedroom. Like in the living room, the glass wall slides open to a redwood balcony. The bed is rumpled, covers thrown all over the place. The fireplace across from it is cold and unused. Jordan sits on the bed. He's completely relaxed, which tells me something. This is *his* bedroom.

My insides jitter. I can't move any farther into the room. Overwhelming emotions swirl through me. Confusion, anxiety, and something a little naughty I don't want to name. My heart beats in my ears.

"The bathroom's right there." He points.

"What?" I'm anchored in the doorway.

"Your hands."

I look down. I was so caught up in Jordan and the girl that I forgot that I was covered in paint. "Right. I'll wash them," I say, like I'm expecting praise for coming up with such a brilliant idea.

I shut the bathroom door. My face resembles a bruised tomato in the dim white illumination provided by a single skylight. I scrub the paint off and let my hands drip over the sink.

I'm in Jordan's bathroom, attached to Jordan's *bedroom*. I don't know what he expects to happen now. We've spent months talking. I like him—a lot. I trust him. But we still haven't even kissed. I don't know where we stand. And I'm definitely not ready to jump all in.

Jordan knocks on the door, and my heart almost explodes from the force of its beating. "Let's take a walk," he says, and I exhale in relief so loudly that he probably hears it through the door.

My coat is in the Jeep, and I'm not prepared for the blast of cold, wet mist that hits me when Jordan slides open the door. I cross my arms and try to hold in my body heat. Jordan, who is usually Mr. Observant, doesn't notice.

A staircase leads off the balcony down the cliff to a path that winds through a smattering of trees to a small dock on the water.

Gravel crunches under our feet. "Gracie's my sister. Half sister."

"Your sister?" I don't want to be judgmental, but I'm so relieved that she isn't his daughter. That's the kind of thing you have to be up-front about. If she were his daughter and he didn't tell me, I wouldn't have been able to believe another word he said.

"Yeah. It's complicated. I never see her. We're practically like strangers to each other."

That explains her shyness toward him.

"Remember how I told you that my mom fell apart after my dad died? How she moved out here by herself? She was really messed up, and she had an affair with one of the doctors at the hospital where she was working.

"My uncle was so pissed when she got pregnant. He didn't want her to keep the baby. But Mom was caught up in some fairy tale about living happily ever after with the doctor. I don't know if the doctor ever really cared for her, but he didn't want to leave his perfect life to be with Mom when Grace was born.

"She tried to take care of Gracie, but she couldn't do it. The doctor petitioned for custody. She's lived with him and his wife ever since."

"Wow." We've reached the dock. I look back and the house has disappeared in the mist. I lean against the swollen wood railing. My shirt is almost soaked through, and my fingers are numb. I suppress a shiver.

"Mom's still not completely back to her normal self. I don't know if she ever will be. She never talks about Gracie. Sometimes I think she's forgotten all about her."

"No," I say forcefully. "She hasn't." Even when my mom was at her rock bottom, I know she didn't forget about me. She wouldn't have been able to get clean and turn her life around—sort of—if she had. And I know that little Gracie hasn't forgotten about her mother, either. Even when I was with Marie and had everything I needed, I always wondered where Mom was and worried about her.

"It's incredible that the doctor's wife would agree to raise another woman's child like that," I say. Maybe Grace has a Marie in her life.

Jordan waves a hand. "She's his second wife. The first one dropped him once she found out about Gracie."

"Oh." Now I'm worried about this little girl. If I hadn't had Marie . . .

Jordan sees it on my face. "Gracie's in good hands. So really"—he looks away—"she doesn't need me or Mom at all."

"That's not true. You're her big brother. I would have given anything to have had someone like you when I was her age."

Jordan's eyes meet mine. "Really?" He steps forward until our foreheads are almost touching. Then he pulls away a few inches and sweeps his eyes around my face, like he's taking in all the details. "I've never had a girlfriend like you before."

Girlfriend. The word echoes through me. I want to call him my boyfriend. Hear how it sounds aloud. Let him know that I feel the same way. But before I can, Jordan brings his lips to mine.

I close my eyes.

He kisses me.

A slow, lingering, delicious kiss. I lace my fingers around the back of his neck and pull him closer. The cold turns warm, and my damp clothes and hair feel dry. Nothing exists but the two of us and the sound of ocean slopping against wood.

"We should get you inside," he says while his lips are still brushing mine.

Hand in hand we walk back through the glass door. He

disappears into the walk-in closet. He tosses a blue T-shirt at me. "Here, you can wear this. I'll put your clothes in the dryer."

I hold the shirt in front of me. Am I supposed to go into the bathroom or strip right here in the middle of his bedroom with a glass wall behind me?

Jordan stays in the closet, so I pull off my wet top and jeans and put the T-shirt on. It comes down to my midthigh. "Um, okay?"

He steps out wearing only a pair of gray sweatpants. "Whoa," I say when I see his bare chest. He gives me a cocky smile and flexes his muscles. His rippling arms and sculpted chest are worth an exclamation, but that's not what I'm looking at. I step forward and raise my hand. I glance up at him, and he nods. I touch the smooth skin on his chest and trace my finger along the outline of a carp the color of the carrot juice Carol Alexander always has in her fridge.

He beams with pride.

"It's gorgeous. I've never seen anything like it." The pigment is so intense, like it's been painted on his skin. The carp's tail swirls over his heart. Its eye, lifelike, peers up at me curiously.

"It's for good luck and strength."

I can't stop running my finger over the electric carp's body. "How . . ."

He laughs. "It was done using an ancient Japanese technique. It hurts, but it looks great."

Drake clears his throat in the doorway. We both jump. I drop my hand.

"Jordan," he says. His eyes stay on the floor to avoid witnessing more of our half-naked moment.

"I'll be right back." Jordan pulls on a shirt and kisses me on the forehead.

As soon as I'm sure they're gone, I twirl around and flop down on the bed. I can't wipe the smile off my face. And I don't want to. I feel too good.

My clothes are still crumpled on the floor. I get up and shake them out. My jeans dislodge something shiny from the carpet. I pick it up. It looks like a diamond earring that has been stepped on and bent at one end.

Jordan comes back into the room. I drop the earring. A new emotion fills me. Of course he's brought girls back here before. He said he had never had a girlfriend *like me*. Not that I was the first and only one to see his life here.

"Are you okay?" he asks.

"Sure."

"I know I hit you with a lot today. I didn't know that Gracie would be here." There's sadness in his eyes when he says her name.

"I have an idea." I shimmy back into my damp jeans. "Come with me." I grab his hand and lead him out into the living room. "Stay here." Jordan smirks in amusement.

I go down the dark hallway to Grace's room. She's still on the floor playing with the toys. Drake sits on the bed watching her with a cold intensity. I was coming to get Grace anyway, but seeing the way Drake looks at her makes me feel a primal panic. I want to get this girl away from him.

He glances up at me. I ignore him. "Hey, Grace, can you bring your picture out to the living room?" I say cheerfully. I don't want to scare her.

She looks at Drake, but then picks up her paint-soaked paper and follows me.

Jordan smiles when he sees the two of us appear around the corner. His phone is on a side table. I pick it up and find the camera app.

Jordan rests his hands on Grace's shoulders. "Hold your picture up." I snap a photo. Then I dash behind them and hold the camera in front of the three of us. "Say *cheese*."

After the last day of school before Thanksgiving break, I use my key to let myself into Marie's. She's still at work, and her little bear will be at some sort of afternoon activity. Her old computer takes forever to start up. I focus on the monitor and try not to let the ghosts of living here invade me and make it even harder to go back to Bluebird Estates.

The log-in screen pops ups. The password is *littlemouse*. The breath hitches in my throat as I type it in. I pull up my email and look at the photos I sent to myself from Jordan's phone. Grace looks so happy to be with her big brother.

I print two copies of the photo of them together. One for me and one for Jordan. Marie has the printer set up to put the date stamp on everything. She likes to chart the growth of her little bears that way. I don't want to hang around any longer than I have to, so I leave it and print a copy of the selfie with the three of us. My head is overly big, and I have a stupid expression on my face, but it reminds me of the moment—and of Jordan kissing me on the dock.

I can't stomach taking these happy memories to Bluebird

Estates. I pry open the wall space in the guest room and stick my copies inside where they will be safe and waiting for me to come back for them. And I will. On the day I make it out of Clairmont.

Carol Alexander opens the door with a dish towel thrown over her shoulder and a ruffled half apron tied around her waist.

"Happy Thanksgiving," I say, and push a box of cheap chocolate-covered cherries at her. It's a hollow gesture, and we both know it. But it's a boundary. She's invited me to dinner. I'm a guest who contributes to it.

"Paige is upstairs." She smiles, but I can tell as she subconsciously backs away from me that Paige has told her about our fight, about my quitting the dance team. Carol's afraid she will say or do something wrong.

In her room, Paige is painting her nails with earbuds blasting. She uses her shoulders to shrug them out when she sees me.

I sit on the edge of her bed. Paige continues with her nails. The microwave beeps downstairs.

I want to tell her everything about Jordan's house and his sister and the kiss, but my lips stay closed, like if I say the words aloud, they will somehow become less important. Less *mine*.

I glance up at the ballerina poster that's still on the wall over her bed. I turn to Paige, and our eyes meet.

I see something in hers I've never seen before. Embarrassment. I've made her painfully aware of how much she has compared to me. If I don't fix this right now, the damage I've done is going to be permanent.

"Paige, you're my best friend. You've changed my life. I don't know where I would be, *who* I would be without you." Her eyes get glassy. "Please," I beg, "I can't lose you." Jordan has filled up so much of my life, but he can't replace Paige.

"I don't want to lose you, either." She sweeps a finger carefully under her eye to catch a tear before it messes up her mascara. "I'll do better. I promise."

My heart breaks into even more pieces. "No. That's not what I meant. I want you to keep being you. Sometimes I just need a little space to figure out who *I* am."

"Okay," she says, but the next tear rolls down her cheek. I bite my lip. I don't know if I fixed things or made them worse.

"Girls, dinner's ready," Carol calls up the stairs. Paige grabs a tissue and dabs at her face. She blinks hard, like she's trying to erase all that just happened. She stands with a bounce.

When we get to the dining room, Carol Alexander gives me the biggest, fakest smile I have ever seen.

My box of cheap cherries is displayed prominently on the sideboard between the pumpkin pies.

CHAPTER 15

BETSY

Adrian's fingers dig painfully into my shoulders.

"I have to go." I shove the black monster out of sight.

He propels me to my feet. "Who were you talking to?"

I hunch over and curl up to confine the pending blows to the smallest area possible.

"Answer me," he seethes though his teeth.

"My mom."

His face is blacked out, but I feel its fury. I know what happens now. I end up duct-taped and tied up in the shack. Or worse.

He drags me down the hill. I fumble to put the monster back into my pocket.

"What are you doing here, Betsy?"

The jig is up. I might as well come clean. I jerk away from him, stumble, and barely catch myself before I end up on my knees. I spin around. "I won't let you hurt them."

His face changes to some sort of mock innocence. "I'm not hurting anyone. Get out of here. Go home."

"I'm not leaving them here with you." We stand face to face as the wind whips sand around us like two Old West gunfighters waiting for the other to flinch.

"Betsy." Adrian breaks the silence. Anger makes his voice shake. He reaches out like he's going to grab my arm again. Coughing fills the night air. It's a deep, painful, hacking sound. Adrian's face crumbles. He turns and races back to the shack.

I follow him.

The larger of the two figures stirs. It's a woman. Her hair is matted around her face. She picks up her head and takes a labored, wheezy breath. She holds a coughing bundle.

When the blankets fall, I see a little boy who's probably about Rosie's age. His small body spasms with each cough, but his eyes stay closed. Tears course down the woman's face.

Adrian shuffles around among the debris surrounding them and holds up a bottle of cough syrup. Even I can see in the moonlight that shoots through the holes in the shack that the bottle is empty.

"Adrian?" I take a step toward him.

His head snaps around. "Betsy, go home. I have it under control."

I take another step forward. "Adrian, he needs to go to the hospital." I make my voice soft and soothing, like I'm trying to coax a kitten out of a tree.

"They can't go to the hospital," he spits back at me.

"Whatever you've done, we'll work it out. You're still a minor. It won't be that bad. But we have to take them to the hospital before this gets any worse."

"What I've done?"

The boy's wheezing intensifies. Misery doesn't begin to describe the expression on the woman's face. It's more like grief and terror and resignation all rolled into one.

"Adrian," I say again, "if that boy dies, it will be on your head. That's not something you want to live with."

"I've kept them alive so far. I can do this. He's getting better."

I place a hand on his shoulder. It's a daring move. The knife is on the ground. He could pick it up at any time. "Let them go," I say.

"Go? Where are they going to go? She can't take a sick child through the desert."

I can't wait, can't negotiate any longer. I dive for the knife. My fingers wrap around the handle. It's lighter than I thought. Like a steak knife from C&J's. I don't think I can do much damage with it. But I will use every ounce of my strength to do whatever I can.

I get to my feet and hold the knife in front of me.

Adrian looks surprised. "Get away from them," I say with a burst of confidence.

I don't know what I expect to happen. Maybe that he'll surrender and let me march him back to town. He doesn't. He, with irritation playing over his brow, swipes the knife from my shaking hand and picks up the duct tape.

"Go home, Betsy."

The little boy whimpers. The mother gathers him back into her arms. Tears form in my eyes. I don't know what to do. I can't save my own life, much less someone else's.

Adrian pulls out a strip of duct tape and starts wrapping it around the woman's left shoe. He stops and looks at me. His eyes widen. "When you followed me, did you walk in the tire tracks or did you sneak around behind the hill?"

I don't know what he's talking about. But then I hear it. The crunch of a vehicle approaching.

"Dammit, Betsy. You tripped a ground sensor." He grabs me by the arm. "Come on."

He hauls me out to the back of the Bronco. "Don't say a word," he warns. He's dropped the knife, but he's still stronger than I am. I have nothing to defend myself with, not even nails to scratch him.

The vehicle is on the other side of the hill and coming up fast. Adrian grabs the back of my neck and forces my face against his. Our lips crash together. I try to pull away, but his fingers clamp down to hold me in place.

When the headlights illuminate us, Adrian steps back. He holds his hand up to shield his eyes. The doors open, and two men in dark green uniforms step out. "Ah, man. We can't catch a break," Adrian says. He squeezes my hand. I try to smile. I have to play along. Uniforms are bad. Maybe even worse than Adrian.

The two men move into the light. One is young. He has a nice face. Bright and enthusiastic.

The other is old and crusty. His gray hair blows up off his head. "Border Patrol," he says, and shines a flashlight in our faces. "ID."

I swallow hard.

"Come on. Me and my girlfriend just want to be alone. We aren't breaking any laws. And we're *Americans*." Adrian makes his voice sound like he's a dumb jock with an even dumber girlfriend. I shrug and wrap myself around him. He flinches.

Crusty's annoyed with us. He shines his flashlight directly onto my face. The young guy walks around the Bronco, checking the inside. When he's satisfied by his search, he comes back to where we are. We make eye contact.

"Is everything okay?" he asks.

I nod. Crusty glares at Adrian. "I'm going to need to see ID, son," he says.

Adrian digs into his pocket for his wallet. The light flicks to me. "You too."

I go absolutely still. My lungs constrict. My heart doesn't beat in my chest. My fingers don't throb beneath Adrian's. My worthless driver's license is in my back pocket. One call on the radio and my life is over.

If they check my ID, I'll be arrested, imprisoned, probably given the death penalty.

If I tell them there are people in the shack and Adrian gets away, he'll kill me.

If Adrian doesn't get away, everyone will know who I am, they will know it was me who turned him in. And I'm dead anyway.

Everything I have been through has led up to this moment.

That little boy in the shack gets to have a chance.

I grip down hard on Adrian's hand and turn my head to the young guy. I make sure he sees me. I flick my head over my shoulder at the shack. He pauses, eyes locked onto mine. Then realization washes over his face. He takes off running.

Crusty, confused by what has happened, takes longer to get it. Then the light drops off me and onto the ground. His feet crunch rhythmically away through the gravel.

A shriek comes from the shack. A scuffle. Codes barked into radios.

Shadows black out the top of Adrian's face. I can only see his mouth tighten, but I know if he had that knife in his hand, he would drive it through my heart.

More vehicles approach. Adrian drags me to the Bronco. I don't know if I should fight or go with him. It comes down to who I would rather have kill me. I cooperate. At least with Adrian, it will be quick. If the feds catch me, my death will drag out for years.

We leap into the Bronco. Adrian throws the truck into gear and sends a spray of dirt over the white-and-green Border Patrol SUV. We careen out into the desert with the lights off, bumping over bushes and rocks. The approaching SUV can see us, but they don't give chase.

When they have passed, Adrian comes to a stop. The paved road is only a few hundred feet in front of us.

"Get out." He is so beyond furious his voice comes out calm and controlled.

I open my door. "You can do what you want with me now. But I wasn't going to let you place another death on my head." I step into the sand. He drives away.

I collapse to the ground.

I'm still alive.

For now.

CHAPTER 16

KAYLA

Even though Albert's a dick who treated us like his servants, not having a job sucks. I sit alone in McDonald's and sip water. I talked to the manager. He said that if they had an opening, he'd consider me for it. But until someone quits, I'm stuck here drinking water. I can't afford niceties like coffee or soda anymore.

I can't go home. Mom doesn't know I got fired. If I tell her, she'll worry. She'll start wringing her hands and pacing. She'll walk down the hall. Finn will open his door. Who knows what will happen after that. I don't want to find out.

Over winter break, I went to every business within walking distance of Bluebird Estates. Most of them told me I had to be eighteen to work there and then showed me the door.

A crusty old man in a vacuum cleaner repair shop with a NOW HIRING sign in the window demanded to know my work experience. I told him, and he seemed interested. Then he asked me why I quit No Limit Foods. I told the truth that

I had gotten fired. His face crumpled into a scowl. I should have lied.

If I knew that Jordan would be around forever to drive me home, I could get a job anywhere. But I can't count on that. Things are great with Jordan—perfect, even—but what happened with Paige taught me how quickly relationships can unravel. What if next week Jordan meets a nice community college girl and realizes that I'm just a poor, unemployed high school student?

The only option I have left is Carol Alexander. She could get me a nice job in a nice office. And I would never be able to look at myself in the mirror again. I have to find another way.

Jordan is in Florida helping his uncle again. He didn't know how long he would be gone, so he made arrangements for Drake to pick me up and take me home when my shift would have ended. I've already done my homework, as well as the extra credit, and read ahead for all my classes. Not having anyone to talk to makes the night drag on forever.

A tall, pimply-faced guy with a crooked uniform walks around with a rag in his hand. I flag him down.

"Can I help you, miss?" he asks, like he isn't used to girls of any kind talking to him, much less former dance team members from Clairmont High.

"Where's the girl who's usually here? The pretty one with the nose stud."

"Shonda?" He blushes. It's cute. He twists the rag around and around between his fingers. "She didn't show tonight. Manager's pissed."

"Thanks," I say, and release him from having to speak to

me any longer. He takes off and hides behind the fry cook, who looks like he couldn't give a shit about anything.

I could only drink so much water inside McDonald's, so I'm sitting on the curb outside. In the corner of the parking lot, Elton has the back of his station wagon open. He smiles at the things inside. It's nice. It's the first time I've ever seen him look anything but miserable.

Drake's Camaro pulls up. He's talking on his cell phone. Whoever is on the other end is making him angry. He hangs up as I open the passenger door. His face is etched with exhaustion. Lines that weren't there before create patterns around his eyes and mouth. They make him seem old and worn.

After the cold way I saw him look at Grace, I don't want to get into the car. But what choice do I have? I can't walk home alone, and I don't want to disappoint Jordan, who set this up so I would be safe.

"Thanks for the ride," I say. Drake nods, like his head's too heavy and he's struggling to return it to its upright position.

A couple of raindrops hit the windshield. It's not even a sprinkle. "Why is it always raining?" Drake mutters.

He turns onto a heavily wooded side street off Bluebird Lane.

The car stops. "Um, Bluebird Estates is the other way," I joke, hoping that my tone hides the fear creeping up my body. My heart pounds. I try to keep my breathing even so he won't notice. My best defense is to stay calm, casual.

When his head turns, his eyes burn holes in me. He leans forward, and for a second, I think he's going to kiss me. I automatically jerk back against the car door. "I can walk from here. Thanks for the ride." I flash my Clairmont Explorers Dance Team smile, trying to look nonthreatening, and reach for the door handle.

"Wait." His tone is forceful but filled with some kind of desperation that makes me pause. He blinks hard. I shiver in my jacket and notice he's wearing only a T-shirt. The snake on his arm flexes as he grips and releases the steering wheel. Grips and releases. "Stay away from Jordan," he says.

"What?" I ask. "Why?" Are they having a fight? Is he getting back at Jordan for ragging on him about the rent?

He rubs the bridge of his nose. "Just do it." A command mixed with irritation.

"Um, okay," I say. I want out of this car. I pull the door handle. The door releases and lets in a blast of cold, wet air.

He grabs my shoulder. My heart pounds again. "I'm serious," he says. I don't doubt that, and I also don't want to spend another moment with him. I pull away so hard I end up on my butt on the sidewalk. My backpack crashes to the ground behind me. Drake's face changes instantly. He seems confused by my reaction. Worried. "I'll see you tomorrow?" he asks, his voice light and hopeful.

I nod and smile, humoring him, like his rapid change is totally normal. But I'm never getting in a car with him again.

I shut the door. The Camaro pulls away. I wait there in the darkness until it turns the corner.

A noise comes from over my shoulder in the trees. I slowly stand up. Memories of the man in black flood back. I'm ready to run. A moan. A brushing on the ground.

I know I should be silent. For some reason, Drake picked here to stop the car and act crazy. For me to get out and be alone in the darkness.

The moan again. Agony and terror rolled into a soft sound.

"Hello?" I call into the trees. I take a step forward. Leaves crunch under my feet and send sparks up through my body. I take a couple more steps. The moaning stops. Something instinctual drives me faster and deeper into the dark.

But I already know what I'll find.

I almost trip over her body lying crumpled and cast aside in the mud, one leg propped against a tree trunk. I fall down on my knees next to her head. I touch her swollen face. "Can you hear me?"

Her eyelids flutter. Relief almost knocks me over. She's still alive. Terror picks me back up onto my feet. The guy could still be here, and she needs help *now*.

I curse at myself for not activating that flip phone from Carol Alexander. I feel around on the ground, hoping against all odds that I will find a cell phone. When I don't, I lean back over her head. She whimpers. I try to sound calm. "I'm going to get help. I'll be right back. You're going to be okay." Lie. Even if she lives, she'll never be okay.

After quitting the dance team, I started sitting on my ass all day. By the time I hit the parking lot of Bluebird Estates, my lungs are burning and my thigh muscles twitching.

"Help!" I scream over and over. No one comes outside. No curtains move in windows. It's as if I'm the last person left in the world. "Help!" I scream again. Nothing.

I push on the lobby door. This time it's locked. I reach for my bag. It's not on my shoulder. It's still sitting on the sidewalk where Drake left me.

I pound on the door. The glass rattles under my fists. "Help!" I try again, but my voice is weak. I slide to the ground. My eyes fill with tears. Sobs rush out of my mouth.

A blurry figure comes down the stairs. He lights a cigarette, opens the door, and steps around me without looking, like I'm some kind of bad memory he doesn't want to acknowledge.

I slip my fingers around the door before it slams shut. My legs quiver, but I haul myself forward. I'm crawling when I reach the top of the stairs. Apartment 21 opens. "What's up, Tracey's girl?"

Seeing him gives me the extra energy I need. I shove past him into his foul-smelling dump. I knock a pizza box off the table, dig my hand under the couch cushions, and kick at a newspaper on the floor.

"Whoa, what are you doing?"

I find it. Under a discarded sweatshirt on the kitchen table. I dial 911.

The woman on the phone is irritated with me. I'm talking too fast, not making sense. I repeat myself three times before she understands. Even then I'm not sure she believes me.

"Hey, where are you going?" Finn calls. I'm walking with his phone. I have his sweatshirt shoved under my arm.

I explain over and over again where the girl is, but the operator keeps telling me I'm at Bluebird Estates. "I know. She's not here," I try again. "I'm going to her now."

"No, don'—" I hang up. I'm not going round and round

anymore. The cops will come. I will flag them down from the side of the road if I have to.

My feet take me right to her. She's cold. Her breath is raspy. She's stopped moaning. She doesn't have much time.

I can't make out much about her. She's young. Dark hair and skin. Her clothes are ripped to shreds and covered in blood. I have the sweatshirt. I know I'm supposed to apply pressure, but I can't figure out where. I drop it in a pile of wet leaves and touch her hand. She doesn't react.

"My name's Kayla." The gentleness of my voice surprises me. The dam of emotion behind my eyes could break at any time and shower us both in tears. "The cops are on their way. You're going to be okay." That same lie again.

I want to move her leg off the tree. When I lean forward, I can see it's propped up at a funny angle. My stomach is empty, but bile forces its way into my mouth. She must be in agony. There's nothing I can do. I have never—not even the last time I called 911, when I was five years old—felt as helpless as I do in this moment.

Sirens. I put her hand down and grab the sweatshirt. "I'll be right back."

They drive past the street. Three cop cars, a fire truck, and an ambulance. I run to the middle of Bluebird Lane and jump up and down, waving the sweatshirt. "Here," I yell. "Here!" They don't stop. It's starting to drizzle. My hair sticks to my face. I run screaming, as if I'm possessed.

The ambulance stops. "Please," I say. My arms shake. They won't flap over my head anymore. Tears run freely. My knees give out. I fall onto Bluebird Lane.

The cop cars swing around. They come back. I hold my finger up and point into the trees. I can't get out of the road. They miss hitting me by inches. But they see where I'm pointing. The cars empty, and dark-suited figures scatter into the woods.

A soft grip on my shoulder. "Are you hurt, miss?" I can't shake my head, can't breathe, can't see through the water pouring from my eyes.

He lifts me to my feet and sits me down in the back of the ambulance. "Help her," I manage to whisper.

"The cops will clear the scene, the paramedics will go in and get her, and then we'll take her wherever she needs to go." He doesn't say *hospital*. My face crumples again. A blanket wraps around my shoulders. A device latches onto my finger.

He's a large man; rotund. He wears a food-stained, white, button-up uniform shirt and black pants. He examines a tablet in his hand. "Your pulse is pretty high. Can you take a deep breath for me?" I try. "Good," he says. He has kind eyes. Eyes you don't see on Bluebird Lane.

The radio at his hip crackles to life. He listens to the unintelligible voices on the other end and brings it to his mouth. "Ten-four," he says.

"What's happening?" I leap to the ground and paw at the thing on my finger.

"Easy," he says. "They've stabilized her. It will still be a few minutes before they can bring her out."

"She's still alive?"

He smiles. "She's alive."

"Miss?" I turn around. A cop, in jeans and a black slicker with POLICE across the back in neon yellow, holds up the badge hanging around his neck. "I'm Detective Cavallo. I need to take your statement."

I pull the blanket tighter around my shoulders. "Do you live nearby?" he asks. I point at Bluebird Estates. "Are your parents home?"

"My mom," I squeak.

"Maybe you'd feel more comfortable talking with her there?" I wouldn't, but I nod anyway.

He leads me to his unmarked car and opens the door. The front passenger side. Not the back, where they put the bad guys. An officer wearing blue rubber gloves runs up holding my backpack. I take it from him and let it plop into my lap.

A car is pulled over at the end of Bluebird Lane on the edge of the parking lot. A Camaro. Drake leans against it. Even in the dim yellow light, I can see that his face is tense and colorless.

"This is it, right? This is where you live?" I haven't gotten out of the car. The detective looks at me with concern. I can't tell if it's concern for my mental state or concern that my mental state might affect his investigation.

Now the front lobby door is propped open. The detective examines it as if it might be a clue. I keep going.

Finn meets me at the top of the stairs. "Where's my phone?" He steps forward into my face, but his eyes flit over my shoulder. They expand. The glint of the detective's badge under the zinging fluorescent lights propels Finn backward. His apartment door slams.

Apartment 26 opens. Mom stands in the doorway with her arms crossed. The look on her face stabs me in the heart. All the disappointments of her entire life focus on me. Me, her daughter, being dragged home by the cops.

The detective introduces himself and asks if he can come in. Mom glances nervously over her shoulder. There's nothing in the apartment except dust and dirty dishes, but old habits die hard.

He sits across from me at the table. He's middle-aged but fit, muscular. His dark brown hair is neatly parted and swept to the side. But his most eye-catching feature is his nose. It's two sizes too big for his face.

He shifts his weight on the unsteady, mismatched second-hand chair that's too small for his bulk. He's uncomfortable.

Join the club.

Mom hovers over us. Now that she has determined I didn't do anything, she's trying to be maternal. It doesn't suit her. She offers him something to drink. He declines. She brings me a mug. It contains lukewarm tap water, but I accept it and pretend to be drinking something soothing.

The detective flips open a notebook. "Can you tell me what happened?"

"I was on my way home from work"—I glance up at Mom—"and I heard a noise in the woods. I went to see what it was, and I found her."

"You were walking home from work alone? This late?" Mom wrings her hands behind his back and watches the door. She's waiting for him to cry neglect and for social services to come charging in.

"My boyfriend picked me up. But, um, we got in a fight,

and I took off. It was stupid." It's a half lie. I focus on the stained tabletop.

He asks me other questions about where I found her and my call to 911. I tell a prettied-up version of the truth, but I leave in the important parts.

He closes the notebook. I've done it. I've made it through. Mom relaxes. "One more question." The tension in the room rises into the red zone. "Have you seen anyone strange hanging around? Anyone in the woods?"

Three girls. This guy has attacked three girls. I was almost one of them. I look at Mom. I have a choice to make. A horrible choice. If I tell him about the man in black, it might help the investigation. It might save another girl. But what if Mom is accused of neglect for making me walk home late at night? For letting me almost get attacked? They would take me away. It would be Mom's last strike. She wouldn't have anything to live for. She'd go back to using.

I could go back to Marie's.

I'm going to be sick. I gulp the metallic, bleachy water. The detective waits. He's had practice with this. He will sit at our broken table all night if that's how long it takes for me to answer.

My eyes lock on Mom's. I shake my head. The lie seeps out of my pores like sweat.

He can smell it. He flicks a business card onto the table. "You can call me anytime."

Mom thanks him for getting me home safely. When he's thumping down the steps, she closes the door and presses her back against it, as if he's going to try to break back in.

I stand up from the table and go to my room. I can't look at her.

I still have Finn's phone and sweatshirt. I shake a stray leaf off the sweatshirt and try not to think about where it came from. I pull it on over my damp clothes and dial the number I memorized when I was five. Marie made it into a song, so if I ever got lost, I would just have to hum the tune and the number would come to me.

I feel so lost.

She answers on the third ring. Her voice is scratchy, full of alarm at being woken in the middle of the night.

"It's me," I say. The full weight of what happened crashes around me. My knees give out. I hit the floor. The dam breaks. I sob into Finn's sweatshirt.

"Kayla? Where are you? I'm coming to get you." I hear rustling. She's shoving her shoes on, scrambling to find her keys.

I manage to regain enough control to tell her no.

"What's going on?" she asks in the same tone of voice she used my first day with her. Calm, loving, but afraid to say the wrong thing.

"It's not me." My voice is small, fragile, like the squeak of a little mouse.

"Kayla, honey, you're scaring me. What's happened?"

"There's another girl. I found her. I didn't want you to think it was me."

"Oh, Kayla, I am so sorry." I hear the tears in her voice. It sets me off again.

"I would like to speak to your mother, please," Marie says,

now with determination. It's the voice she uses with teachers who accuse her little bears of being disruptive.

I crawl out of my room. Mom is still against the door. Holding it up. I hand her the phone.

Marie will be polite, businesslike, and distant. She will tell Mom that she is here for us. She has resources. But Mom will get the real message. She's being scolded.

Mom doesn't say anything. She listens and hangs up the phone. She hands it back to me, eyes wide and overwhelmed.

She has no idea that tonight I've given up going back to Marie's to keep her clean and safe.

I don't sleep. At five a.m., I turn on the TV. An attention-grabbing jingle plays, and the screen turns red with the flashy breaking news graphic. Another girl. Number three. She was found in the woods. The police think she was grabbed on her way to work. At McDonald's.

CHAPTER 17

BETSY

"What were you thinking, Betsy?" Teddy yells. "You can't wander into the desert at night on some kind of crusade. Do you know what could have happened to you?"

The woman and child have been consuming my every thought. Those that aren't about Adrian killing me, at least. Finals distracted me for a week, but then I had all winter break to think. I have to know what happened to them. And to find out, I had to tell Teddy.

I didn't tell him everything, just the basics. I followed Adrian out into the desert. There were people in a shack. Border Patrol came and took them away. That's it.

I don't respond to his anger. I stand still with my hands clasped in front of me and wait for him to finish.

His face is red. His mustache twitches. "I'm not going to tell your mother about this. It would only scare her." He points a finger at me. "And you're not going to do anything like that again."

I nod. I knew he wouldn't tell Mom. He wants to protect her. Make her world a land of unicorns and rainbows. One where her delinquent daughter gets straight As and helps old ladies cross the street.

"Will you find out what happened to them?" I ask, and look down at my hands. "Please."

"Don't put me in that position, Betsy. What am I supposed to say if someone asks why I want to know?"

"It's for Adrian." I look up at him through my lashes. Everyone loves Adrian. But really, it's for me. And I need someone else to see what he was doing out there.

Teddy shakes his head. "I'm not encouraging that boy. What he's doing is dangerous and illegal. He could get in real trouble."

"What do you think he was doing?" I ask. Teddy of all people should see what's going on here. Why am I still the only one who has figured Adrian out?

"What did *you* think he was doing?" He narrows his eyes. I imagine a command to go to my room would come next if he could get away with it.

I shrug. "He was acting strange." Please figure it out. Please release me from having to hide from Adrian every day, from pretending to agree with everyone when they tell me how nice he is. What a good boy he is.

Teddy's not buying it. I hold my body so rigid my muscles shake. "*I* need to know! I need to know if another child died." A tear of frustration splashes off my face and lands on my crewneck sweater.

Teddy's shoulders go slack as the anger leaves his body. "Betsy," he whispers.

I hold my hand out. I'm back in control. "No. Don't say anything. Just find out what happened."

I go to my room and slam the door. I pull out the black monster. It hasn't rung, but I send a text anyway.

Fuck you.

In my head, I see him raise an eyebrow and chuckle to himself. The monster buzzes.

Tsk. Tsk. Such language. Careful you don't get your mouth washed out with soap.

I toss the phone and pick up the sweatshirt it used to nest in. I press it against my cheek. It smells like cardboard and dust. Anything that used to be there is long gone.

Teddy's still pissed, but he comes through. I muster up my courage to enter C&J's. I haven't been here since before Thanksgiving. Just because Adrian hasn't come after me yet doesn't mean he won't. And I've been avoiding Happy. I don't want her to get hurt. It's better if I just slip out of existence than have to say goodbye.

I get through the door that doesn't jingle, but no farther. I hover between the in and the out, with the door against my back, letting the warm, oily air escape.

Angie glances up, but she doesn't hop to the door with a menu. Disgust is all over her face. Adrian probably told her I stole the money from the table, but she can't prove it. She's going to keep a close eye on me from now on.

Adrian is in the back near the kitchen door, rolling silverware into napkins. Seeing him sends a chill down my spine. I don't want to do this.

Happy takes a drink of juice and waves to me from our booth.

I don't see Rosie. It's the extra boost I need. I step inside. Happy waves again. She has her good-luck charm sitting on the table.

I avoid Adrian's eyes and slide into the booth across from her. "Hi." I try not to look at the fish.

"You came back." She smiles broadly and makes me feel like crap for disappearing on her, even if it was for her own good.

She looks around the empty restaurant, leans over the table, and whispers, "I'm glad you know now. I wasn't allowed to tell anyone."

I sit back. "Know what?"

"About Adrian," she says.

My heart races. Happy can't know the whole truth if she's still smiling. I wonder how Adrian sucked her in, how he made her believe in him. Made her look the other way.

I clap my hand over my mouth and try to breathe through my nose. When I've forced my stomach to settle, I remove my hand. "The woman and the kid from the desert are okay," I whisper.

"That's good," Happy says. She picks up her fish and swims it on the table. "I thought Adrian was in over his head with them. But you know Adrian." She chuckles.

"What do you mean?" I have to ask, even if I give something about myself away. I have to know what she knows, and I desperately want someone to talk to.

"They usually leave food and water out there, but then Adrian found the sick kid and the mom. He was determined to make the kid better, so they could keep going." She rubs her protruding belly. "If it were my baby, I would want to take him to a hospital, even if I got sent back." She looks up at me and shrugs. "But who knows why they left to begin with." She takes a sip of her orange juice, like this is a normal conversation.

"That's what Adrian told you?"

She crinkles up her brow. "He's been working with that immigrant aid group since we were, like, fourteen. He's kept it a secret for a long time. Only me and Tomás knew." She smiles. "I hate keeping secrets."

I melt into the torn seat. "Yeah, I know what you mean."

Helping people cross the desert? That's Adrian's cover story? I almost laugh. He's good. Impressive. Because who's going to follow up if "immigrants" go missing? Who's going to suspect a nice boy trying to help?

Adrian has had months to kill me. He could have done it after the birthday party or in the desert. He could have had someone else do it. Sneak into my window in the middle of the night and *poof!* I disappear forever.

But he didn't.

I'm not wrong about him. I can't be. I've seen him do too much. Being wrong is what gets innocent people killed.

I slide out of the booth. "I'll be right back." I have to know why I'm still alive. I'm going to poke the beast.

Adrian doesn't look up as I approach him.

"I need to talk to you," I whisper.

He treats me like a ghost or an echo of a person. Without acknowledging my presence, he picks up a gray dish tub and walks through the flapping doors.

Angie straightens paper placemats on a table, pretending she isn't still watching me. I take a deep breath.

I go through to the kitchen.

Mr. Morales is up to his elbows in suds. He scrubs a giant stockpot while singing softly to himself. When he sees me, he smiles, like I'm his favorite person, and winks. "Hello, Betsy," he says in his deep, warmly accented voice.

A piece of my frozen heart melts. I want to bounce to the sink, pick up a towel, and help. But my feet stay planted. My face is still and without expression.

Adrian grabs my shoulder and spins me around. "You can't be back here," he snaps.

"We need to talk about what happened."

His eye twitches. He glances at his father, who has resumed his singing, and pushes me into the walk-in.

I stand between two clear bins of tomatoes and wrap my arms around myself to protect my slight body from the cold. Adrian leans against the stainless-steel shelving that lines the walls. His body shakes with barely contained fury.

"The little boy had pneumonia. The mom was severely dehydrated." I push my lips up into a smile to provoke him. "But they're safe now."

It works. He clenches his fist, like he wants to take a swing at me. "They'll be deported. Do you know what they were running away from? They might have still had a chance. But now you"—the tip of his pointed finger lands inches from my heart—"have sent them back."

His hands grip the first container they reach, one full of shiny, green jalapeños. He hoists it up and storms out of the walk-in.

I drop my arms and let the cold seep into my body. I don't understand. Adrian seems to really care about the people in the shack. Like on a human level, not like something is in it for him. What if Happy is right? What if Adrian is a nice guy who tries to do good things?

Or maybe he's a really good actor.

I step out into the steamy air. Adrian chops peppers with a huge, deadly-looking knife. He pauses, his eyes meeting mine, the tip of the knife pointed at my heart. It's a message. One I understand.

Mr. Morales still washes but has stopped singing. I try to smile at him, but the corners of my mouth just twitch. I exit the kitchen and leave behind the sound of Adrian's rhythmic chopping.

Angie tracks my progress across the dining room. I pass Happy in the booth. She slurps up the dregs of her orange juice and scoots herself out. She bounces behind me. "Wanna go for a walk?"

I shake my head. Happy ignores it. "The doctor said I should take a walk every day."

When I open the door that doesn't jingle, she's hot on my heels. The sun is going down and taking the warmth with it. "It's too cold for a walk," I say.

Happy considers this for a second. "No, it's still okay out here." She hooks her arm around mine. "Let's go to the park." Even though she's several inches shorter and moves with a pregnant waddle, she's still strong.

She drags me past the flower shop, where Mom has the phone up to her ear. She laughs and makes notes on a pad. It isn't the brightly lit shop that makes her glow. I sigh deeply without realizing it. Happy squeezes my arm.

She leads me around the back of the strip mall into the old but well-cared-for neighborhood where the Morales family lives. At the end of the street sits a square of open space. The grass is brown; the few trees stand naked. Strips of color peel off a play structure. Happy digs her toes into the ground and kicks at a rock. She hasn't said a thing since we left.

"Are you okay?" I ask. Happy looks at me, startled. I glance over my shoulder. We're the only people in the park.

She plops down on a bench, legs parted, belly balanced on top of them. "I'm Happy," she says. "I don't get to be anything else."

I sit down next to her. I don't know what to do with my hands. They fold in my lap, and unfold, and fold again.

"You probably think I'm stupid," she says. My head shakes, but too quickly, too emphatically. She laughs. "It's okay. Why would you think anything else? I'm sixteen, I'm pregnant, and I walk around acting like I won the lottery." She leans her head back and closes her eyes against the sun.

"Adrian gave me the name Happy. In first grade. Maybe I was happy then. Now I'm just living up to expectations." She rubs her stomach. "When I told my grandma, she said she wasn't raising no baby, and she kicked me out."

I force words from my mouth. "I'm sorry."

She opens one eye. "Yeah," she says. "Tomás isn't a bad guy. You probably think he is. I know he deals, but what are we supposed to do? We're alone in this. Any day, I could be all alone."

I watch in horror as my hand pats her baby bump. She opens her other eye. Instead of irritation at my complete invasion of her personal space, she smiles.

"I never knew my father," I say. It's the only true thing I have ever told her. Right now, after everything with Adrian, I feel like I need to grab on to something. Something that's *me*. "There was this guy when I was little, but he didn't stick around."

Happy nods along, like she's heard this story before. Then we sit in silence. I'm afraid if I open my mouth again, the entire first sixteen years of my life will come tumbling out.

"Adrian really is a good guy," she says.

I pull my hand away. "I don't want to talk about Adrian." How can Happy believe him? The orange fish, the group of little girls at the party, the woman and kid in the desert. The knife and duct tape in his truck. Everything is adding up. Still, when I look at Happy's face, doubt creeps all around me.

I did the right thing, didn't I? That boy was going to die. If it wasn't because of Adrian, it would have been because of the pneumonia. Even though it exposed me further, getting him help was the right thing. Or not. I don't know anymore. I'm not even sure there is a right thing.

"Listen," Happy says with a sternness that throws me for another loop. I concentrate on her face to show her I'm paying attention.

"There was a girl named Raina. She lived here with her mom while her dad was working on an oil rig in the ocean. She went to private school, but in eighth grade, she transferred to our school.

"She was really pretty, like a model or someone on TV. She had blond hair and blue eyes, and she was tall and skinny." Happy can't help but look down at her belly.

"Adrian fell for her hard, like really hard. He was always in a good mood and had this stupid, goofy smile on his face all the time. Then one day he went over to her house. Her dad had come home for the week, and he answered the door. He told Adrian he couldn't see Raina anymore. Ever. He didn't want her bringing home any brown babies."

I suck in a sharp breath. Happy shakes her head. "I know, right? Raina and her family moved to Houston after that. Adrian never got over it, and he hasn't been the same since." She pauses to make sure I'm still listening. "But I wanted you to know, inside he's a good person. The best."

"I did something," I blurt out. "I made a choice." Happy looks at me with interest. "I did what I thought was right, and it maybe wasn't."

Happy nods. She rubs her stomach. "Me too," she says.

Our eyes meet. The sunset is reflected in hers. The wind blows against my ears, turning them cold. But I feel warm inside, and for a fleeting moment, I feel like everything might be okay. Then the sun disappears below the horizon, and Happy's face is plunged into the shadows.

CHAPTER 18
KAYLA

The girl at the mall wouldn't do it. She crossed her arms and told Paige absolutely not. She was barely older than us, and yet her face was covered with almost as many piercings as skin. No way did she get all of those after she turned eighteen.

Carol Alexander and Paige had a disagreement about what Paige could get for her seventeenth birthday. Paige wanted her nose pierced. Carol gave her a coffee-colored cashmere sweater.

Since Thanksgiving, Paige and I have been trying. We see each other at school, and we've hung out a couple of times, but there is an awkward tension surrounding us like a dark mist.

Plus, I found the cashmere sweater in my locker with the tags still attached.

The place we're in now is Seedy with a capital *S*. Sierra's sister knows a guy who will pierce anything. No ID. No questions.

I stand over a glass case and peer at a thousand pieces of metal that can be poked through numerous body parts. Paige grabs my hand. "This is so exciting!" she squeals.

I lift my head and catch sight of myself in the small, smudged mirror on the counter. My skin has a strange cast to it. My eyes are sunken, lips pale. I look gray, like someone who missed four days of school because of the "flu." It's going around, you know. But really, I couldn't face the hallways full of people whose biggest concern is what to wear to the winter formal next month. Not after what I've seen.

Every time I close my eyes, there she is. On the ground, bleeding. Girl Number Three. She has a name. Shonda. I don't like to think about that. It's easier to call her Girl Number Three, like the robot reporters on the news.

When I open my eyes, I can still see her.

"What do you think of that one?" Paige points into the case. "A star? For Explorers?" She realizes her mistake and looks away. We don't talk about my quitting the dance team.

"Which one?" I ask, and try to seem engaged.

"The third from the top."

I follow her finger. It points at a tiny silver star on a metal post that curves at the end. *Like an earring that has been stepped on and bent.*

In the mirror, my skin turns green.

I smile and nod. The guy comes out. Paige puts her money—cash up-front—on the counter.

She screws up her face and cringes as the guy prepares to shove metal through it.

It's a coincidence. Hundreds of girls have nose piercings, not just Shonda. Even straight-laced Paige is about to have one.

Jordan brought a girl with a nose piercing back to his house. She took it out and put it on the bedside table. It fell on the floor. A simple explanation. Pain hits me in the gut. Fear? Jealousy? I don't have words to describe what I feel anymore.

Paige glances at herself in the rearview mirror for the hundredth time. A pinpoint of sparkle shines off her splotchy red nose. "Mom is going to freak," she says, satisfied.

We pull up to Bluebird Estates. I don't think Paige ever cared about it before, but this time, now that I've wrecked our friendship, she sees it for what it really is. Her eyes are alert and her hands clamp down on the steering wheel, like she's nervous. The faster she can get out of here, the better.

"Thanks for the ride," I say.

She smiles at me. She looks like her mother. Polite, but fake, hiding the disgust. The gap between us in the car becomes a crevasse, a canyon, a gorge. I don't know if there's a bridge long enough to cross it again.

I creep up the stairs. It's too early for Mom to be staked out at the peephole. I stop in front of apartment 21.

It's Saturday, which would have been a workday for me at No Limit. I have nowhere to go. Jordan's still not back, and Mom is already suspicious that something is going on. If I go to apartment 26, I will have to confess. Confess that I have no job, I have no dance team—I have nothing.

I can't go to McDonald's. Anyone could be waiting for me there.

I tap on the door with my fingernail. Finn opens it wearing boxers. He steps back. I walk past him but hesitate to sit on the couch. His phone rests on the coffee table. I shudder when my mind flashes to holding it. Dialing.

The TV is on. Some loudmouthed talk-show host yells at her guests. Finn sits down and picks up a pipe. He offers it to me.

I almost take it.

A tear traces down my face.

He sighs and puts the pipe down. He pats the sofa cushion next to him. I sit. "What's going on, Kayla?"

I jump in surprise. "You remember my name?"

He shrugs. "I gave it to you."

I pull my right leg underneath me and turn to face him. "What?"

"You were a pudgy, red, squalling thing, only a few days old, when your ma brought you here. I hadn't seen her in years. I don't know where she was living, but they wouldn't take a baby.

"She got clean when she found out she was pregnant, but when you arrived and were an actual baby to take care of, your ma didn't know what to do. She hadn't even given you a name. So I gave you one." He picks up the pipe again and runs the flame of a disposable lighter under the bottom. "I thought Kayla was pretty."

"What happened to her?" I ask.

He takes a drag off the pipe, holds the smoke in his lungs,

and gazes up at the ceiling. He releases. "She tried hard for you, but once you've had a taste, it never goes away."

He lays his head back on the torn upholstery. "I loved her. Always have, always will." He smiles his little-boy smile of approval—Drake's smile—then his eyes close and flutter under his lids in starry oblivion.

Drake's smile. It's been nagging at the back of my mind since I found Shonda. It was his car that sped past me the night of the first girl. His boots that were covered in mud the horrible night it was almost me. He was the last person to see Finn's hooker. He's always hanging around, watching people go in and out.

Shonda left with him from McDonald's.

If I hadn't gotten out of the car that night, would I have been next?

I don't want it to be him. I want it to be anyone else on the planet but Drake. It would destroy Jordan to know that his friend was the man in black.

It would destroy me. If I hadn't met Jordan, if Jordan hadn't brought Drake to McDonald's . . .

I led him right to Shonda.

I ditch school. After the way I looked at the piercing place, Paige will tell everyone I'm still sick. Not that they'll ask. After quitting the dance team and generally avoiding everyone, I'm running out of people to care about me.

It takes three buses to get to the hospital, but I have to know if Drake attacked Shonda.

When I step into the white, antiseptic-smelling lobby, my stomach growls and my butt's sore from the hard plastic bus seats. A receptionist sits at a round desk under a sign that says INFORMATION. I give her my big Clairmont Explorers Dance Team smile. "Hi, which room is Shonda in?"

She types into her computer. "Last name?"

"Uh, I don't really know. I go to her school. I have her homework." I motion to a nonexistent backpack on my shoulder. My lying skills suck.

The woman clicks her tongue. "Can't do anything without a last name." She stares me down. I've lost.

"Excuse me."

I turn around. A thin, older African American woman holding a cup of coffee runs her eyes over my face. She looks like she's dressed for church in a bright blue suit and hair in neat curls. Her lips part. She breathes in deeply.

"Are you the girl who found her? My granddaughter?"

That night runs like a movie on fast-forward over and over again in my head, weakening my knees. She leads me over to a chair and presses the coffee into my hand. I gulp it and burn my tongue.

I want to ask her a thousand things, but I can't speak. My hand covers my mouth. I can't stop seeing Shonda crumpled and bloody on the ground. I look at the floor, afraid her grandmother will see the picture reflected in my eyes.

"She hasn't woken up yet. The doctors say the rest of her will heal. She just has to wake up."

"I'm sorry," I say with my head in my hands.

The woman wraps her arms around my shoulders. "Thank

you for helping my baby." She stays that way, squeezing me tight until I stop crying.

I give her Finn's number. She promises to call when Shonda wakes up. I know now what I have to do.

An ancient, much-abused pay phone is stuck to the wall outside. I dig Detective Cavallo's card out of my pocket.

There's an ice cream shop around the corner and across a busy street from the hospital. I step inside. A bored guy in a stupid paper hat barely acknowledges me. It's not even lunchtime. Too early for ice cream. I pick a table in the back corner. It smells like bleach with an undercurrent of sour milk. I'm the only one here.

Ten minutes later, Detective Cavallo comes in. He wears a sharp gray suit with a yellow tie. When he leans over the ice cream case, I catch a glimpse of his badge and gun.

He licks a sample spoon of something blue. He smacks it between his lips and nods. He points at me. "You want something?" I shake my head. He waves away Paper Hat Guy, who looks relieved at not having to work.

The detective sits across from me. His huge nose shines under the bright lights of the shop. He seems different than at Bluebird Estates. Happier. Maybe everyone does.

"I hate taking notes. I'm a terrible speller." He laughs and pulls out a digital recorder. My stomach twists. I don't want to do this.

"Take your time, don't leave anything out. Even a small thing could be important." He smiles. And I realize something. I can see it in the set of his shoulders, in his finger tapping the table, the way he glances over his shoulder at paper hat guy. It's a well-practiced act. The ice cream shop. The Mr. Happy routine. Really, he's hard, cold. He's doing what he has to do so I'll feel safe, talk, rat someone out.

And I will. I'll do it for Shonda. And I'll do it because if I don't, I might be Girl Number Four.

"I think it was Drake." My voice is weak and mouselike. As soon as I hear the words, I'm afraid I'm wrong. What if I'm wrong?

Cavallo leans forward. "Last name?"

I blink hard and look down at the table. Someone has carved their initials into the sticky wood. "I don't know."

"Address?" Cavallo tries again. I shake my head. I can't tell him where Drake lives. I can't get Jordan caught up in this.

"What's he look like?"

I give him a description of Drake that's so generic it could be anyone. Cavallo nods along, humoring me.

"What about a car? What's he drive?"

"A black Camaro with a Florida license plate," I whisper.

"Uh-huh." Cavallo nods again, but a spark has appeared in his eyes. "Any identifying marks? Scars? Tattoos?"

"He has a snake tattoo on his arm."

Cavallo sits back and turns off the tape recorder, looking satisfied. "Thank you, Kayla. That was very helpful. You've confirmed another tip we got."

"Really?" I can't breathe. It was Drake. I gulp air, trying to get my lungs to work. "What happens now?" I squeak.

"We'll put an APB out for him as a person of interest. If officers see the car, they'll pull him over."

That will take too long. All Drake needs is another night to find another girl.

Cavallo stands up to leave. "Wait." I reach my hands across the table, as if to grab him and pull him back. "I know where Drake's supposed to be tonight."

Cavallo's eyes widen. "Stay here," he says. His purposeful footsteps echo through the empty ice cream shop. He exits and pulls out his cell phone. The guy at the counter glances at me. I feel my face burn. My insides are all mixed up. Cavallo all but confirmed that it was Drake, but part of me is still hoping that it isn't, that I'm wrong.

Cavallo sticks his head in the door. "Kayla, I'm gonna need you to come with me."

CHAPTER 19
BETSY

A pink slip summoning me to the counselor's office appears during Life Skills. What if Miss Jones is still trying to find my school records? What if she asks why no one in North Dakota has been able to produce them?

I've always been bad at charades. I forget that I'm not supposed to talk and end up giving the answer away. Maybe today is the day I lose this game I've been playing.

The class titters when I walk up to the front. At the doorway, I turn around and survey my classmates, like it might be the last time I ever see them. Happy waves.

I take a deep breath and put one foot in front of the other until I reach the giant smiley face on Miss Jones's door. She looks up. The smile on her face is plastic, even more unbelievable than the poster.

"Please, sit." She motions to the chair wedged between boxes of college brochures.

I sit and focus on my knees.

She leans forward and folds her hands on the desk. "I wanted to check in with you and see how the new semester is going. Is anything too easy? Too hard?"

I shake my head. "It's fine."

"Good. Have you made friends? I see you with Happy and Adrian a lot."

I shrug.

"They're good kids," she says wistfully, as if she isn't only, like, seven years older than us.

I shrug again.

"So." Her fingers tap against the fake wood top of the desk. "I heard a rumor that Lawrence proposed to Angie." She lifts her right hand and rubs the back of her neck. "Is that true?"

This is why she called me out of class? She wants me to dish? Tell her how last weekend Lawrence kneeled down in front of Angie and produced a paper saying he got his GED? How he popped a ring out of his pocket and the whole restaurant gasped? How Angie cried? How her face twisted when she saw me in the corner—like I was a bad omen for her happy marriage?

No such luck, Miss Jones.

I shrug a third time.

She sighs. "You should probably get back to class." Her face contorts into that plastic smile, but her eyes look like she wants to cry.

Angie has the flu. Mom and Mrs. Morales sit at a table in C&J's covered in bridal magazines. They coo over every page.

The wedding has been set for mid-April, and even though she's the most junior member at the florist, Mom will be doing the flowers. Mrs. Morales insisted. Every surface in our house is covered in practice bouquets of various colors.

They make me sneeze.

"That neckline is gorgeous. Look at the beading." Mom points to a page. Mrs. Morales leans in to inspect it. Rosie grips the back of her chair and pulls her feet up until she's hanging.

"This is boring," she whines.

I sit with my chair pushed back from the table. My legs and arms are crossed. I examine my chewed-down-to-a-stub nails.

I feel all the eyes focus on me. I look up.

Mom shows her teeth in a wolflike grin. "Betsy, why don't you take Rosie to the park?" Mrs. Morales nods enthusiastically.

The kid is gone in a flash through the flapping kitchen doors. A second later, she reappears, one arm in her pink puffy coat.

Her clammy fingers wrap around mine. "Let's go, Betsy." I glance at Mom. She smiles like an angel looking down on me from heaven.

When I stand, Rosie almost yanks me off my feet. "Come on!" She hops up and down like she has to go to the bathroom.

I follow her outside. She releases me, takes off running, and leaves my sight. I jog to catch up.

"Hand," I say automatically when we reach the curb. Her

eyebrows knit, but she takes my outstretched hand and allows me to usher her across the street.

I sit on a bench. Rosie tears off to the play structure. "Betsy, watch!" she calls, and flies down the slide.

A basketball game is happening on the other end of the park. Seniors I recognize from school shove one another and wrestle for the ball. One backs away from the melee. He gives me the San Justo head nod.

"Betsy!" Rosie calls again. I ignore her. The angle of the winter sun turns the sky a dusty light blue. I unzip my jacket, close my eyes, and try to suck its weak rays into my pale skin. It's quiet. Almost peaceful. I feel some of the tension ooze out of my muscles.

I don't know how long my eyes are closed. Maybe I even fall asleep. Car doors slam behind me and bring me back to the world. I open my eyes. The basketball players drive away in dented, rusted hand-me-downs.

My lungs take in a deep breath of chilly air. I almost feel okay today.

The empty space where the basketball players' cars were reveals a black sedan. With tinted windows. Just like the one that followed me and took my picture. It sees me and rolls away unhurried down the street and around the corner.

As I watch it go, I realize something that makes my pounding heart stop cold in my chest. Rosie's feet aren't tromping through the sand or up the play structure.

"Rosie?" I jump up. "Rosie?" I spin to all four corners of the park. A puffy pink coat lies cast off on the grass.

"Rosie?" My voice is high-pitched. Desperate.

I pound up to the top of the oiled-wood platform of the play structure. The slide reflects the sun into my eyes. The park is still. Dead.

"Rosie?" I whisper.

My feet carry me down to the sand. I force them to move one in front of the other in the direction the car went. My head goes dizzy. Spots of black appear in my vision. My hands are wet. I look down at them. They're covered in blood. I rub my eyes, smearing the blood onto my face. I stagger to the bench. My chest heaves. An animalistic scream leaves my mouth. I curl into a ball and force the world to go black.

"Betsy?" A soft, warm voice. And crying. Crying in the background. "Betsy?" the voice asks again. I shove my hands behind me. My eyelids flitter. They're too swollen to snap all the way open.

Adrian leans over me. I shriek and pull myself into a ball to protect my soft belly. Adrian steps back. That's when I see Rosie standing behind him, clutching her coat and sniveling. I uncurl and look around. He's not taken me to the shack in the desert. I'm still in the park. Alive.

"Do you want me to get your mom?" Adrian asks. I shake my head. He glances at Rosie, who's taken two steps forward and is peering down at me. "She has a favorite hiding spot over there." He points to a narrow space between a blue metal trash can and a prickly evergreen bush. "When she couldn't wake you up, she ran home and got me." He looks at me accusingly. Blaming. Judging.

Now that the burst of adrenaline is fading, I feel cold. Rosie still stares down at me. Her eyes and mouth are set in a look of curiosity. I lift my head to see what's so interesting to her.

I grab the sides of my jacket and slap them across my chest. There's a rip in the cheap fabric of my shirt. In my panic, I must have snagged it on something. The ragged slit runs from my neck to the now-exposed left cup of my bra.

I peer up at Adrian, and his eyes move slowly to my face. I can't read his expression. It's blank. Too blank. It's the look of someone pretending not to know what they know. I sit up and turn my back to him. Tears course down my face. I can't stop them, and I can't stop him from seeing.

"Let's go, Rosie." He doesn't take her hand. He walks away. She follows, pink coat dragging on the ground behind her.

A chipped, off-white diner mug of hot chocolate with something spicy added to it steams in front of me. I can't force myself to not drink it. The cup shakes as I bring it to my lips. My hands are clean. They were never bloody. Not today, at least.

I'm in a booth, alone, with my jacket zipped as high as it will go. Mom sends worried glances in my direction. She's still surrounded by magazines, but Mrs. Morales has abandoned them to serve a laughing couple seated against the wall.

My eyes won't focus on anything. My ears feel like they're underwater. Distorted, whalelike sounds surround me. My feet are numb. My fingers tingle.

I don't see Adrian until he's sliding into the booth across

from me. I look at his face, familiar and alien at the same time. Stray dark hairs poke out between his eyebrows. His nose has a patch of blackheads on the tip. His left front tooth slightly overlaps the right. His lips are chapped.

"Feel better?" he asks. I don't know if it is a true inquiry or a demand. *Feel better.*

I nod but push myself hard into the back of the booth, like he might jump over the table and grab me by the throat.

"Good." He stands up. He takes a step. Then he turns around. "Oh," he says. "I think you dropped something in the park."

I slap my hand against my empty pocket. Oh. My. God.

Adrian's face changes. This is not the faux-concerned Adrian from the park. This is the Adrian I've been expecting.

He dangles the black monster in front of my face. "You have a pink phone," he says. "I know because Happy wishes she had a sparkly pink phone *just like yours.*" He taps the monster on the table. "This one is black."

I try to grab it, but he whips it away from me. He scrolls through the screens. "There's only one number on here. One number over and over again." He looks at me. "A number with a Washington area code. Who are you talking to in Washington, Betsy from North Dakota?"

He reaches into his pocket and pulls out his fish. He rubs it between his fingers. "I've been to Seattle. It's a nice place. Rains a lot."

He lowers his voice. "In the desert, you said you didn't want another death placed on you. What did that mean?"

"Nothing. It meant nothing." I can't catch my breath. Did I say that to him? How could I be so stupid?

"Stay away from my family, Betsy."

The black monster comes to life in his hand. He glances at it and places it on the table in front of me.

"You should answer that. It might be important."

Adrian starts to walk away again, and then he turns and motions toward his heart. "Sorry about your shirt."

CHAPTER 20
KAYLA

It will be an undercover op to get Drake. Cavallo took me from the ice cream shop to the police station. I spent all afternoon describing Drake over and over again to a parade of sketch artists, cops, and special agents while Cavallo ran around flapping papers and yelling at those same people.

Now I sit in his office. It's spare. A gray metal desk, a computer, neatly stacked manila folders. A sweating can of Coke and a ham sandwich in plastic sealed with a gas station sticker are brought to me, but I can't eat. It's happening too fast.

I can't be sure that Drake will be there. It's been a week since I dove out of his car. Has he still been going to McDonald's, even though I haven't shown? Jordan would have told him to pick me up no matter what. But would Drake care if Jordan got pissed at him for ditching me?

Cavallo charges in. "I'll have an officer take you home now." He moves back to the door.

"Wait," I call out. "I'm not going with you? Drake's supposed to pick *me* up at the McDonald's."

"It's taken care of, Kayla. This isn't my first time doing this. You're a minor, and we can't use you in an operation. And I'm certainly not using you as bait."

"But I want to. I want to help. Please," I beg. It's the only thing that will make me feel better. Make up for my part in leading Drake to Shonda.

Cavallo's face softens. "Kayla, we never know how these things are going to go down. I don't want to be the one who has to tell your mother that the guy pulled out a gun and started shooting."

"Please," I whisper.

Cavallo sighs and crosses his arms. "Fine. If your mother agrees, you can sit in the back of an unmarked car on the other side of the parking lot. You don't get out. You don't say a word. You don't do anything to interfere with the operation. If it looks like it's going bad, you're out of there." I nod in agreement.

A uniformed officer is dispatched to Bluebird Estates to talk to Mom. Explain the situation, get her consent. She'll consent. She'll want to seem cooperative. She'll do anything the cops ask.

When Cavallo comes back, he's changed into his jeans and a black slicker. He's all business. "Let's go."

He deposits me into the backseat of an old silver car. The driver is a hipster wannabe with a full golden beard and tight-legged, too-short pants. He ignores me.

We wait behind the bus at what was my usual stop in

front of No Limit Foods. A girl—although she can't be; she has to be over eighteen or what's the point of me sitting in the cramped backseat of this car inhaling the cloying pine air freshener that hangs from the rearview mirror—steps out onto the sidewalk. She has my hair color, and it's up in a ponytail that swishes as she crosses the street. Up close she looks to be twenty-five, but from the back, from a distance, I guess she could be mistaken for me.

We pull into a space near Elton's station wagon. I won't be able to see anything from here. I undo my seat belt and move forward until my head rests between the two front seats. Hipster cop glances at me and raises an eyebrow. I sit back hard and cross my arms.

He sighs and reaches under the passenger seat. "Here," he says. It's the first time I've heard him speak. He hands me a pair of heavy black binoculars.

My heart warms. "Thanks," I say. He stares straight ahead again, like I'm invisible.

And we wait. And wait. And wait. Being a cop must be really boring. Everything had to be in place hours before Drake is supposed to arrive, in case he was checking things out.

As it gets darker, I can clearly make out the usual people inside McDonald's. The pimply boy leans on the front counter. More than anything I want to jump out of the car, run to him, and tell him Shonda will be okay. But I don't know that. A shiver pulses through my body.

I was sad and angry about the first two girls, but Shonda is different. She's a real person to me, not just a glimpse at the bus stop or a segment on the news. If she dies, it will be my fault for leading Drake to her. I will never forgive myself. If she dies, there will be nothing to stop me from going to Finn's and taking something to forget. Then doing it again and again. There will be nothing to stop me from turning into my mother.

The fake me sits with her back to us in plain view of the parking lot. Since I haven't shown for a week, Drake needs to see "me" when he first pulls up. Otherwise, he might keep driving. Cavallo doesn't want to have to chase him.

A woman sits between fake me and the door. She's dressed like everyone else—faded, old jeans, red hoodie zipped up to her neck—except she's absolutely gorgeous. Her shiny dark hair, reaching almost down to her waist, is pulled back in a low ponytail. She has eyes like a manga character. She's small, but I bet if she stood up, she'd appear as tall and leggy as a supermodel. She reads a well-worn paperback. Every male eye in the restaurant is focused on her.

She's a cop.

The muscles in my arms shake from holding up the heavy binoculars. I put them down. Hipster has barely moved since we got here. I wonder if he's asleep. I lean forward to check, and he eyes me in the mirror. I lean back.

The anticipation is exhausting. The sky grows even darker, and the amber lights that hover over the parking lot click on. My mind flashes back to lying on the cement, waiting for the man in black to show up. And he did. I just didn't know it then. Drake could have done whatever he wanted to me that night. No one would have known. He could have left me in the woods to be found days or weeks or months later. But he didn't.

He could have been trying to gain my trust, make me like him. Make *me* go to him. Or maybe it was because of Jordan.

Or maybe it's because I'm wrong.

I swallow hard.

The cop answers her cell phone. Her eyes flit to fake me. Every muscle in my body seizes up. Headlights bounce through the window. It's the Camaro. He showed. I duck.

The cop puts her book and her phone into her bag. She yawns dramatically. It's a sign to the others outside. They won't move in until she raises her arms and stretches, which she'll do when she has confirmation that it's Drake.

Something's wrong. Both doors of the Camaro open at the same time. Two people get out. Drake out of the driver's side and out of the other . . .

Jordan.

He sees fake me lit up in the window. His face explodes into a smile. I grab Hipster's shoulder. "No. They can't . . ." It's too late. The woman cop lifts her arms over her head. I drop the binoculars.

Two marked police cars with lights on screech up to the McDonald's. One stops behind the Camaro, and the other pulls up next to its left side. Four officers spill out with their hands on their holstered guns. Two approach Drake.

Two approach Jordan.

Hipster starts the car. We pull forward to the exit that will take us to Bluebird Lane. I push my nose against the window as we pass McDonald's. Drake's back is to me. His hands are spread on the Camaro. One of the cops pats him down.

Jordan is on the other side of the car. Cavallo has come out from the back of McDonald's and is examining Jordan's driver's license. The car passing makes them both turn their heads.

Jordan's eyes meet mine. I see something in his that makes my heart stop dead in my chest.

I've betrayed him.

Hipster delivers me all the way to my mother. She opens apartment 26 and wraps her arms around me. Hipster nods at us. Mission accomplished. He'll sit in the parking lot for a couple of hours until Cavallo has everything wrapped up.

I let Mom pull me inside and hold me, rocking me back and forth. "I'm sorry," she says into my ear. "Was it bad? Should I have told them no?"

I shake my head. She pulls away and looks at me. Really looks at me, like she's never seen my face before. I should be in tears, wiping my nose with the back of my hand. But I'm not. It's all too big. Shonda, Drake, Jordan. I'm feeling too much. Everything is shutting down.

Mom hugs me again. "I think you're very brave," she says.

It's late when the knock on the door comes. We aren't asleep. I wonder if I will ever sleep again.

Hipster stands in the hallway and holds a cell phone out to me. I place it to my ear.

"You were great, Kayla Asher," Cavallo bellows. "Drake, or whatever his name is, gave us a fake ID. They're running his prints now. Once we know who he really is, I'll question him. Until then, I've got him in a room. I'm gonna let him sweat awhile."

"What about the other guy?" I ask.

"Other guy?"

"Jordan," I whisper.

"Oh, that guy. Wrong place, wrong time. He seemed to genuinely have no idea what was going on. We asked him some questions and cut him loose."

The aching deep between my rib cage and belly button eases up.

"You did a stellar job, Kayla. Good night." He hangs up.

I don't feel so stellar. Back when school started, I had a job and a best friend. I was on the dance team. I met a boy and had an honest-to-God, real boyfriend. And now? I have nothing. No job. My relationship with Paige is strained. I got Jordan's friend arrested for assault and murder.

Stellar, Kayla. Absolutely stellar.

I sit on the floor of my closet and break open the box that contains the phone from Carol Alexander. I don't want to use it, but what choice do I have now? I have to try to fix things with Jordan.

I go through the steps to activate it and then punch in the number from the scrap of notebook paper that I have stared at a hundred times since Jordan gave it to me. I type a text.

I'm sorry.

CHAPTER 21
BETSY

The phone, the fish, my ripped shirt.

Adrian knows.

I can't calm down. I still was holding on to a little bit of hope that Adrian hadn't figure it all out. That he thought I was just some strange girl who lied about being from North Dakota. But not anymore. Adrian knows *everything.*

Mom whisked me out of C&J's and brought me home. She declared everything to be okay.

That didn't make me feel any better. I pace back and forth, wring my hands, cry, hiccup, gasp for air.

Mom forces a pill down my throat to make me sleep. It doesn't work. I wake up at two a.m., sweating, sick to my stomach.

Adrian knows.

I check the black monster for the millionth time. It hasn't rung again since the restaurant. I hang over the side of the bed and nestle it back into the duffel bag. I won't need it anymore.

I can't clear my head. Horrible things keep dancing in front of my eyes. I don't know what's real. I don't want to die. But I don't want to keep living like this, either.

There's one thing that I know will help. Make it stop. Give me some peace, even if it's fleeting. I've hit rock bottom. It's all I have left.

Lime-green strappy sandals that match one of my overly cute school outfits are the first shoes I find. I slide them on. I pull on a jacket. My toxic-pink phone is in the outer pocket and knocks against my hip. I don't take it out. If I do this wrong and die, the phone will make it easier to identify my body.

Mom took a sleeping pill too. Hers worked. She doesn't hear me creep down the hall to the kitchen. In the bottom cabinet, behind assorted pots and pans, is another duffel bag. Inside, tucked into the lining, is a stack of hundred-dollar bills. I peel off three of them. Mom's probably forgotten all about the bag. Not that it will matter tomorrow. She'll have bigger things to think about than missing money. Mom. She's almost enough to stop me. To send me back to my bedroom. Almost. I turn and go out the front door.

The desert night is bitterly cold. A thousand stars explode over my head. My toes are numb. I pass the strip mall and the school. One foot in front of the other until I come to the land of chain-link fences. A dog barks. "Shut up!" rumbles out of a leaning, paint-peeling mobile home.

At the end of the dirt road, Tomás and Happy sleep in their blacked-out house. I'm not going there. I stop at the first house on the right. The house I saw Tomás dealing to.

The porch light is on. They're up. Of course they are. Bad

things come out in the dark. I walk around to the back door. Music's playing. Not thumping party music, something old and mellow.

I knock. The sound of stumbling inside. The door opens a crack, and a patch of red hair demands, "What?"

I hold up the money.

The door opens wider. His pupils are huge. There's another person in the house. A woman with dishwater-blond hair falling in greasy clumps around her face. She's stretched out on the floor, leaning against the couch. She moans in ecstasy.

I tip my head at her. Red understands. He lets me in.

Pipes, half-smoked cigarettes, and a vodka bottle litter the coffee table. I move toward it.

Red makes a grab for the money. I pull it away. "After," I say. He agrees, because he knows that once I've done it, he can rob me blind. Do whatever he wants. He positions himself behind me. His hands rest on my shoulders.

I sit on the floor. I've seen this done before, of course. It always looked so easy. My hands shake. I feel a mix of emotions I don't have a name for. Relief that I might get to forget what I did. Terror of what I'm about to do. A new guilt for something I haven't even done yet.

There's a syringe in front of me on the table.

I reach for it but pull back. I need a moment to collect myself. Before I do this thing that can't be undone.

I look around the room. Over Red's shoulder, three pictures in dusty frames stand on an empty bookcase. The first picture is a formal family portrait. A mom, a dad, and two cute little blond girls, all in their Sunday best.

The second is of the blond girls as teenagers. They're standing on the side of a river, fishing poles in hands, arms thrown around each other.

The third is a picture of one of them all grown up. She has a little girl of her own. They smile, but the tension is already there. The foreshadowing of something bad about to happen.

That woman is next to me on the floor. A dark, ghostly shadow of her former self. I don't see anything belonging to a kid in the house.

"What happened to the kid?" I whisper. Red places his fingers against the side of my neck. I push him off. My eyes spin around the room. "Where's the kid?" I twist around and grab his face, forcing him to look me in the eye. "Where's the kid?"

"What kid?" His cheeks burn with irritation. His lips sneer.

I let go and try to stand. He pushes me down to the floor. "Where do you think you're going?"

I glance back up at the photos. "I'm not going to do this." I get one foot under me.

"Money," Red demands.

"No," I say. "You can keep your drugs." I push the wad of bills farther into my jacket pocket.

I never make it up to my feet. Red uses his body to pin me to the floor. He gropes my jacket. I slap him hard across the cheek. He automatically raises a hand to assess the damage. It's enough for me to shimmy out from under him.

I get halfway to the door before his fingers grip my upper arm. I kick at him, landing a blow to his knee that sends my shoe flying.

"You fucking bitch." Red's fist swings. It hits me on the side of the head. My teeth rattle. I see stars. I can't stop myself from falling onto the couch. Red crashes down after me, grabbing for the money in my pocket. I can't breathe.

I want to give up.

No, a little voice says inside me. *No.* I've given up too much already. This is *Mom's* money. My stomach churns with a million regrets. I'm not giving it to him so he can use it to slowly kill himself. Mom wouldn't forgive me for that. I wouldn't forgive me.

I muster up all the will in my thin body and lift my knee hard. It makes contact with Red's groin. He groans and rolls onto the floor. The woman's head slams into the side of the coffee table, but she's too far gone to notice.

I run. Splinters from the decaying wood stairs stab my bare foot outside the mobile home. My entire head aches. The night blurs in front of me.

"You fucking bitch!" Red roars. A chorus of dogs bark and snarl. He's coming after me.

My foot is ripped to shreds. I run behind the house next door. A light comes on. I want to knock, beg them to let me in, but they might deliver me right back to Red. If he catches me, I don't know what he'll do.

I keep going. Happy and Tomás are at the end of the road. If I can make it to their house . . . I stop. This is my mess. I did this. Happy and Tomás are innocent. Innocent people get hurt.

I make a quick jag to the left. A Rottweiler slams into the fence. I back into the shadows of the house. The dog keeps barking as Red approaches. The porch light flips on. A man comes out. A menagerie of crude tattoos covers his arms. He lights a cigarette.

Red freezes in the pool of light. The man whistles to the dog. It stops barking and runs to his feet. "Everything okay?" he asks.

Red nods. The man on the porch doesn't move. He takes a slow drag off his cigarette. The dog dances around, thrilled with the late-night company.

I stay frozen in the shadows while a quiet standoff takes place. Red in the road, swinging his arms. The man blowing a long stream of smoke up into the dark sky.

Finally, Red breaks and stomps off. The man stubs out his cigarette and pats the dog on the head. He glances into the darkness where I hide. He nods. The porch light goes out. The dog settles down onto its belly in the yard as I creep into the desert and pull out Toxic Pink.

Teddy doesn't say anything. He looks me up and down, assessing the damage. Checking to see what I've done to myself. He nods, satisfied that at least I'm not high.

My adrenaline has worn off. Tears stream down my face. "Please don't tell her," I whisper. "Mom is doing so well. It would kill her."

He stops the truck at the end of my road and turns off the ignition. "I'm not going to tell." His eyes stare straight ahead into the night.

I dab the water off my cheeks. "You're not?"

He shakes his head. "Betsy, shit happens to people. Shit

that's their fault, and shit that isn't. That's life. You only get a say in what you're going to do about it."

I pull my one shoe and my bloody foot up to the seat and wrap my arms around my knees. "Why are you here?" I ask.

He laughs. It's sad and full of despair. "You mean why do I live by myself at the ends of the earth?" He sighs. "There was a woman. She was scared. She called me three, four times a day. Nothing was ever really wrong. One night she called, and I couldn't do it anymore. I ignored her. I watched a football game with my feet up." He rubs his face. "When they found her body, she was still clutching the phone. My number was the last one dialed. After that, the only peace I could find was at the bottom of a bottle. I lost my job—I lost everything. Then I got offered a deal. I got sober. And here we are."

"Do you regret it? Making a deal?"

"I used to. Until you and your mom came along." His face shows such an earnest intensity I have to turn away.

"Betsy, nothing can change the past. I know you're hurting, but if you look around, you'll see that unexpected good things can still happen. There's got to be at least one good thing you have now that you wouldn't have if you'd never come to San Justo."

He pauses, like he's waiting for me to answer. I can't. I can't see anything beyond the darkness right now.

To appease him, I nod. As I open the door, he rests his hand on my arm. Even though it's gentle and kind, I flinch. "It wasn't your fault, Betsy. You're a kid. They used you."

"Adrian knows," I say, and reclaim my arm.

"Put some ice on your face," he calls after me.

———

I break the seal on a bottle of foundation Mom bought me when we first got here. I smear it over the dark splotch of bruise appearing on my left cheek and stretching up toward my eye.

When I'm done, I look ghostly. I flop my hair over my face.

Mom makes pancakes with blueberries. She draws a smiley face in syrup on mine. She sits down across from me.

"I talked to Teddy." My fork freezes in midair and a drop of syrup splashes to my plate. "He says that everything's fine. There's nothing to worry about." Mom smiles tightly, like she doesn't quite believe it, and picks up a bouquet of yellow and white roses tied with a red silk ribbon. "What do you think of this? Would pink be better?"

I eat my pancakes. Agree that pink would be better. Smile like the girl Mom wants me to be. Not like a girl who still has three hundred dollars in her jacket pocket. Not like one who almost did what I almost did.

When she gathers up her flowers and leaves for work, I limp to my bedroom and drop down to my knees. I liberate the black monster from its dark prison.

It flashes with a text message. A complaint about the weather. He's taunting me. Waiting for my reaction. I respond politely and pretend that I'm the same as before Adrian knew everything.

I press send.

The monster stays dark and asleep.

It lets me live another day.

CHAPTER 22
KAYLA

I ride the bus from school to No Limit Foods. The bus driver smiles at me, as if going back to our old routine makes all the universe right again. He's wrong. Jordan never answered my texts. His phone went to voice mail whenever I called. I told him I would be at No Limit. I have nowhere else to go.

I get off at my stop and scan the parking lot for Jordan's blue Jeep. It isn't there.

When I walk past the McDonald's, the manager dashes out. "Hey," he calls. I stop and turn to face him. He flaps a piece of paper in my face. "We have an opening. You just need to fill out the application."

"Thanks," I say, take the paper, and almost throw up in the parking lot. I fold the application and stick it into my back pocket. I don't have a choice. I will have to fill it out. I'll find a way to trick myself into believing the fry cook quit and that I'm not taking Shonda's job.

Even though I know Jordan isn't there, I slink through the doors of No Limit.

It still smells like old produce mixed with stale bakery goods. If someone told me months ago that smell would make me want to burst into tears, I'd have thought they were high.

Albert's nosing around the front, watching my replacement. She's flustered. Her line's impatient. She runs her finger over the laminated card, searching for the code for bananas. Bananas. Everyone buys them. It's the easiest one to remember.

Elton flips through a magazine by an empty register. He looks up, and surprise passes over his face. "Hi, Elton," I say to break the awkward tension filling the space between us. He doesn't respond. His mouth hangs open slightly. His eyes lock onto me. I turn around and feel him stare straight through my back.

I slip down the cereal aisle before Albert sees me. There's only one place I can think of to go. I dodge a woman with three whining children and a cart piled up to the top with frozen dinners, canned goods, and brightly colored junk food. I pass the dairy and the meat cases and enter the red glow that surrounds Albert's stupid castle of cherry cream soda. The one that hid small children all last summer.

It's exactly the same. Not a single six-pack is out of place. I lean against it. If I were two feet shorter, I would curl up inside its little door and never come out again.

Jordan doesn't magically turn the corner or appear eating M&M's. It was wishful thinking, but still I wait. Albert is on to me. When he walks by for the tenth time, I, for the tenth time, pretend to examine the calories on a can of cherry cream. By the time it gets dark outside, I've almost convinced myself I want to drink one.

"Do you have a ride home?" Albert's voice is soft, almost caring. His manager's vest is slung over his arm.

"Sure," I say. My voice is flat. I don't even make an attempt to cover the lie.

"I'll drive you home." The *manager* is back in his tone.

"I can walk."

"No. That creep is still out there."

I narrow my eyes. "I thought they caught him. Arrested him in front of McDonald's."

Albert shrugs. "A cop buddy of mine said they let him go. He wasn't the guy."

"Oh." I turn back to the soda. My heart beats with equal parts excitement and terror. It wasn't Drake. That's good. Maybe Jordan will eventually forgive me. But if the guy's still out there, so is Girl Number Four.

"Let's go," Albert says. It's an order. Even though he isn't my manager anymore, I follow him out to his car.

It's a standard vanilla, off-brand car with a spotless cream-colored interior. It's so Albert.

"Bluebird Estates?" he asks, and double-checks all the mirrors and hits the automatic locks before putting the car in reverse.

Bluebird Lane is to the right. We go left. "Um, Albert?" I point behind us.

"I didn't want to fire you," he says. We make a right onto a street crowded with car dealerships. It glows like daytime. "But there are rules. I have to follow the rules."

"Albert?" I try again. "This isn't the way."

"The new girl can't keep up. She'll never be as good as you." He makes another right turn. "I miss you."

"Albert, please stop the car." I don't let my voice betray how freaked out I am. Albert is Albert. He's a pain in the ass, but he isn't violent. *Is that what all those other girls thought?* A nice, straight-laced, rule-following grocery store manager offered them a ride and they never came back?

"Albert, please." I unlatch my seat belt and paw the door, searching for the lock. We make another right turn. The car comes to a stop. I pop the door open without taking my eyes off him. I'm not going down without a fight.

He stares. "If you walk the way we went, you'll stay on well-lit streets with lots of traffic. It's farther, but it's safer."

My heart thuds in my ears, so I'm not sure I hear him right.

He points. "I grew up here." I follow his finger. Bluebird Estates looms over us. "Apartment 32. The water never got hot on Tuesdays." He laughs.

My face must be glowing electric red. I can't believe I thought for a second that Albert could be the attacker. He's so Albert, with his vest laid out on the backseat so it doesn't get wrinkled.

His phone rings. A frown passes over his face. "I have to get this," he says.

"Thanks for the ride."

"Hey, Kayla? We might have some openings for stockers this summer. . . ." He trails off. Albert is willing to break the rules for me. My heart rises in my chest. Shonda will get better and go back to McDonald's. I'll go back to No Limit. The world will be almost right again.

"Thanks." This time I mean it.

"Kayla," Finn whispers through a crack in apartment 21. "Kayla."

"Not now, Finn." I keep walking.

Mom doesn't open the door when I approach. Voices come from inside. I turn the knob and push the door open enough to stick my head through. Detective Cavallo is perched on the same too-small chair. Mom sits across from him. They look like two people on a blind date who have run out of things to say.

Mom jumps to her feet when she sees me. "There you are," she almost shouts. The smile on her face is manic. She pushes me into a chair and disappears to her room.

Cavallo glances at his watch and then raises an eyebrow in what I assume is a fatherly gesture.

"You let him go?" I ask to take his attention off me.

The color leaves his face. He picks at a torn piece of skin on the side of his thumb. It isn't an act. This is real.

"It's not him."

"Are you sure? You said he gave you a fake ID. Did you do the fingerprints and DNA and stuff?"

He glares. "I'm sure. The dispatcher typed his driver's license number wrong when the officer called it in. It was a simple mistake. Everything checked out in the end."

"Then why are you here?" I see Mom peek her head out from her room in my peripheral vision.

Cavallo sees her, takes a deep breath, and lowers his voice to a whisper. "I shouldn't be telling you this, but you need to stay away from Drake and his, uh, associate."

"Associate? You mean Jordan?"

He nods. "You're young, Kayla. You have your whole life ahead of you. Study, go to football games, kiss high school boys."

Another fatherly gesture. Cavallo talked to Jordan once under circumstances that were my fault. Now he thinks Jordan's too old for me? Wrong for me? He may be a cop and all, but he's not my father. He's known me for, like, ten minutes. He doesn't get to tell me how to live my life. I stand up. "Is there anything else?"

He shakes his head. I show him to the door.

Mom creeps out like a scared cat. She glances around and straightens up. "What was that about?"

I shrug. She doesn't need to know.

A knock on the door echoes through the apartment and sends Mom scampering away again.

I open the door. Finn shoves a piece of paper at me. "I'm not your secretary," he growls, and storms away.

Shannon is awake

"Do you mean Shonda? Shonda is awake?" I yell at his closed door. He opens it and gives me the finger.

I can't sleep. With Albert and Cavallo and my excitement over Shonda waking up, I hadn't stopped to think about what

I did. I got an innocent man arrested—dramatically—in front of a whole restaurant of people. I feel like shit. Worse than I have felt about anything—other than finding Shonda.

Plus, the man in black is still out there.

I slip on my shoes and pull my coat over my pajamas. Mom is a sound sleeper, so she doesn't hear me sneak out the front door. In the hallway, thumping music echoes from upstairs and hides the sound of my footsteps, not that anyone is sober enough to wonder why I'm leaving in the middle of the night.

I push open the lobby door and see the Camaro parked along Bluebird Lane, right where I thought it would be. I knew Drake would go back to dealing. He has to pay rent somehow. After what I did, who am I to judge him.

He's on the phone. I knock on the window. He jumps and drops the phone, like I've disturbed a call he doesn't want anyone to know about. When he registers that it's me, he rolls the window down. I step back and cringe.

"What?" he barks.

I take a deep breath. "I'm sorry. I know you probably hate me, but I wanted you to know that I'm sorry about what I did." There. I said it.

He glances around me, but we're alone. "You did what you thought was right." I jump at the sound of his voice. It's soft and low, not filled with anger like I expected. "You did what you thought would help that girl. I respect that." He reaches his fist out the window. "We're cool." I hesitantly bump his fist with mine. I feel tears forming in my eyes. I don't know what this niceness is about, but it makes me feel even worse about what I did. It would be better if he yelled at me.

"Tell Jordan"—my voice cracks—"tell him I'm sorry." Drake nods. I start to walk away.

"Kayla?" he calls after me. I turn around. Now he's animated, exasperated. "Stop wandering around by yourself in the middle of the night."

CHAPTER 23
BETSY

I hold a letter in my hand. A folded, forbidden missive. An explanation. An apology. If I have to write my final words, I would want them to be these. I hold it in front of the teasing gap-mouth of the blue mailbox. My fingers need to let go, and it will be off. Flying to a place that seems a million miles away now.

My fingers won't release it. They hold firm. My feet bounce back and forth, unclear about the directions they're receiving. Stay or go.

The mailboxes are a patchwork of darker shades of blue, wherever graffiti has been covered up. They stand in a line on the main street that runs through town.

This block is empty. The storefronts boarded up. The stucco cracked.

The letter in my hand flutters in the breeze. *I have to let go.*

A red truck pulls up to the curb next to me. The window rolls down. I slam the letter behind my back and automatically flop the hair over my face to hide the bruise on my cheek.

The driver leans out. His eyes are obscured by mirrored sunglasses. His smooth, deep brown arm reaches for me. From his fingers dangles my lime-green strappy sandal.

My heart pounds. My lips roll under. The letter crumples in my fist. Tomás motions the shoe at me. "From that asshole's description, you're the only person this could belong to."

I step forward. My hand shakes as I reach for it.

"Thanks," I whisper. I think. Or maybe it's in my head, because Tomás doesn't say anything. He doesn't move. I stare at myself reflected back where his eyes should be.

"I, uh . . ." I don't know what to say. I'm afraid the memory of what happened with Red will make me collapse to the sidewalk.

"I'm not a narc," I blurt out.

Tomás's composure of steel breaks. He laughs. "Yeah, I kinda figured that." His face turns serious again. He points to my shoe. "If he gives you any more trouble, let me know. I'll take care of it."

"Please, don't tell—"

He raises his palm to stop me. "Not my business."

"Why are you being nice to me?" The words burst out of my mouth like an accusation. I can't hold back the waterworks anymore.

He shrugs. "Happy likes you. You're real with her. Not like those bitches who act nice and then say she's a slut behind her back."

I don't even know what the word *real* means now, much less how to be it. I use the hand that's clutching the letter to wipe my face. The ink smears.

"I've never had a friend like Happy before." It's true. I know if I were to tell her—tell her my story—she would listen. She would laugh at the funny parts and cry at the sad ones. She wouldn't judge me or roll her eyes or tell me how stupid I was.

Tomás smiles. Not smiles—beams. He loves her. I can tell. It's real love, too. Not some knockoff version of love, the kind of love you use when you want something.

Tomás rolls the window up and pulls away.

I shove the soggy, wrinkled letter into my pocket. The shoe hasn't done anything to me. It covered my foot and then got left behind. I dump it in a trash can anyway. I won't be able to look at it again. It's a reminder, a symbol of what I almost did to myself.

Shit has happened to me. Lots of it. I haven't felt in control of a single moment of my own life. I'm tired. My feet hurt. My eyes may never be dry again. But I want to do better. I have a friend. Mom is happy. We are part of a *community*. People look out for one another here. I've never had that before.

I'm not letting anyone take it away from me.

I stick my head into C&J's. Mrs. Morales is jotting down notes at the front podium. "Hi, Mrs. Morales. Do you think I can talk to Adrian outside for a second?" I flash her a million-watt smile. She smiles back with motherly pride and yells for Adrian to come up front.

I step outside and press my back against a pillar that blocks me from being viewed from inside the restaurant. While I wait, I try to channel the nastiest, most evil, manipulative bastard I can think of.

Adrian steps in front of me. "Bet—"

I hold a finger in front of his face. "No. It's my turn to talk now."

He crosses his arms and grins. We'll see how long that lasts.

"Yes," I say. "I have two phones. You got me. Maybe that makes me an escaped convict, or a Russian spy, or maybe that makes me exactly who you think I am. But I"—I place my finger on his chest and let it slide down seductively—"have never been caught red-handed in the desert."

His face falls a little. "Those Border Patrol agents got a good look at you. I bet they'd love to know what good little Adrian was doing with a woman and child in an isolated shack. And you know what would happen after that? *Everyone would find out.* Your parents, your teachers, the whole town."

I sigh dramatically. "Sure, some of them would pat you on the back for it. But what about the ones who don't? What about the ones who stop eating at your parents' restaurant?" I pause and go in for the kill. "What about the fathers who tell their daughters to stay away from you?" He flinches. That was it. That was the nerve.

I smile. "So here's the deal, Adrian. I'm going to do whatever I want, talk to whomever I want, and you won't be able to do a thing about it. Because if you take me down, I'm taking you with me." His face goes white. "Nod if you understand." He moves his head almost imperceptibly.

"Now smile pretty. Everyone's watching."

His lips turn up. He shows some teeth.

"Good boy." I place my hand on his shoulder and slide it down to his wrist as I turn away. I wave to Mrs. Morales in the window and walk down the sidewalk.

When I'm at the end of the shopping center out of view of C&J's, I throw up into a trash can.

Mom sits in a pile of white ribbons and red roses. Her calloused fingers loop the ribbon around the flowers in a fast, practiced motion. She holds up the bouquet. A white trail runs down her arm. "What do you think?"

"Looks great. You're getting good at that." I smile. Mom is caught off guard. She examines me for hints of substance abuse or delirium. Finding none, she smiles back. It lights up her whole face.

I have a grocery sack hanging from my wrist. Inside is a box of store-brand chocolate cake mix and a can of frosting. It isn't as fancy as I wanted, but it was all my piddly allowance could buy.

I place the groceries on the counter and search the cabinets for a cupcake tin. I catch a glimpse of the disturbed duffel bag. I push a stockpot in front of it and glance up at Mom. She's humming to herself in the garden of roses that was once our dining room table. I find the cupcake tin and set it next to the sack on the counter, like I do this every day. Like this is a normal thing. Making cupcakes on a sunny afternoon.

I feel a buzz in my pocket. I turn on my heels. Mom

glances over her shoulder as I run to my bedroom. I shut the door and pull the back monster out. It's silent. The phone didn't vibrate. It was my jumpy imagination. I expect him to call, expect him to read my mind from afar. Expect him to know about the money, the letter, Adrian.

I put the crumpled letter into the bag with the sweatshirt under my bed. They can keep each other company. I lie down and listen to my heart beating.

A few minutes later, Mom knocks on the door. "Betsy, are you going to bake something? Do you want me to preheat the oven?"

"Yes." It comes out as a strangled whisper.

I texted Happy to meet me at the park. When I pull up and wrestle the Tupperware of cupcakes out of the car, she's sitting on a bench with her back to me. Her short legs that don't touch the ground swing back and forth. If you didn't know who she was, she would seem like a joyful, carefree child.

When I walk around the bench, her belly comes into view, then the dark circles under her eyes, then her mouth, hard, pinched, and unsmiling.

"Hi," I say, and sit down next to her. She tilts her head with curiosity.

I take a deep breath. "I know that you have a lot of friends, and they've probably thrown you a baby shower." My lungs have trouble exhaling all the way, forcing me to suck in another shallow breath to keep talking. "But here." I shove the cupcakes at her. "These are for you."

I'm no good at this. Her eyes meet mine. I feel my face get hot. "You're my good thing," I say. "You're my good thing that happened because I'm here in San Justo." I feel stupid and clumsy. This is not how I imagined this going. I wanted to thank her for being my friend, even though I have been a terrible one back. Thank her for talking to me that first day of school, for introducing me to the Morales family and Tomás and treating me like the human being that I'm not sure I am.

She peels the top off the box. "Wow," she says.

There's another thing. I can't chicken out now. I place a card in her hand. I couldn't find anything else to write on, so it's one of Mom's business cards. I blacked out her information and wrote on the back.

"'Good for babysitting whenever you want,'" Happy reads aloud. "Really?" She's right to be skeptical. I nod.

She turns away. This was a stupid thing to do. I have made a colossal fool of myself. I should go before I make things worse. I move to stand up, but Happy looks back at me. Her eyes are glassy.

"This is the nicest thing anyone has ever done for me."

"Really?" I ask.

She nods as she wipes her face. "Hormones," she says, and dives into the cupcakes, smearing chocolate icing on the sides of her mouth.

If it's true that food takes on the emotions of the preparer, these cupcakes probably taste like blood and dirt and tears, but Happy doesn't seem to notice. She eats three, blissfully smiling to herself.

CHAPTER 24

KAYLA

A guard is posted outside of Shonda's room. His long limbs and pale, skinny body are folded like a praying mantis into a small, white chair. He holds a comic book up with one hand.

When he sees us walking toward him, he stands and blocks the door. "She's not allowed visitors."

Even though both he and I tower over Shonda's grandmother, she maneuvers me around him and into the room.

She pulls a chair next to Shonda's bed and motions for me to sit.

The guard follows us in. "Ma'am, you can't . . ."

She raises an eyebrow. His mouth shuts.

"I'll give you your privacy," she says, and pulls the curtain across the room. Her heels clack along the sterile white tile into the hallway.

Shonda's eyes are closed. I sit and reach for her hand. The same one I held in the woods that night.

She stirs. One of her legs is suspended above the bed in an

elaborate contraption. The opposite arm is enclosed in a pink cast. Oxygen tubes limit how far she can turn her head, but her eyes slide to the side to see me.

"Please," she whispers, "don't be mad at me."

"What?" I ask.

"Don't be mad at me for kissing your boyfriend."

At least one of the many machines and tubes she's hooked up to must contain some pretty heavy pain meds.

"I'm Kayla," I say. "I used to see you at McDonald's."

Her eyes droop closed again. "I know. You're Jordan's girlfriend. Don't be mad at me."

I squeeze her hand. "Shonda, what are you talking about?"

"At his house. I tried to kiss him."

"When were you at his house? Was the guy with the snake tattoo there? Did he do this to you?" All the horror of the woods rushes back to me.

"Drake?" she asks. "He gave me a ride home once, so that I would be safe."

She tries to moves her head to look at me, dislodging one of the oxygen tubes. She lifts the pink cast, but it drops back to the bed. Her eyes close.

I fix the tubes and say her name forcefully. I can see the effort she puts forth to keep her eyes open.

"Who did this to you?"

"I don't know. He hit me from behind. I don't remember anything except being cold and hearing your voice tell me I was going to be okay."

I look away. I don't want her to see my face crumple.

"I told Jordan I had never seen the ocean before. He said

he had his own ocean, but I didn't believe him. He took me to his house and down to the water. It was beautiful."

"I think I found your nose stud in his bedroom."

Her eyes slide away from me again. Her broken arm reaches her face this time. She touches her nose and winces. She turns back to me. "I tried to kiss him. He was nice about it. He didn't make me feel stupid. He told me he had feelings for someone else. I asked him if it was the pretty girl from McDonald's, and he said yes." Her hand squeezes back against mine. "Please don't be mad at me."

"I'm not mad." I can't process it right now. I can't feel happy or excited while staring at a girl who almost died. A girl who, after all she has been through, is worried I will be upset with her over kissing my boyfriend. Or former boyfriend. He still won't talk to me.

I stand up and let go of her hand. "I hope you feel better soon." I move the curtain back. She's so fragile and tiny like a baby bird in a nest of white sheets, metal, and plastic.

"Thank you," she whispers. Her eyes, now focused, look directly at my face to convey the full meaning of her words.

I smile my big Clairmont Explorers Dance Team smile, so I won't start to cry. "You know the tall guy at McDonald's, the one who works the register?" I don't want to mention his bad skin or the still-blank McDonald's application sitting on my desk at home.

"Jerry," she whispers.

"Yeah, Jerry. He totally has a thing for you."

She smiles.

———

I'm not going to look at the No Limit Foods parking lot. The bus jolts to a halt at a red light. I glance up at the ceiling, down at my hands, and at the woman playing with her phone in the seat across from me.

We wait through three red lights. Traffic is backed up. The hazards on a stalled car blink, adding to the annoyance of the other drivers with each flash. Even though it feels like a sign, I'm not going to look at the No Limit Foods parking lot.

The bus inches forward. Once we're beyond the car, it will be clear sailing all the way to Bluebird Estates. I've had two other buses from the hospital to wrestle my mind into not thinking about Jordan. How he said he had feelings for me. How I blew it. I'm not going to look for his Jeep in the parking lot.

I look.

The bus breaks free of the backup. The driver hits the gas to try to make up time. I pull the cord. Over and over and over again. The driver slams on the brakes and shoots daggers at me through her giant rearview mirror.

I stand up and make my way to the front. Jordan isn't the only person who drives a blue Jeep. It could be a coincidence.

"Are you getting off?" the driver asks. Her tone is not polite. I hover in front of the open door that blasts me with muggy, exhaust-filled air. I force myself forward, but the bus starts to go before my back foot has cleared the last step. I stumble onto the cement.

A pair of hands tentatively grabs my shoulders and steadies me on my feet. Elton's cane hits the ground. His breath is minty on my face.

"Thanks," I say. We both peer down at his cane. "Let me get that." I bend over and lift the piece of black painted wood. It's heavier than I would have expected. The paint is chipping off in places where it has been nicked.

I put the cane in his hand. "Thanks again," I say, and tear across the street toward Jordan.

The doors whoosh open. If Jordan isn't here, my heart will explode and I will die at the foot of Albert's cherry cream soda castle.

I search aisle after aisle. He isn't here. I steady myself on the cherry cream turret. This is it. It's over.

A crinkle in my ear. The smell of sugar. "Hi."

It's as if he can walk through walls. Even I, who wanted to see him more than anyone, missed his calm, quiet stance behind a mound of clearance chocolate Valentine's hearts.

He tosses an M&M into his mouth.

My knees go weak, my stomach hurts, and my head pounds. I move my lips, but the apology that was queued up behind them doesn't come out. I'm so happy to see him, so sorry for what I did, so scared of what I feel.

We stare at each other. My eyes flutter around his face, taking in every feature. His brown eyes, slight stubble appearing on his chin, a scar on his temple that's brought out by the fluorescent lights.

He takes a step forward and opens his arms. I propel myself into them. My mouth finds language, and I pour apologies into his ear. He pushes me away and places his finger against my lips. Then he kisses them.

Albert clears his throat behind us. We break apart, laughing. "I brought you something," Jordan says. He reaches into his pocket and pulls out a rubber alligator key chain. Its jaw flops comically open and it has FLORIDA painted in red block letters on the stomach.

He rubs the back of his neck. "I know it's kind of stupid."

"It's great," I say, and pull him back for another kiss. Albert slams a case of canned corn down.

The backseat of the Jeep isn't comfortable. My head rests against Jordan's chest. Outside in the park, a group of boys whoop and chase one another around with sticks.

"Has Grace come to visit again?" I ask.

"No." He sighs. "I put the picture you took on the refrigerator. Mom didn't say anything, but I caught her looking at it."

I suppress a grin. I don't want him to think that I'm smiling at his unhappiness, but he's reminded me of that day at his house, kissing on the dock.

I sit forward and place a finger over his heart. "Can I see it?" I ask, shy, embarrassed. He glances out the window. The boys run into the distance. The Jeep sits alone. We're the only people in the universe.

He pulls his shirt off. The carp glows in the fading light of the sunset. I trace it with my finger. I feel his eyes on me, burning, lusty.

"Carps swim upstream against the current. No matter how hard it gets, they keep going. In legends, they swim up waterfalls and become dragons. They're strong. They never quit. This"—he points to his chest—"reminds me to keep going.

"And when I have a bad day remembering my dad, or when Mom disappears or pulls some other crap, or Grace"—he swallows hard—"I think about the carp, and it reminds me that I can make it through."

I sit back, cross my arms, and grab the bottom of my sweater. I pull it over my head. Static sends my hair flying. I toss the sweater aside and sit facing him in my cheap cotton bra.

"I want one," I say. Jordan looks confused. I point to the pale skin over my heart. "I want one right here. A carp that glows like the sunset." I need a symbol of power, a reminder to keep going. Every second of my life.

A darkness paints his face. I've done something wrong. He's realized how young I am, how innocent and inexperienced. I turn away and reach for my sweater to cover myself. I'm such an idiot.

"Right here?" He leans in and kisses the spot where my finger was. A shock passes between his lips and my skin. He laughs. "I guess that must be a sign."

"My birthday's in March," I blurt out, and feel like an idiot again.

He moves his kisses up my neck. "Then I'll have to get you a present."

CHAPTER 25
BETSY

Happy and Tomás had a fight. A bad one. For a week, Happy's been sleeping in Adrian's room while he sleeps on the couch. I haven't seen her much. I've been avoiding Adrian like he's a rabid bat swooping for my hair. We may have an understanding, but I don't want to provoke him.

I also don't want to stop feeling free. Having Adrian off my back has changed things. The black monster still rings, but breathing is easier. My death doesn't consume all my thoughts. I don't restart the countdown to it every morning.

Happy looks like she's stretched beyond what a human body should be able to handle. She lies on my bed. It's the first time anyone other than Mom's been in my room. It makes me nervous. But Happy doesn't seem to care about the unicorn and rainbow curtains, the lack of photos stuck to the mirror, the blank walls.

Another thing makes me nervous. The black monster is sitting on my desk. Happy came over unannounced. I didn't have time to hide it. If I stuff it in my pocket now, she'll see.

"How much longer?" I point to her stomach.

She sighs deeply. "A couple more weeks."

"Oh." I sit on the floor, keeping my eyes away from the desk.

The front door jiggles and flies open. Laughter and the swish of plastic shopping bags float down the hallway. Two different laughs. Teddy is here.

Happy sits up. She comes from a world where teenagers politely greet their elders and make conversation.

Mom sticks her head in. "Betsy, can you help unload the car?" Then she sees Happy and takes a step back. A huge smile spreads across her face.

Happy tries to stand. "Stay here," I say. "I'll bring you a snack."

Outside, Teddy has most of the grocery bags in his arms. I pick up the last one and slam the trunk shut. I try not to meet his eye. I don't know what I'm supposed to say to him now.

I follow him into the house. Mom has her head stuck in the freezer, moving around the food that's already in there so she can stuff more in. It's like she's afraid if she doesn't buy all the food now, the store is going to run out.

Happy laughs. She comes into the living room talking. Talking into the black monster.

Teddy and I look at each other.

"No, Happy's my nickname," she laughs again. "I know, right? Okay. Just a sec."

She holds the phone out to me. "It's your dad," she says, a confused look passing over her face.

I rip the phone out of her hand and turn my back to Mom. Teddy leaps in front of her and hoists up all six shopping bags he still carries. "Who wants ice cream?" he asks in an overly jolly tone.

The words *ice cream* propel Happy's bulk into the kitchen like a dog drooling at the sound of a bell.

I don't turn around to look at Mom.

I walk to my room and shut the door. "You told her you were my father?" I whisper-screech into the monster.

"Would you rather I tell her the truth? And why is someone who isn't you answering your phone?"

"It was an accident. I went outside for a second."

"I'm getting tired of your *accidents*, Betsy. It's like you have an actual death wish."

"I don't," I say. And I mean it. Before, I would have thought about that, twisted it around in my head, decided if I wanted or deserved to keep living. But now I know for sure.

"Do I even have to tell you to not let it happen again?"

"No." I hang up the monster and push it under my bed.

I wander out to the living room. I can make up something to explain to Happy, but what am I going to tell Mom?

Happy already has a bowl in front of her. Teddy thunks a heaping scoop of rocky road into another one. He glances up at me. I flit my eyes over to Mom. Teddy hands me the bowl with a full, mustache-lifted smile. Code for "I'll take care of it."

I sit down on the couch next to Happy. "Who was that?" she asks.

I roll my eyes dramatically. Probably too dramatically. "Just another old friend who thinks he gets to tell me how to live my life." I put as much teenybopper attitude as I can into it.

"Another piece of your mystery," Happy says. I detect the slightest bit of annoyance in her voice. It makes me feel horrible. I can't afford to lose my one and only friend.

Happy goes back to her ice cream. Mom and Teddy finish unpacking the groceries. I lick my spoon and let the sweet coldness wash around my mouth. Mom's melodic laughter fills the room.

"They're in love," Happy whispers. Her eyes follow them around the kitchen, like she's watching one of those Mexican soap operas Mrs. Morales sometimes has on in the background at C&J's.

"No. They aren't," I say. Teddy's a good actor.

"Maybe you should tell them that."

I see them through her eyes. Mom, pretty, still young with a smile as big as her mouth will allow. Her eyes are dreamy, and she tosses a lock of hair over her shoulder. Teddy's eyes are focused on her lips, like he would kiss them if Happy and I weren't in the room.

I'm not sure what I'm supposed to feel watching them. Hope? Sadness because I know it's all a charade?

Happy turns back to me. Her face falls, as if their happiness has reminded her of the darkness seeping into her world.

"Tomás wants to talk."

"That's good, isn't it?"

"Did Adrian tell you why I left Tomás?"

I shake my head. Happy is under the well-crafted illusion that Adrian and I have become friends. That we are all one big happy gang.

"After you brought me those cupcakes, I realized something. This baby deserves better than a drug dealer for a father. It deserves a good thing. So do I. I told Tomás I didn't want to see him again if he was still dealing."

I nod. I want to congratulate her. Tell her she made the right decision. Pat her on the shoulder like the supportive friend I should be. But I don't. I have no right to say anything about relationships. I sit on my hands. Happy turns back to the dopey couple in the kitchen.

"Will you come with me?" she asks.

I try not to look at Adrian trying not to look at me. The tension between us is so thick I'm surprised it doesn't knock down customers. Just seeing him makes my fear come back with a vengeance. My death countdown clock restarts.

Tomás was supposed to be here by now. Happy and I sit in our booth. The table is empty. Our red cups of soda and juice haven't magically appeared. Happy's too miserable to drink anything, and without Mrs. Morales around, I'm still on Angie's blacklist. If Happy hadn't led the way, Angie might have turned me away at the door.

We've waited in silence for twenty minutes. During that time, Adrian has cleared and reset tables, pushed in chairs, straightened pictures on the wall—anything to keep an eye on us. I'm not sure if he's watching out of concern for Happy or out of ire for me.

"Forget this, let's go," Happy says. Her voice contains an edge I haven't heard before, like she's standing on a precipice about to jump into a lake of snark and attitude. She can't go there. If Happy goes over that edge, what hope do any of us have? How will I ever climb back up?

I grab her arm. "Give it a couple more minutes." I feel Adrian's hard stare warm my face.

We wait another ten. I see Tomás first and do a double take. His dark glasses and baggy pants are gone, replaced by khakis and a yellow T-shirt that says SAM'S CAR WASH. He pulls a matching yellow visor off his head and holds it over his heart. It's the first time I've seen his whole face. Standing in the doorway, he looks so young and vulnerable. If I were a different person, I would want to reach out and give him a hug.

When Happy sees him, her mouth drops. He glances at me and then motions with his head for her to follow him outside.

When they slip out the door that doesn't jingle, I feel cold and unwelcome. I don't want to disturb their moment by going out after them, so I sit staring straight ahead. The muscles in my neck grow so tense that my head aches.

I feel Adrian moving around the restaurant. Every time I catch a glimpse of him, it makes my insides roil. I don't regret what I had to do to get him off my back. It was the way I did it. The person I have become. Even if I end up living a long life, I will always hate that part of myself. The part of me that did that to another human being.

Outside, Tomás and Happy kiss so passionately I feel my face redden as I watch them. He leads her to his truck. She goes without a backward glance to the window where I sit.

They pull away, and I'm back to my original state. Alone and friendless.

The walk home takes forever. It's only February, but green buds decorate the trees along my path as they wake up from a winter where the sun never stopped shining. My turtleneck itches. I'm not looking forward to being covered up when the heat hits again.

Teddy's truck is parked out front. Even though we're okay now, I still feel uneasy around him. I guess I'll get over it if he keeps hanging out with us, which, now that *he's in love with my mother*, seems likely.

I can't imagine Mom truly being in love with anyone. I want her to be happy, but it's only ever been us. A third person feels like an interloper in our private battle.

I go inside. Mom's on the couch, leaning against Teddy. He has his arm around her. I try to sneak past them, but Teddy's head snaps up. The look on his face tells me something is wrong—very wrong. Mom's face is red and puffy. When she sees me, it crumples into a sob.

I drop to my knees in front of the couch. "What? What is it?"

Teddy pulls Mom closer. His voice is soft, but slow and clear. "There was a fire. Where you used to live. A lot of people died."

"Mom?" My voice cracks and goes up an octave.

She closes her eyes and nods. She reaches out. I let her take me in her arms.

Did I do this? Is this my fault too? Teddy reads the terror on my face.

"It was electrical. Poor maintenance," he says.

"Really?" I don't believe him. He would say anything to protect Mom.

"I talked to the investigator myself. They're sure it wasn't arson. It was a tragic accident."

"That place was a death trap," Mom says. Her voice goes cold. Colder than I have ever heard it. She wipes the tears off her now set and stony face. "Time for dinner."

She shoots to her feet and moves into the kitchen. I glance at Teddy. He's as confused as I am.

CHAPTER 26
KAYLA

Bluebird Estates looks shinier than usual. Extra broken glass from Friday night's benders glitter in an abstract mosaic in the parking lot. I told Mom I have a school event. It will last all day. She doesn't ask.

I wait on the curb for Jordan's Jeep. The air is starting to warm. The sun peeks out from behind puffy white clouds. He wouldn't tell me where we're going, just that it's an early birthday present.

He pulls up wearing sunglasses—the first time I've seen him wear any. They're opaque. I can't see his eyes. I get in, and he leans over to give me a peck on the lips. Two coffees sit in the cup holders. He plops a fast-food bag in my lap. Inside is a stack of rapidly cooling breakfast sandwiches.

"Road trip," he announces.

I've only been to Seattle twice. Marie brought me the week before I started middle school to go clothes shopping. She pretended like it was a special treat, but now I know that she realized I'd be fighting a battle as the free-lunch foster kid at the rich school.

The second time was right after I was returned to my mother. Carol Alexander brought me along on her mother-daughter weekend with Paige. We stayed in a fancy hotel, wore their fluffy robes, and ordered room service. Carol kept offering to buy me things. Clothes, necklaces, a giant stuffed puppy I thought was cute. I know now that was how she coped. Why talk when you have money?

I press my nose against the window and look at the sparkly buildings, the cars, the people. Jordan smiles at my glee. Even with both hands on the wheel navigating traffic, he seems freer, like he's floating. A thought so intense that it makes my whole body convulse in a shiver cuts through my head. *Is this what love is?*

We drive straight through the city into the suburbs. I try to hide my disappointment. I pictured walking hand in hand with Jordan through the tourists and weekend shoppers, having lunch at a café, blending in. Feeling normal.

Jordan pulls the Jeep into a gas station parking lot. He doesn't turn it off. This isn't our destination.

"You have to be absolutely sure. Tell me you're absolutely sure you want this."

This? Does he mean him? Us? Is he still mad about me getting Drake arrested? We haven't talked about it. It's like it never happened. But I can't forget it; how can he? His expression is hidden behind the dark glasses, but my panic must show. He tugs down on the neck of his shirt, exposing the carp.

"Are you absolutely sure you want one? I have to hear you say it out loud."

Relief flows through me. We're okay. "I'm absolutely sure," I say. Maybe he understands why I did what I did to Drake. Maybe he has truly forgiven me.

"Okay." He puts the Jeep back into drive.

"But," I say. He slams on the brakes. My head knocks into the back of the seat. "I'm not eighteen." I hate that I have to remind him of that, especially after he brought me all this way.

"It won't matter." The Jeep moves forward.

Jordan stares into a small black camera mounted over the front door as he rings the bell. We're in a suburban neighborhood with manicured lawns and trimmed bushes. The house is elegant, with clean lines and crisp white paint. It smells like money.

The door is opened by an Asian woman. She smiles politely and opens her arms to invite us to pass through.

I've never seen the inside of a house like this. Its light-colored wood floors stretch from room to room without being interrupted by carpeting. A few modern-looking chairs that match the floor so well they seem to be growing out of it are placed purposefully around the front room. It's so uncluttered and immaculate I find it hard to believe that someone could live here.

My eye is drawn to a black lacquered table against the wall. Above it hangs an elaborately etched samurai sword, and a scroll painted with thick black characters.

Jordan takes my hand and leads me to the back of the house that has been cut off by a floor-to-ceiling bamboo screen. This section is bathed in light. It's like being outside, except I don't see any windows or skylights. The wall is covered with a mural of green bamboo. There's the sound of running water. It's incredibly peaceful. I feel myself relax as soon as I step in.

A man sits on the floor in front of a large white cushion with his legs tucked under him and eyes closed. Surrounding him are metal containers containing brightly colored powders.

When he hears Jordan approach, he stands and then bows. Jordan bows as well, but not as deeply as the man.

The woman enters behind us. Jordan squeezes my hand and lets go. The men leave. The woman motions for me to take off my top and lie on the cushion. She wraps my hair to the side and places a crisp piece of white linen across me. I don't even have to tell her where I want the tattoo. She leaves the skin over my heart exposed.

When she's satisfied everything's in order, she kneels down and glances over her shoulder. "Are you sure you want this?" she whispers. Her accent is heavy. "You can still stop. You can stop right now."

"I'm sure," I say yet again. When Paige got her nosed pierced, the guy didn't even talk to her. He just did it.

She leaves the room.

The men come back in. They position themselves on either side of me. Jordan takes my hand. The man—the artist—wipes down the area with alcohol. He dips a metal barb into a dish of iridescent ink.

"This will hurt," he says in an accent as heavy as the woman's. He plunges the metal barb into my skin.

Breath seizes in my throat. My body shudders. The metal barb punches in and out of my flesh. It burns and tears. Hot blood dribbles out from the wounds.

"Don't move," Jordan says. His eyes are focused on the barb, not on my face or my pain. He squeezes my hand. "You're doing great."

When it's over, I catch a quick glimpse of the carp before the man places a bandage over it. It's smaller than Jordan's, more feminine and better suited to me. It's beautiful. The men leave the room. The woman helps me put my top back on. The ache is overwhelming. I'm light-headed. I ask for the bathroom. I throw up three times in the sparkling white toilet.

The towels are too clean and pretty to touch. I wash my hands and wipe them on my jeans.

Jordan is waiting outside. He kisses me on the forehead. "You were really brave. You didn't scream or cry. You're a true warrior." He is full of pride, but he doesn't ask if I'm okay. I've never expected or wanted him to take care of me, but right now, a sympathetic smile, some acknowledgment of my pain, is what I need.

I climb into the Jeep. Jordan is still beaming. This doesn't feel right. I've never had a real boyfriend before, or a tattoo. But I don't think this is how either is supposed to feel.

We drive back into the city. Jordan takes me to lunch. I slurp two ibuprofen down with my ice water while he's engrossed in the menu. I feel better. We go to the aquarium. Jordan kisses me while fish shimmer like jewels floating in midair above us.

He tells me to wait for him by the otters. I press my hands against the glass. The fuzzy creatures spin and twirl in the water. One swims up to my face. Its whiskers twitch as it examines the strange being that is me. I laugh. It tugs at the skin on my chest.

I hear my name. Jordan waves to me from behind a throng of people. I push through them with my arms gripping my shoulders, protecting the skin over my heart. He reaches out for me and places a hand on my waist. His other hand is behind his back.

"There's something I need to tell you," he says. He leads me to a corner. All those bad feelings come back. My neck and shoulders throb with tension. "I don't know how to say this." His face is tight, as if the metal barb is being plunged into the skin over his heart. It makes me take a step back into the walkway and knock into a group of children. One of the mothers tsks at me and pulls her child away.

"Kayla." Jordan takes my hand. "My life isn't easy. It never has been. There haven't been a lot of people I could trust. I've never had anyone to love." His gaze is over my shoulder. He blinks and focuses on my eyes. "But I think I'm in love with you."

I swallow hard. The ache on my chest becomes a new sensation. A warmth spreads out from my heart itself. Through my arms, down my legs. It's the feeling of having what I've always wanted. Someone who knows me—all of me—and loves me for it. Someone who I love back.

"Me too," I say.

From behind his back, he presents me with a stuffed carp from the gift shop. Its black beaded eyes and cute mouth smile. Jordan wraps his arms around me and pulls me against him. The carp is trapped between us as we kiss. My hands reach behind his neck until we can't be any closer. The fish, the water, the glass, the disgusted snorts and whistles disappear.

It's just us.

CHAPTER 27
BETSY

My stomach flips over when Adrian stomps up to my locker. I force my body to go perfectly still. I won't let him notice my pounding heart or my shaking hand on my algebra book.

"Happy's in labor," he says curtly.

"When? What happened?"

"The middle of the night. They're at the hospital now. She made me promise I would tell you."

He turns fast. "Wait," I call after him, but he's already disappeared into the crowd.

The day drags by. I'm jittery. I can't pay attention. I keep thinking about Happy and her baby. I keep fearing for Happy and her baby. What if something happens to them? Happy is my only friend in the world. If something happens to her, I won't make it. I won't be able to keep going.

Finally, the last bell rings. I try to catch up with Adrian, but he vanishes as soon as the classroom door is thrown open. I need to know how Happy is. I jaywalk across the road to the strip mall. Mom's car sits in the parking lot. She's been working overtime to get everything ordered and arranged for the wedding.

I walk past C&J's without looking through the plate-glass window. But I feel them. Watching me from inside—Adrian and Angie—dreading that I might come in. I don't. I keep going until I see Mom concentrating hard in the window of the florist.

She lights up when she sees me. "How was school?" she asks, and pokes a white, fragrant lily into a vase already stuffed with a colorful assortment of flowers.

"Happy's in labor."

"Good," Mom says. "That poor girl has been miserable these last few days." Mom looks up and sees the anxiety on my face. "She'll be fine. Women give birth every day. She's young. She'll snap back quick. When I had you . . ." Her words trail off. The lily is perfectly placed, but still she messes with it, trying to find something to do with her hands.

The sadness she has been hiding since she found out about the fire is back. I feel like crap for reminding her of the past.

"Well," she says, and plasters on a fake smile, "the rest of these flowers aren't going to jump into the vases by themselves."

"Do you want help?" I volunteer.

"No. Go be with your friends," she says. She thinks I have friends. I have *a* friend, and she's in the hospital. Anything could be happening to her right now. She could be bleeding to death. Having a stroke. Her heart stopping. She might already be dead.

A vise grips my chest. I can't suck in air. I feel dizzy. I stumble and hit the door of the flower shop with my shoulder. It opens and tosses me outside. I have to know what's happened to her.

The door to C&J's still doesn't jingle. I'm hyperventilating now. I suck breath after breath in through my open mouth. The dark wood and red booths are blurry. I put a hand down to catch myself. The table rattles.

I feel people watching. But I'm out of control. I can't stop the pictures in my head. The same ones that appear whenever Rosie is around. Flashes of blood and rain and the gun. The look on his face when he almost—

Soft hands touch my shoulders. Mrs. Morales's kind brown eyes float in front of me. She lowers me into a chair. Adrian and Angie huddle together in the corner, watching from a safe distance. Their mother barks orders at them in Spanish, and they scatter. Adrian returns a moment later with a red cup of water.

Mrs. Morales holds it up to my face until I take it and sip. The cold water sends an icy chill down my throat. It momentarily distracts my lungs, allowing them time to fill with air.

I grab a napkin off the table and wipe my face. Blow my nose. "Thank you," I whisper. Mrs. Morales pats me on the back and sends a warning glance around the restaurant to the smattering of customers. They quickly turn back to their food.

She walks away, and I suck down the water like it can fill all the empty spaces inside of me.

The door doesn't jingle, but I hear Rosie's scattered footsteps the second she's inside. She races over, making me flinch. "Betsy! I have a baby cousin."

Angie strides across the restaurant, her face full of expectation.

"It's a boy," Lawrence says. Angie whoops and leaps forward to kiss him.

Rosie grabs his hand and jumps up and down. "I want to show Betsy." Lawrence gives her his phone. She manipulates it with expertise and shoves it in my face.

On the screen, a disheveled and splotchy Happy holds an equally disheveled and splotchy infant with closed eyes, a head of black hair, and a wrinkled face on the verge of wailing. Tomás hovers over them, looking a combination of awe and bewilderment.

Seeing Happy alive lifts a thousand pounds off my shoulders. "His name is Manuel. They're going to call him Manny," Rosie says. She leans in and whispers conspiratorially, "He isn't very cute."

Angie taps her lightly on the back of the head. "Hey, don't you dare say that around Happy. He's beautiful." She takes the phone out of my hand, as if I'm intruding on a private family moment I have no business being a part of.

Adrian hangs back at the kitchen door. This is his family moment. I'm keeping him from it. I stand and walk out. No one except Adrian, whose eyes follow me across the restaurant, notices me leave.

"I'll wait here." Teddy picks up an ancient magazine and sits down in the waiting room chair. They're keeping Happy in the hospital for an extra day of observation.

I still feel a little shaky. When I called Teddy, he didn't ask why I couldn't go on my own. He just dutifully picked me up and drove me to El Paso. I'm starting to like him.

Mom sent along flowers, of course. A beautiful arrangement of white and yellow carnations surrounded by baby's breath. It matches Happy exactly—cheerful and young.

I'm pointed down the hall to her room. Outside, a woman, who is thin and meticulously dressed and made-up, talks on a cell phone. She glances at me. Her face shows indifference, as if I'm a food tray or an IV pole being wheeled by.

I take a breath and collect myself before I go in. Images of Happy unconscious and hooked up to tubes and machines keep flashing through my head. I almost turn around and run back to Teddy. But I make myself go in.

Happy is sitting up, awake and tube-free. In her arms she holds a wad of white blanket with pink and blue stripes at the bottom. Tomás, wearing his car wash uniform, is sound asleep, sprawled out at a painful-looking angle in a chair in the corner.

Happy tips her head at him. "He's too new to take any time off." Her voice is full of sympathy, but her eyes beam with pride.

I set the flowers down on a side table. "These are for you," I say, like it isn't obvious. But then I look around. The room is sterile. No cards. No balloons. No well wishes of any sort. The only other thing that sits on the side table is Happy's little orange fish. If I could knock it to the floor and push it under the bed where it would be lost forever, I would.

"Thanks," Happy says. She pushes the bundle toward me. "Want to hold him?"

I do. I really do. But my feet won't step closer. My arms won't reach out. I don't want to hurt him.

Happy leans toward me. Her belly still protrudes from under the covers. She pushes the bundle against my chest. "Hold him," she says. What I didn't notice when I walked in was that a dark glaze has formed over her eyes. New lines carve up her forehead. Her jaw is tense.

I take the baby.

He lets out a little mewl as he lands in my arms. I pull back the blanket to see his face. Wide unfocused eyes stare up at me. A brand-new soul. He doesn't know me, doesn't know anything about the bad things in this world. I want to throw my body over him and protect him from it. My arms shake. I sit on the bed to brace myself.

The woman outside on the phone cackles. Tomás stirs in the chair but resettles without waking up. Happy leans back against her mound of pillows. "My stepmother," she says. "This is her idea of a visit."

Happy closes her eyes, leaving me alone with the baby. I straighten the little blue cap on his head, and he grabs my finger. I rock him back and forth, until he too closes his eyes.

I have never felt so alone and so unalone.

A nurse with big hips and wildly patterned scrubs bustles in. "Time to feed," she says, and unceremoniously takes the baby from me. Happy blinks the sleep away as the nurse, holding the baby like a football in one hand, undoes the top of Happy's gown with the other.

I stand up to leave and give them privacy. "Stay," Happy pleads. I do. I wait with my back to them until the baby is affixed and Happy is covered with a blanket.

When I turn around, she grimaces. "I'm not doing this when I get home," she whispers. From the other side of the room, the nurse shoots her a judgmental look. Happy smiles back sweetly.

I realize something. That smile is Happy's defense. Mine is to shut my mouth, look down, and wish to disappear. But Happy . . . She kills them with innocence and kindness. Makes the world love her. See things that aren't really there. Happy isn't happy. Happy is sad—and desperate.

The whole room changes. I see it as the nurse sees it now. A teenage girl nursing a baby she doesn't know what to do with, her teenage dropout boyfriend—who may or may not still be a drug dealer—and her wreck of a friend who could crumble into a million pieces at any moment.

"They're good people," I say in an old voice I haven't heard in a long time. The nurse glances at me. "They're good people," I say again, looking her directly in the eye. She shuffles from foot to foot.

"I'll be back in a few minutes," she says to Happy, and bolts.

Happy tears up. She grabs my arm. "I don't think I can do this."

I take hold of her hand and squeeze. "Yes, you can. You're not alone. Tomás loves you. Angie and Mrs. Morales are going to spoil Manny to death. Adrian would have given birth to that baby for you if he could have." As soon as the words are out of my mouth, I know it's true. Somehow Adrian manages to love people—really love them—even while he's in bed with the devil. I jump at the realization. Does that mean someone else dark once loved me, too?

Happy is waiting for me to finish. "And"—I look away as my voice cracks—"I might not be much help, but I'll try. I'll try as hard as I can, I promise." Happy squeezes my hand back, and then she lets go to wipe her cheek.

"Thanks," she says.

Tomás smacks his lips and blinks. "I think I fell asleep," he mumbles.

Happy laughs. This time it's real. It's a beautiful sound.

CHAPTER 28
KAYLA

It still hurts, but it's healing. I don't want to cover the tattoo up. I want to show it to the world and yell, *Jordan loves me!* But I can't. The carp has to stay hidden. I'm not supposed to have it.

Mom would freak if she knew about Jordan. Marie would freak if she knew about Jordan or the tattoo.

I pull on a high-necked shirt. In one year and a couple days, when I'm eighteen, I can show it and Jordan off, and there's nothing Mom or Marie can do about it.

I give the stuffed carp a squeeze and put it back in the middle of my bed. It adds a shock of color to its gloomy surroundings. An island of happiness in a sea of gray. It's Jordan sitting in the middle of my life.

I told him I have birthday plans with Mom. That's a total lie. Mom will tell me happy birthday and then spend the whole day feeling guilty because she can't buy me a present. I don't want to be around for that. I told her I had plans with Paige.

But I'm going to surprise Jordan. Really, really surprise him.

"Can I help you?" A woman with a sharp nose and clothes that probably cost more than all the money I ever made at No Limit Foods waves me over to the counter. I take the five steps, like I belong there. Like the coffee-colored cashmere sweater in my hands could be mine and not a cast-off from my rich friend.

"I'd like to return this." My voice betrays my lack of confidence. The woman glances at it and at me. She probably thinks I stole it. She picks it up and examines it for defects. "The color doesn't look good on me," I lie. She raises an eyebrow, but she scans it and punches at the screen on the register. The drawer pops open.

I walk out with a wad of cash, feeling giddy, like I won the lottery—or robbed a bank. This money could help Mom and me a lot. It could supplement our food stamps. We could eat nice, nonclearance, unexpired food for a month.

I have had to think about taking care of Mom for seventeen years. This time is for me. With the carp under my shirt, I feel strong, determined. I know exactly where I'm going and what I'm going to buy.

The second I walk into the store, with its lace and smell of perfume, I melt like chocolate in a hot car. My strength, my confidence, my feeling on top of the world, all lie in a puddle around my feet. I feel twelve years old again, standing outside and giggling at the headless mannequin in the black lace teddy displayed in the front window. *There are crotchless panties hanging on the wall above my head.*

I can do this. I walk up to the salesgirl and hope she can't see my nervousness. "Hi," I say. She slips the strap of a huge leopard-print bra onto a mini–plastic hanger and turns around. She has a gold ring dangling from her nose. I flinch. Maybe this was a bad idea.

I start again. "Hi, I'm looking for something, uh, simple." I cringe and wait for her to sneer at my virginal innocence.

But she doesn't really see me. I'm another faceless customer standing between her and her break.

It's awesome.

A few minutes later, I'm in the dressing room with a collection of slick, satiny things. The first one I try on is a black bra with white polka dots that pushes my boobs painfully up to my neck. It comes with matching panties so tiny I can't figure out which side is the front. The second set I try on is equally revealing.

I work my way through the hangers, rehanging the ones I don't want. This is a stupid idea. Who am I kidding, trying to buy fancy underwear to surprise my boyfriend? I should take my cash, get back on the bus, and buy Mom a nice dinner.

The last one is more conservative, a bright red satin bra thickly trimmed with lace and matching lace-trimmed boy shorts. It's probably this store's version of white cotton granny panties. I try the set on. It fits. It's kind of sexy.

Even though the salesgirl couldn't care less about me, I'm embarrassed when I put the lingerie on the counter. I make a couple of surreptitious glances over my shoulder. The world passes by outside in the mall. Everyone is too wrapped up in their own heads to notice my purchase.

"Here." Paige hands over a paper shopping bag from the expensive organic grocery store.

I peek inside. I don't know if it's a real sign of friendship or if she's just going through the motions, but it's exactly what I asked for. "Thanks," I say. "I'm just borrowing these. I'll give them back next week."

"Whenever." She lingers, looks down at the floor, bites the inside of her lip. She wants to know, and I want to tell her, but that's not who we are anymore.

"Do you want a ride?" she asks.

"No, I have some things to do." I point over my shoulder at nothing.

"Oh." She slides her bracelet up and down her arm.

I put the shopping bag down, and I hug her. She's surprised. Even though the dance team is a huggy group, it's never really been our thing.

"I'll see you on Monday?"

She nods. As I walk away, I hear her whisper, "Happy birthday."

When I pass apartment 21, a bloodshot eye examines me through the cracked-open door. "No," I say, and hold up my palm.

Finn sticks his head out. "I didn't say anything."

"Whatever you were thinking, the answer is no. The answer is always no."

He feigns being hurt, and then I realize I better be nice to him. I'm going to need his help.

"Hey, Finn?" I say, all sweetness. "Tomorrow's my birthday. You know what would be the best present in the world?" He perks up. "If I could borrow your car." And he perks down. That's not what he was hoping for.

"Come sit with me for a while first," he says.

"Okay, but that's it. I'm not doing anything."

"Did I ask you to do anything?" he snaps. "Just come and sit. Keep me company."

I believe him, because I know he's lonely.

Mom will have heard our voices in the hall. Right now, she's standing on her toes, hand braced against the doorknob, eye straining against the peephole.

I choose myself over her discomfort. "Okay," I say to Finn, and go inside.

He busies himself sweeping debris off the couch. "Sorry it's such a mess." I laugh, but then I see the hurt in his eyes. Deep down inside, Finn is a sensitive little boy.

I sit down. A black cockroach crawls along the windowsill across from me. I stamp my feet to stop the ones hidden on the floor from getting any ideas. How long do I have to stay before I can ask for his keys and get the hell out of here?

"Do you want something to drink?" He opens the fridge and peers inside, but I know his is emptier than ours.

"No thanks." He closes the fridge. There's a smile on his

face. I don't know what he took today, but it has made him cheery and bouncy.

"I found something." He disappears into the bedroom. Maybe I could find his keys and take them. But there's so much crap on the floor and on the table. It would be like turning over rocks in the woods. Any number of disgusting things could be lurking underneath.

Finn sticks a beat-up gray teddy bear with a well-chewed bow around its neck under my nose. "This is yours," he says.

I take it by the ear. It's the bear he gave me a thousand years ago now, or at least, that's what it feels like.

"Thanks," I say.

He steps back and examines me. I fidget on the couch. "You've grown up real good." He beams, as if he had something do with it.

The first knock on the door is so soft I think the sound is coming from a pile against the window. The second is loud enough to send Finn into a panic, shoving his pipes and plastic bags in between the couch cushions next to me. If it's the cops, he can claim they're mine. Classy.

His movements send a set of keys sliding along the coffee table. As soon as his back is turned, I pocket them.

He opens the door and sucks in a deep breath. I jump up, afraid it really is the cops.

"Send my daughter out," Mom says. I've never heard firmness in her voice before. She's more of a let-the-world-push-her-around kind of person.

"It's nice to see you, Tracey," Finn says. His cheeks are red, and his eyes look down to the floor.

Mom's face twists, as if she's feeling a thousand emotions at the same time. "Send my daughter out." Her voice shakes. This is the hardest thing she's ever had to do. Her demons live with Finn in this apartment, and she's facing them. Trying to protect me. Guilt slashes through my guts.

I pick up the shopping bag from Paige and hold the teddy bear by the ear. "Thanks, Finn." I step out into the hallway. Mom grabs my arm and pulls me to apartment 26. She pushes me through and slams the door. I watch her with curiosity, wondering if she's going to yell at me. That's never happened before. She's always been afraid that if she did, I would run off, get high, and relive her life story.

She doesn't yell. Her back slides down the door until she hits the floor with a thump. She rests her head on her knees. I place my hand on her shoulder. "That was brave, Mom. Thanks."

I shove the old teddy bear into the back of my closet and toss Finn's keys onto the bed. He won't even notice they're gone. The look on his face told me that as soon as his door shut, he was going to crawl into the crack between the couch cushions and not come out for days. If he ever comes out at all.

CHAPTER 29
BETSY

Angie stands in the corner of C&J's, rocking Manny and cooing softly. Lawrence watches nervously. Rosie bounces around him, whining that it's her turn to hold the baby.

Happy, half dead with exhaustion, props her head up with her hand and picks at a plate of enchiladas. Adrian examines me, like I'm a science project that has yielded disastrous results.

Mom sits at a table ringed with flowers, oblivious to the rest of the world.

It's a lazy Sunday afternoon. The restaurant is empty. Mr. Morales serenades us with his beautiful voice. Mrs. Morales paces back and forth between the kitchen and the dining room, lost in the list in her head of what still needs to be done for the wedding.

I have a taco in front of me. I've been doing well. My baggy clothes almost fit me. No one has to fear any longer that feeding me might cause an eruption.

But not today. The taco, my favorite thing on C&J's menu, is unappetizing and gray.

When I woke up this morning, there was a pink Gerbera daisy lying across the top of my pillow. I picked it up and twirled it in the brilliant late-March sunlight. For a brief moment, I forgot. I was happy. Full of feelings of promise.

Then the March sun made me remember. I stumbled into the kitchen. Mom smiled at me sadly and placed a giant, cakelike blueberry muffin from a bakery in El Paso in front of me.

She didn't say anything.

I break off a piece of taco shell and put it into my mouth. Happy's eyes are so heavy I'm afraid she's going to face-plant into the salsa.

"Hey," I say, "do you want to go lie down or something?"

She glances up at the baby. She's become fiercely attached to him, and I know she doesn't want to leave him. "Angie's not giving him up anytime soon, and everyone else is waiting for a turn. You won't get him back until closing time."

"Okay," she concedes.

I retrieve the keys to Mom's car as Happy pushes herself out of the booth. She's asleep before we even pull out of the strip mall.

The sun is in my eyes, but it feels nice on my face. Soothing, like I could curl up and take a nap too.

I stop at a red light. Everything is quiet. An older, chunky couple on motorcycles tools by, but otherwise, there isn't any traffic.

As the light on the cross street turns yellow, a bright blue hatchback pulls up behind me. I glance in the rearview mirror. The driver is a man wearing a baseball cap and dark glasses. He could be anybody.

I pull through the intersection. Happy's head is cradled in the top of the seat belt. I slow way down and gently roll over a collection of potholes to keep from waking her up.

The lane next to me is clear. I expect the driver of the blue hatchback to use it to speed past me and mumble obscenities about my old-lady driving. But he doesn't. He slows down too, keeping a car length of distance between us.

He's got my attention now. My skin itches. I try it again. I come to a dead stop in the middle of what is usually a busy road. Again he doesn't pass me; he doesn't raise his hands in the *come on!* gesture; he doesn't flip me the bird. His left elbow rests on the doorframe. His right hand is relaxed on the wheel. He bobs his head, like there's music playing in the car.

My imagination is in overdrive again. The spring air has made my skin prickly, made my body jump at every noise, made me look over my shoulder. Happy is still asleep, peaceful.

I turn right. The car follows. I drive at a good clip down the residential street. A few people are out working in their yards. They raise their heads and wave before they realize they don't know me. I turn right again. The car follows. That's two right turns. What are the odds that he happens to be going exactly where I'm turning?

There's only one way to find out. I turn right again. The street with the potholes comes into view in front of me. We're back where we started. He's following me. My head clears. Now that I know it isn't my imagination, I feel calm and in control. I turn left. Back to the strip mall. I watch him in the rearview mirror. I tighten my grip on the steering wheel. I'm ready to hit the gas. Take Mom's little car out into the desert. Activate every Border Patrol sensor between here and Mexico.

This isn't Adrian's doing. He would never put Happy at risk. I glance over at her and then dig out the black monster. No buzzing, no flashing, no missed calls. It hasn't done anything for days. I've never had silence like this before. I hoped it meant that I was being a good girl. That somehow I was living up to his expectations.

Maybe not.

The hatchback stays put at the stop sign for an unreasonably long time. Then it slowly turns to the right. Its bumper disappears into the distance behind me.

I suck in a shaky breath. Happy stirs. "Go back to sleep," I say in my most soothing voice. She obliges.

I was going to take her home, but not now. If someone's coming after me, I'm not leading them to her. I take a twisty path up and down streets I've never seen before. The blue hatchback never makes a reappearance.

I drive past my street and check the curb for any unknown vehicles. There aren't any. I throw the car in reverse, back up, and whip around the corner.

When I stop in the driveway, Happy wakes up again. She seems confused as to why we're at my house, but she's too tired to ask. I walk her inside, and she crashes on the couch. It's warm in here, but I cover her with an afghan anyway.

I slip my shoes off and dash to my room in my socks. I dial the number—the only number—on the black monster. It rings twice. "Who's following me?" I yell the second it picks up. There's a chime on the other end. A pleasant robot lady tells me the number has been disconnected.

I check the number and try again. Nothing. Where is he? I don't know what this means. Does it mean I'm free? Or does it mean it's over. That I'm over.

No echoes through my head. No, this wasn't the deal. No, I've been a good girl. No, I was just starting to figure out this life.

It's getting dark when Happy finds me curled up on my bedroom rug. She stretches out a crick in her neck. "I feel so much better." Her eyes narrow. "Did you fall asleep there?"

I hoist myself up to sitting and rub the carpet mark on the side of my face.

"Tomás can sleep anywhere too," she laughs. "Can you take me back now? Manny is probably hungry."

"Sure." I look at her face and *see* it. I memorize the dimple in her chin; the crinkles around her eyes from smiling; her dark hair, staticky from lying on the couch.

I glance at the black monster peeking out from under the bed.

It's flashing.

"Are you okay?" Happy asks.

I try to smile. I try to make my face look like all the horrors of my entire life aren't passing through my head right now. "Yeah, I'm just tried."

She snorts. "I so get that. Most of the time I don't know if I want to laugh hysterically or cry."

I nod. Right now I want to burst into tears. Happy reaches her arms up to stretch. I shove the black monster into my pocket.

"I need to go to the bathroom," I say, and slide past her.

The black monster has a text from an unknown number.

Time to pay the piper.

Mom's car was covered in dirty spots from when it attempted to rain a few days ago. No one looked twice when I pulled up to Sam's Car Wash. I wait on the other side of the dark mouth where the car will reappear all shiny and clean. Tomás stands across from me, holding a squirt bottle and a rag. He gives me a polite head nod.

My stomach churns. This isn't the way to treat friends. People who have been good to me. But I don't have a choice. I'm doing this to protect them. To protect all of us.

I dash over to Tomás. "I need to talk to you."

He's surprised, but he must see the desperation in my eyes. "My break's in ten minutes." He uses his head to point to a chicken place next door.

Tomás buys a soda and sits down across from me. He looks so tired. His head bobs, like it doesn't want stay on his shoulders.

"I need your help," I say. I lower my voice. "There's a

reason I'm in San Justo. Something from my past." I glance around. "I need to be able to protect myself."

Tomás nods sagely. He slurps up soda. I don't think he cares about my problems. But he loves Happy, and I've become part of his extended family that is San Justo.

I open my mouth to explain. Tell him everything. But he raises a hand. "I get it."

I take a gasping breath. "I won't get caught. I promise."

Pain stabs into my stomach. He has a kid and a girlfriend to support. I'm putting him at risk of losing everything. I truly am the most selfish bitch on the planet.

I still have the money I took from Mom's duffel bag. I wouldn't give it to that junkie, but I'm doing this for her. For all of us. I slide it across the table. Tomás palms it. "Give me a couple days."

The night is still. I flick the match head across the strip. I had to light the candles a final time. I light the ones left for the first little Manuel. Then I light the red one for another little angel whose life was cut way too short.

I sit back in the dirt. A wisp of cloud floats among the stars. In the distance, coyotes call to one another. Miles and miles of desert stretch in front of me. I wonder how long I would make it. If I started walking now, how far could I go before thirst and exhaustion overtook me? Would someone leave me supplies or take me into their home?

No. Running is a pipe dream. They'd find me.

I laugh aloud. I don't even know who *they* are. I might get thrown into a van, never to be seen again. Or I might turn a corner and come face to face with a lone gunman who won't blink before ending my life.

Whoever it is, they won't stop until they've got me.

I stand up and brush the dirt off. I blow a kiss to the candles. To the little angels.

I parked Mom's car on a quiet residential street without much lighting so no one would see me out here.

I'm bathed in shadows when Adrian's Bronco drives past. It slows and comes to a stop along the curb, two houses down from where I stand.

Adrian gets out. He holds a bag from the toy store where I bought Manny a stuffed giraffe. It's almost empty and floats along behind him as he walks to the front door.

I creep forward until I'm directly across the street. I step behind a tall, wild bush and peek out.

The porch light is on. A pair of small purple flip-flops sits in the yard. I can see the top of a metal swing set in the back.

All terror I had tamped down roars through me. *Anything* could be happening in that house.

I want to be the kind of girl again who disregards her own safety and charges in there to save someone. But I'm not.

Now that I have decided I want to live, I can't move. I'm rooted behind the bush. Self-loathing rolls over me.

Adrian comes out carrying a Walmart bag. From the way the bag is shaped, it looks like its contents are well wrapped in paper or cloth. I can't get any closer to see.

Adrian doesn't glance around as he walks to his Bronco. His gait is cocky and confident.

I pull myself farther into the bush as he drives away. I turn back to the house, hoping to get a glimpse of what's going on inside. To summon the courage to pound on the door and come to the rescue.

The porch light turns off.

I slink to Mom's car like the coward I've become.

CHAPTER 30
KAYLA

"Come on!" I smack the steering wheel of Finn's car. It's a boat. Older than me. Probably older than Finn. Cars don't even come in this shape anymore. It's boxy, with hard corners and two-tone paint that gave up sticking to the sides a long time ago. Now it's light rusty metal on the bottom and dark rusty metal on the top. The interior is torn and saturated with cigarette smoke. I'm too afraid to look through the pile on the backseat.

And of course, the tank was empty.

It gave me trouble in the parking lot of Bluebird Estates and at the gas station. Now, in front of the gourmet bakery, it's threatening to die a slow, lingering death while two red velvet birthday cupcakes sit in a pretty pink box, sucking up the stench.

I also have a coloring book for Grace. Maybe Jordan can use it as an excuse to see her. Maybe I can help him find other ways to see her more often.

The engine catches, and the car roars to life. It makes a

screeching sound, then a low growl, then a constant clocklike tick. A myriad of warning lights shines brightly on the dash, but I only need it to get me to the island and back. It's Finn's problem after that.

I let Paige's tailored tan trench coat fall open as I drive. Under it, I'm wearing her white dress. It's short and tight on me, and when I whip off the coat, Jordan will be able to see the clear outlines of my lacey red underwear.

A shiver of excitement races through me, and I press harder on the gas. The car groans and chugs, and the speedometer almost climbs to the speed limit. There's a line of traffic behind me on the two-lane road. Whenever there's a break in the solid yellow line, they scream past.

The sky loses light. The setting sun is replaced by heavy black rain clouds. I have to make it to Jordan's road before dark, or I'll never find it.

I'm near the water. I can feel the electricity of the storm coming off the ocean. I roll down the window and breathe in the cool, wet air. A raindrop bounces against my forehead, and in a blink, it's pouring.

Finn's window won't go back up again. Even though I slide as far to the right as I can, a dark, wet splotch forms on the side of the trench coat. It doesn't matter. I won't be wearing it for long.

The rain blacks out the sky. My excitement turns to panic. What if I can't find the road? Jordan doesn't know I'm coming, and I have no way of calling him. I left Carol Alexander's phone at home. I used up all the time on it. I'm not letting her pay for more.

I slow down to a crawl and scan the ghostly woods barely touched by Finn's one working headlight.

I almost hit it. The black Camaro rests against the dark trees. I slam on the brakes. Regardless of all the things that have happened, right now I love Drake. He's left his car on the side of the highway, pointing like an arrow to the dirt road. I'm going to give him half my cupcake.

I turn. The car balks at my suggestion that it roll over the muddy road. I push it forward at a crawl, vibrating and bouncing over every rock and rut. My teeth rattle. My butt goes numb. It's nothing like riding in Jordan's Jeep.

The house seems a lot farther away this time. I try to use my excitement to propel the car faster.

Everything goes quiet.

The vibration stops, the engine fades, and the one headlight goes black. I wiggle the key and the gearshift, and stomp on the gas and brakes.

I smack the wheel. Finn's car is dead.

I was in too much of a hurry to get out of the apartment in my sexy underwear to think about an umbrella. I flip open the glove box and flip it right back closed again. I'm not sticking my hand in there.

I don't have a choice. It will be romantic, me appearing at his door, soaking wet in the middle of a storm. Things like that happen in the movies all the time. I shove the pink cupcake box as far under the coat as I can, open the door, and sink up to my ankles in mud. Slightly less romantic, but I go with it.

It turns out that Paige's trench coat is for decorative purposes only. It isn't made to stand up to the deluge falling from the sky. By the time I make it to the edge of the house, I'm soaked all the way to my skin. I could have skipped the dress. When I take the coat off, there will be nothing hiding any detail of the red lace.

My hair drips into my face. My feet, in what were originally my cute—and only—flats, are caked with mud and leaves. The pink box melts in my hands. I hunch myself over it and jog for the door.

All the lights are on, as if the house is meant to be a beacon for lost travelers in the woods. I stand under the sliver of an overhang above the front door and try to clean myself up. I kick the shoes off and use the semiclean bottoms of my feet to try to rub the mud off my ankles. I squeeze out my hair. I check on the cupcakes. They're kind of soggy, but still cupcake-shaped and edible. My stomach growls. I had been too nervous and excited to eat anything all day.

I take a deep breath and remind myself I'm seventeen today. That's 364 more days until I'm a legal adult. I can do this.

I raise my fist and knock. Nothing happens. I knock more forcefully. My heart drops to my muddy feet when no one comes to the door. Jordan's Jeep is parked out front. Someone has to be home.

The rain is loud; maybe they can't hear the knocking inside. I press on the door handle. It gives, and the door opens. "Hello? Jordan?" I call. I hear voices coming from the back of the house.

A horrible thought crosses my mind. *What if Jordan's mom*

is home? He says she always works and rarely comes home, but what if tonight is an exception? With the way I'm dressed, there's no hiding my intentions.

I know my face must be as red as my underwear, but there's nothing I can do about it now. I'm stuck. Committed.

I step across the threshold, cringing at the water and mud I drip on the pristine carpet.

"Hel—" A hand slaps over my mouth. An arm wraps hard around my waist. The pink box flies through the air.

A snake hisses up at me.

I claw at it, my heart racing a million miles an hour. He pulls me roughly through the kitchen and down the hallway. I kick at his shins. My feet connect, but he keeps moving.

He throws me to the floor of a bedroom. Through the blackness overtaking my mind, I hear an odd, prideful voice. *I knew it.*

I snap back to the room. Drake straddles me and pins my arms over my head. He leans over. I stop breathing as his head blocks out the overhead light and casts a dark shadow over his face. My coat is splayed open. My red underwear shines up at him.

"You're a stubborn girl, Kayla," he whispers. I thrash and try to pull my arms away from him. He clamps down tighter. I whimper in pain.

"Here's what's going to happen, and for once in your life, you're going to pay attention and follow instructions. Do I make myself clear?"

I nod—anything to keep him talking.

"I'm going to let you go now. You won't make a sound.

No matter what you hear, you will stay here on the floor with your head down until I come and get you. Do you understand?" I nod again, and he releases the pressure on my arms. Drake stands up and pointedly looks away from my almost-naked body. I don't move, but my chest heaves, trying to suck up air to feed my racing heart.

"Stay," he says, and walks out, closing the door behind him.

CHAPTER 31
BETSY

Mom gasps. My head shoots up. My heart races. *This is a church, for heaven's sake.* They can't come get me here.

She brushes Adrian's shoulder. "I got pollen all over you."

I don't think Mom's slept all week. If she has, she probably dreamed about flowers. She's nervous. This is her big shot. She wants—needs—everything to be perfect.

Tomás came through. I have a yellow fake-leather purse looped around my body. Inside is a gun. Another black monster. It's heavy and cold and beat-up. I try not to think about what it's seen. What it's done.

Lawrence and his groomsmen, Adrian and Tomás, look like they're going to the prom in their rented tuxes with gold cummerbunds and bow ties. When they first came in and Adrian saw me laying a string of pure-white lilies on the altar, he stopped. Tomás ran into his back.

"Sorry, man," Tomás mumbled, and collapsed onto a pew.

Lawrence pointed at him. "Coffee. Now. I don't want you

passing out during my wedding." He hoisted his brother up by the shoulders and led him to a back room.

Then Adrian, always pretending to be a gentleman, dove forward to help Mom with a heavy vase.

She goes to get something to clean the pollen off.

He fingers his shiny bow tie. "What is it with girls and the matchy-matchy? Angie's marriage would still be legal, even if the groomsmen didn't match the bridesmaids."

It's a joke, I think. He's keeping up appearances. But his jaw is clenched, teeth grinding.

I pick up a flower. "I'm here helping my mom," I say. There's no sense in provoking him, not while I'm still alive. While I still have a chance.

I drove past that house he went to. Other than a car that was way too flashy for the neighborhood parked outside, it looked totally normal. I don't know what I was expecting. Maybe a neon sign that said MURDERS INSIDE?

My stomach churns. If I survive whoever is coming for me, I will have to tell someone about that house.

Mom returns with a wet paper towel. She brushes Adrian off while apologizing profusely. When she finishes and heads back out to the van, he turns around. Our eyes meet. He doesn't look away. He stands in the middle of the aisle, and his gaze locks on me. I place my hand on the yellow purse. As much as I want to, I don't look away. I can't show him my fear.

The door opens in the back of the church. Both of us jump. Miss Jones, the Miss Jones from school, teeters in on heels she obviously never wears. She sees me and Adrian.

Her eyes run over my jeans and T-shirt. "Shit," she says,

but then glances apologetically up to the heavens. "Am I early?" Her unsteadiness doesn't seem to be caused by the shoes alone. Her eyes are watery, and her cheeks red.

As Adrian moves forward to greet her, she looks over his shoulder. Her eyes widen while the rest of her face threatens to collapse.

"Ten minutes. He gets to sleep for ten minutes and then his ass better be dressed and ready to stand here." Lawrence comes around the corner talking to no one in particular. He stops dead in his tracks when he sees Miss Jones.

She throws her hands up and giggles. "I'm early."

I adjust a vase in the corner and try to become invisible. My pocket buzzes. I freeze. Lawrence, Adrian, and Miss Jones glance at me. Adrian's eyes narrow.

I slink into the hallway out of their sight. The black monster has been quiet since the last text. I'm terrified of what it will say now.

It's a different number, but still a Washington area code.

Tonight.

I stagger back. I grip my yellow purse. No. It can't happen tonight. I'm around all these people.

I don't have time to react before Adrian's hand wraps around my wrist.

My purse swings behind me and slaps me in the side. Adrian pulls me deep into the dark hallway. I rip my hand away and reach for the purse. He stops. It's just us. I've been given a chance to stop this. I slide my fingers into the purse and wrap them around the gun.

Adrian looks into my eyes. My hand releases on its own accord. I want to, but I can't do it. Even after all I've seen, all that's happened to me, I can't shoot someone in cold blood.

He pushes me into the back room.

"Stay," he whispers. Tomás is asleep in a folding chair with a cup of weak-looking coffee steaming on the table next to him.

My body goes limp in a chair. Its metal bites into my limbs, but I hardly feel it.

Adrian kicks Tomás's foot. "Wake up." Tomás blinks sleepily. When he sees me, he half smiles. The look on Adrian's face intensifies.

"Debbie's here," he announces.

Tomás is up on his feet, like he's chugged a Red Bull. His head whips around the room, searching for something he can't find.

"I'll wait outside." Adrian points at Tomás. "Figure something out."

Adrian leaves. I huddle on the chair. Should I run after him?

Tomás's eyes land on me. "If Angie sees Debbie here, she'll freak."

"Angie?" Haze is taking over my mind. My yellow purse is in my lap. I want to throw it to the floor.

Tomás paces. "A couple years ago, Angie kicked Lawrence out. They were broken up for months, and he started dating Debbie. When Angie told him he could come home, it was messy. Debbie took it hard. If Angie sees Debbie here, she'll call off the wedding."

The haze grows thicker. All I can do is stare at Tomás.

He looks at me, like I stopped understanding English. "Debbie. Miss Jones. From the high school?"

I push away the blur, the yellow purse, and the knowledge that tonight I die. "Angie can't do that," I say. This wedding has to happen. Mom needs this. Needs to feel successful. So she has something—something for when I'm gone.

Tomás has moved out to the hallway and is peeking around the corner. I follow him and look.

Miss Jones swipes a finger under her eye. Lawrence holds her other hand. It's not a romantic gesture—more like comforting someone who has lost a loved one.

She leans forward until their faces are far too close for a man who is about to be married to another woman in an hour. He doesn't pull back. I can't tell if he's humoring her or if he's actually feeling something.

Adrian tears back into the side doorway. Any second, Angie, her friends, and Mrs. Morales are going to come in. Come in and see.

Adrian and Tomás make frantic hand gestures to each other. They aren't going to make it. By the time the two of them figure it out, it will be way too late. Angie will have a complete meltdown.

I leave the boys, still paralyzed by indecision, and dash around the corner. "Miss Jones!" I yell. "Thank God you're still here." Lawrence jumps back and lets go of her hand.

I loop my arm around her elbow and flinch when my purse swings to the side. "I have to change, and I totally need help zipping up my dress." I pull her back a couple of wobbly steps. She won't leave Lawrence.

"You're the only one who can help me. I'm so not having them"—I jut my thumb over my shoulder at Adrian and Tomás, staring with mouths agape from the hallway—"see me in my bra."

The word *bra* brings Lawrence back to his senses. "It was good to see you, Debbie." He gives her a friendly wave and jogs to meet his groomsmen.

I still have Miss Jones by the arm. She's coming with me whether she likes it or not. I almost pull her off her heels, but eventually, she walks beside me. Just as we reach the door, a huge amount of commotion fills the back of the church.

Squeals of "you can't see the bride" and uproarious laugher echo through the hallowed space. Miss Jones stops and stands perfectly still.

"Come on," I say, and take her outside. As soon as we are in the parking lot, she cries big, ugly, screw-up-your-whole-face, drunken tears. She heads for her car. I step in front of her and hold out my hand. She shouldn't be driving. She shouldn't have driven here in the first place.

"Do you want me to take you home?" I ask.

She shakes her head and rubs at the mascara now running down her face. "No," she says softly. "No," she says again with determination. She squares her shoulders. "I'm going to stay. I am going to see him get married. It will be good for me. It will end this once and for all."

I'm not so sure about that, but as long as the wedding happens and Miss Jones isn't out driving around, I will have fulfilled my responsibilities.

Then I can go back to worrying about dying.

"Do you need help with your dress?" Miss Jones asks.

"Um, no. That's okay. I'm not going to be here for the ceremony." And my dress doesn't have a zipper.

She's confused but doesn't say anything. I need to meet Mom at the van so we can go to the high school where the reception will be, but I'm afraid that if someone doesn't watch Miss Jones, she'll do something crazy—like run in, grab Angie's veil, and demand that Lawrence marry her instead.

A black SUV with dark tinted windows comes out of nowhere. This is it. I jump back, instinctively placing Miss Jones between it and me.

Like a human shield.

Then the horror of what I have done washes over me. I step out and push her behind me. She isn't part of this. They're here for me. I put my hand in my purse. I'm ready. I can pull the trigger to save someone else.

The back door of the SUV opens.

Happy bounces out wearing a bright pink shift that clings to the baby weight she's still carrying. I whip my hand out of my purse and grab on to Miss Jones to keep from collapsing in relief. Concern crosses Happy's face. I scan the parking lot. Does she see something I don't?

"Uh, hi, Miss Jones," she says. Miss Jones tips her hand up in a halfhearted wave.

The rest of the doors of the SUV open, and assorted older relatives dressed in their Sunday best spill out. They smile politely at the two pale girls standing at odd angles in the church parking lot.

As Happy gets the baby, my lungs remember how to breathe. I walk over to her and motion behind me with my head. "I have to go help my mom. Will you keep an eye on Miss Jones? Don't let her into the church until right before the ceremony starts. Make sure she sits in the back."

Happy giggles. "If Angie saw her, she would freak."

"Exactly."

Happy ambles across the blacktop and calls, "Hey, Miss Jones, wanna see my baby?"

Mom is rearranging things inside the florist van behind the church. I grab the other side of a box she's struggling with.

"Thanks," she says, and steps back to examine the insides of the vehicle. Her hair is tied back in a scarf. Her face has color. She looks genuinely proud of herself, of her life here.

"What if it had always been like this?" I whisper.

"It's like this now." She places her hand on my cheek. "That's all that matters."

I want to scream. And cry. And bang my fists on the side of the van at the unfairness of it all. Mom's doing great. I'm getting better. We have a house. I have a friend. Mom has an almost-boyfriend. One who's nice. One who will treat her the way she deserves to be treated. One who might actually be in love with her.

Mom looks over my shoulder and blushes.

"Ready to go, ladies?" Teddy is decked out in cowboy chic: Plaid button-up shirt. Crisp, ironed jeans. Spit-polished boots. A bolo tie with a silver clasp around his neck. Even his mustache has been combed. I think this is Teddy's version of wearing a tux.

"Teddy's going to help us move some of the heavy stuff." Mom doesn't even try to hide her feelings for him anymore.

"Why don't you ladies head over to the school? I'll be right behind you."

"Thanks, Teddy," I say, and pat him on the shoulder. He jumps slightly at the unexpected physical contact. "Oh shoot! I got pollen on you. Mom, do you have a cloth or something?"

"Um, I think so." She buries her head in the front seat of the van.

I give Teddy's shoulder a quick brush. Then I stick the black monster into his front pocket.

CHAPTER 32
KAYLA

Like hell I'm going to stay here on the floor waiting for Drake to come back. I roll over onto my knees and search for something to defend myself with. This room has a twin bed with a blue comforter tucked under military style at the corners. A nightstand with a lamp and an alarm clock. A closet sparsely filled with hung-up T-shirts and pressed pants. Nothing on the walls, no personality. This is Drake's room, and I'm getting out of here now.

I turn the knob centimeter by centimeter. When it pops open, I gasp and wait for Drake to charge me, beat me, do what he did to those other girls. The hallway is brightly lit but empty. I step out. The plush carpet tickles my bare feet and masks the sound of my careful steps.

I hear something. Soft crying. A child crying. Oh my God. Grace. It's coming from her bedroom immediately to my right. I have to take her with me. Get us both away from Drake and out to the main road, where maybe we can flag down a car or at least hide until the sun comes up.

I reach for the door, but I hear something else. Heavy, stomping feet. Drake's coming back. I dive into the open door behind me. The bathroom. The light is on. If I turn it off, he'll know. I step behind the shower curtain with the rubber duckies and flatten myself in the tub.

The door to Grace's room opens. Paper rips. Something rattles. "Come on, sweetie, have some M&M's." Not Drake. Jordan. I pull myself up to my knees. Tears of relief drip down my face. Jordan will rescue us, take us away from Drake.

A second set of footsteps. I drop back down to the cold surface of the tub.

"What's taking so long?" Drake snaps.

"Relax, dude. This is the easy part." Soft, tiny footsteps. "That's a good girl. Have another chocolate."

All three of them walk away. I jump up. My foot slips on the puddle I have created, and I have to slam my hand into the wall to keep my balance. I freeze, but then I can't contain the sob any longer. It leaves my mouth like an explosion. I'm sure Drake must hear. "Jordan?" I call out softly. *Jordan, please come and get me.*

But he doesn't come. No one does. I'm going to have to get myself out of here. Get away from Drake. My mind flashes to Shonda in the woods. Drake can't see me leave the house. If I end up beaten in the woods, way out here on this island, no one will be coming to save me.

I step out of the bathroom and creep to the end of the hallway. I'm going out the front door into the dark. I'll get help and send the cops back for Grace.

I peer around the corner into the cavernous, glass-walled

living room. I lurch back. Drake and Jordan stand with Grace in between them. Three men face them. The two on the ends have stylishly spiked hair and wear twin tan suits over black shirts. They are muscular, nervous-looking. Their eyes dart around the room. The man in the middle is shorter. A belly peeks out from under his black suit jacket, but he's solid like a brick wall.

When I look again, Jordan pushes Grace forward. I don't know what I'm seeing. Jordan entertaining guests? Introducing them to his sister?

The man reaches out and lifts Grace's chin. A tiny stub sits in the place where his pinkie should be. He sweeps her bangs off her forehead and twists her head from side to side. Her glassy eyes have a faraway stare to them. She doesn't look afraid. She doesn't look like she feels anything.

Panic rises up inside of me again. Wait. Drake is the bad one. Drake is the murderer. But Jordan stands tall and uninterested as his sister gets checked out like an animal.

Drake glances over his shoulder to where I'm standing. I jerk back into the hallway.

I have to get out of here. I'm five feet from the entrance to the kitchen. From there, I will have a clear shot to the front door. But the jumpy guys will see me. They aren't focused on Grace. They look everywhere but at her.

The man releases Grace and nods.

I'm going to make a run for it.

"Wait," Drake says. Everyone freezes. "Where's the money?"

One of the jumpy guys snickers. Jordan glares at Drake.

The man in the center reaches behind him and slides out a black messenger bag. Drake grabs it, slaps it down on the end table, and opens it.

"Shall we wait while you count it?" the man says.

Jordan grabs Drake's arm. "That's rude," he mutters. Drake closes the bag.

No. My whole world comes crashing down. Jordan, Drake—they're both in on it. Nothing I believe is real. Jordan doesn't love me. Jordan's a criminal. My legs won't hold me up. I slide down to the carpet.

The man takes Grace's hand. My mind spins. I can't let them do it. Can't let them take her. I have to do something. Distract them, grab her, get out.

I'm going to do it. Run out screaming at the top of my lungs. I have so much adrenaline right now I could break down walls with my fists. Outrun them.

Before I can move, one of the jumpy guys looks up at the ceiling. Then the other. The man snaps his head to Jordan. Jordan focuses on Drake. Drake's eyes grow wide. The breath hitches in his throat.

I hear it. Something outside. Not rain. This is a rhythmic chopping sound. A helicopter.

It happens so fast, my eyes have trouble keeping up with the motion. The man reaches for the waist of the jumpy guy next to him. A dark object appears in his hand. He points it at Drake. A pop. Drake collapses to the floor, hidden from me by the white leather sofa.

Grace whimpers. Jordan falls to his knees, his hands prayerlike in front of his chest. "Please. I didn't know. I didn't know."

All my love for Jordan is still there. My insides haven't caught up to what my eyes are seeing. When the gun swings over to Jordan, I scream. Even though the men turn their attention to me, I can't help it, can't control it. It's instinctual to protect someone I love. I race to Jordan and throw myself between him and the gun.

He pushes me away hard. I fall to the floor. The helicopter is deafening.

The man barks something at the jumpy guys. One grabs the messenger bag, and the two of them run out through the glass door into the darkness.

The gun swings around. Jordan, me . . . Grace. Her eyes meet mine. Another pop. She falls quietly, her head landing on Drake's chest.

My mouth opens. The air, the sob, the scream—all back up in my throat. Nothing comes out.

"This is your mess," the man says. "Clean it up." He drops the gun in front of Jordan and walks businesslike into the night.

Jordan picks up the gun. Stands.

I'm on my knees, but I'm not begging. Everything that has happened is like a movie or a bad dream. I feel like I'm floating over the room watching it from afar.

He points the gun at me. "Kayla, I'm sorry," he whispers, and pulls the trigger.

CHAPTER 33

BETSY

When we pull up to the high school, all I can think about are the texts.

Time to pay the piper.

Tonight.

I charge over to Teddy, waiting on the basketball court.

"I don't know what the texts mean," he says before I can ask.

"How can you not know?"

He shrugs. "Don't wander off by yourself. Stay in big groups of people."

"But—"

"You're going to have to trust me. Stay in the middle of the crowd. Do you have your other phone? Is my number still the first one?"

I nod, pull Toxic Pink out of my yellow purse, and show him.

"Good girl," he says. He smiles. "Let's not worry your mother."

Mom steps back to survey the centerpieces on the banquet tables. Everything for the reception is set up on the outside basketball courts. They got lucky with the weather. The sky is perfectly clear.

"Mom," I say in a voice that quavers. She turns and looks at me with the smile of satisfaction still on her face. "I love you."

She sweeps an errant piece of hair off my forehead. "I love you, too. Now let's get this finished before the entire town shows up and sees us in our grubbies."

The gym is open so that the guests can use the restrooms. When I go inside, I imagine a thousand monsters lurking in its dark shadows Every noise sends my heart beating into my throat. Even the sound of my own footsteps makes me whip around and look behind me.

Tonight.

There won't be any more calls or texts. That was it. The last one.

I check every corner of the girls' locker room. There's definitely no one here, but I can't relax. I'm beginning to think maybe the anticipation is worse than what they will do to me.

My zipperless dress came from the old lady section of a department store in El Paso, but it was the only one I could find that didn't have a plunging neckline. I pull the piece of flowered cloth over my head. The top sits at the bottom of my throat. The rest of it falls shapelessly like a sack around me.

I fasten a thin black belt around the middle in an attempt

to make myself look like I have a curve or two. It doesn't work. And anyway, it doesn't matter.

I stuff my feet into equally frumpy flats. I'm not wearing heels. I can't run in heels. I know I can't outrun the demons that want to take me, but at least I can get them away from all these innocent people. No matter what Teddy thinks.

I sit down on a bench in the cool darkness of the locker room. I open my yellow purse and, for the hundredth time, look at the gun. Could I really do it? Or should I just let them take me away? Poof. Disappeared.

This sucks.

I laugh aloud. I have been living with this for a whole year now. Waiting. Moping. Starting to hope that things might get better. That I might make it through.

No such luck, sweetheart.

Something inside me snaps, and I feel calmer. This was all set in motion a long time ago. I didn't have any control then. But I might have some control now. I can keep anyone else from getting hurt. I throw the strap of the yellow purse over my shoulder.

When the first guests arrive, Mom sprints to make final adjustments.

"Teddy," I squeak. He looks down at me. I have to do this without crying. I take in a deep breath. "You make her happy. Will you stay with her? Even if—even after . . ."

"Hey," he says. "Nothing's going to happen. Do you understand me? Nothing is going to happen."

I nod. He smiles a mustache-lifting smile. "Your friend wants your attention." He points at Happy, who is bouncing up and down and waving. I glance back at him. "I'll be around," he says.

Happy has Miss Jones in tow. Before they get to me, Miss Jones peels off toward the bar. Happy looks relieved.

"Everything was fine," she says. "Why would you go to your ex-boyfriend's wedding?"

Miss Jones stands alone, pretending not to be chugging a glass of wine. I shrug. "Love can make you do strange things."

"Yeah, but she's, like, supposed to be a teacher," Happy says with disgust. In his carrier, Manny fusses. "I think he needs a diaper change."

"The bathrooms in the gym are open." She and the baby need to stay as far away from me as possible.

An army of limos pulls up in front of the school. The guests hoot and holler as Angie and Lawrence step out. Rosie follows, throwing rose petals around them, the groomsmen and bridesmaids, the car, random guests. Mom rushes forward to give her a refill.

It's going to be a long night.

Adrian catches my eye and walks toward me. I turn and push through the crush of guests holding up their phones to take pictures.

I hang out on the fringes of the party until everyone is seated and eating. The sun is going down, and a cool April breeze is whipping up. I hug myself and lean against the still-warm stucco wall of the gym. Adrian glances at me occasionally, like he's keeping an eye on me. But I know he won't be the one. He won't do anything to me here. He loves his family too much.

At a table on the far side of the basketball courts, Miss Jones throws her head back in laughter. The wine in her hand sloshes over the sides of the glass. She's being entertained by the man sitting next to her. He leans in close, like she's the center of the universe. I can only see a mass of dark red curls on the top of his head. His left arm is tied against his body in a blue sling. He sits back for a moment, and I catch the profile of his face, the angle of his nose, his lips splitting across his cheeks, the curve of his chin.

My eyes focus on his chest. The sling covers it, but I still see the tattoo. The carp. The color of fire, and just as deadly.

I clap my hand over my heart to keep it from running away. It's my imagination. It has to be.

Happy devours a piece of cake while Tomás gives Manny a bottle. I tiptoe up and crouch between them.

"Who's that guy talking to Miss Jones?"

Tomás shrugs and shakes his head. "I still can't believe she showed." He glances at my yellow purse. I back away from them.

Mom and Teddy are nowhere to be seen. Rosie wanders from table to table, showering the guests with her endless supply of petals. She has now also acquired a second basket full of white roses. Both baskets hang over one arm. As she approaches each table, she places her finger against her lips in a thinking gesture and decides who's most worthy to receive a flower.

I slide along the wall in the shadows, trying to get closer

to the man without being seen. The waiters circulate, picking up plates and pouring coffee. The DJ asks for everyone's attention. All eyes turn to Angie and Lawrence at the head table.

All eyes but two.

It's him.

At least now I know who's coming for me.

It's the gunman.

CHAPTER 34
KAYLA

I open my eyes. The darkness lifts, and they begin to focus. I'm alone. I slap my hands around my body, looking for damage. I don't find any. I dig my nails into the carpet and pull myself inch by inch to Grace. I lift her head. It flops in my arms. Her face is blank. I cradle her against my chest. Her blood creates a red patch that spreads across my white dress and fills in the space between the outlines of my underwear. I rock her while Drake's snake watches with an unseeing eye.

The splintering of wood. Yelling. A hundred charging feet.

"FBI. Get your hands up," a black clad figure yells at me. He doesn't look real. He's another monster in this nightmare.

My hands are yanked behind my back and encased in body-warmed metal bands. They are lifted, jerking my body up. My bare feet drag along behind me. My eyes won't leave Grace. My neck turns and contorts trying to stay with her.

Cold, wet air seeps into my pores. My neck gives out, and

my chin thuds to my chest. A soggy pink cupcake box lies on the floor, its contents ground red and white into the cream-colored carpet like blood and skin foaming at the mouth.

The woman doesn't turn away as I remove my red lacey underthings. She takes them with a latex-gloved hand and places them in a plastic bag on top of the bloodstained dress and coat. She doesn't speak. Her face is blank, as if I'm a specimen in her lab. She hands me a jumpsuit made out of a white papery material.

My body is intact. I don't have a scratch on me. Jordan missed.

I wish he'd killed me.

Hairs are plucked from my head. My nails cut. My cheek swabbed. I'm fingerprinted and photographed and scanned. There's been no time to cry. No time to process what's happened. No time to scream and pound on the two-way mirror watching my every move.

A man—professional-football-player big and bulky—wearing a slicker with FBI across the back enters. The woman nods. He cuffs me and grabs my arm.

The jumpsuit rustles alongside his crisp, clipped footsteps. He walks too fast, and I stumble. His grip doesn't loosen, and I'm dragged, scrambling to put my feet back underneath me.

"I didn't do anything," I whisper. It's the first noise I've made since they threw me in the back of a black SUV in front of Jordan's house. *Jordan's house.* The night comes rushing back to me. I can't breathe. I can't stand. The force of my weight being pulled to the earth causes the agent to lose his grip. I fall and hit the floor. He hoists me back up, but not before I taste the polished linoleum on my lips.

Another SUV. The back windows are tinted so heavily that the streetlights outside glow like alien orbs in a sea of darkness.

We drive for a long time. My head aches. My stomach growls. I have to pee.

We come to a stop in front of a nondescript three-story office building surrounded by neatly trimmed hedges. The parking lot is empty. It's still the middle of the night.

I have no idea where I am. Seattle maybe. Mexico. The moon.

Football Player sits me in a chair in a second-floor conference room. He removes the cuffs from my wrists. Before he leaves, he looks me square in the eyes, conveying the message that if I try anything, the cuffs will go right back on.

There's nothing in the conference room. No photos of sweeping vistas floating over inspirational sayings. No coffeepot in the corner. Just a long table with two chairs. One I'm currently occupying and an empty one across from me.

I tap my fingers on the table. I have to do something to busy my mind. When I sit still, I see her dead eyes staring at the ceiling. Jordan pointing the gun at me. Drake's snake. I tap my fingers until the tips go numb.

The door opens. A man enters. He's short. If I were to stand up, I would tower over him. He wears a black suit with a red tie. The bald patch that takes up most of his head shines under the overhead lights. His face is long, pinched, and weaselly. He clasps a thick, legal-sized manila folder against his chest. He closes the door behind him.

"Kayla, Kayla, Kayla," he says. "How you have disappointed me." He shakes his head. His pointy nose is hypnotizing as it goes back and forth.

He puts the folder down in the middle of the table and sits in the other chair. He clasps his hands and leans forward. "What are we going to do with you?" His mocking tone echoes around the room. I sit back in my chair and bite my lip. This is not the time to start crying.

"My name is Weathers. AUSA Weathers. Do you know what that means?" He doesn't give me a chance to answer. "That stands for Assistant United States Attorney." He slaps his palm on the table. "Assistant."

He picks up the folder and rifles through it. "You were supposed to be my secret weapon, Kayla." He stops and my eyes meet his piercing glare. "Until you turned around and shot me in the foot.

"You seemed too good to be true. I've dangled pretty girls in front of Jordan before. Even some pretty boys, but he never took the bait. Then he found you all on his own and seemed to get genuinely attached." An ache spreads through my chest, coldness surrounding my heart.

He slides a photo across the table. A young man in a starched navy-blue shirt with a matching tie. His expression is serious, but you can see the life and excitement in his eyes. It's a younger, shinier version of Drake.

"Agent Liam Christiansen. The best of the best. Do you know how many years it took to get an agent into that house?

How many towns Christiansen had to slog through, playing along as Jordan hunted for kids? The bowing and scraping he did for that little pipsqueak?

"Then Jordan walked into a dumpy little grocery store in Clairmont. Maybe it was your perky smile or the way you ran soup cans over the scanner. Who knows. But you were the answer to our prayers. Jordan was so distracted that I was able to put together a whole operation under his nose, and he never suspected a thing."

He leans back in his chair. "I helped out. Made sure Christiansen knew where you were. Kept his eye on you. Drove you closer and closer to Jordan. Got Jordan to drop his guard, get sloppy. But you"—he waves a finger—"turned out to be more trouble than you're worth. Accusing my agent of being a murderer? You almost blew the whole operation. I had to let that big-nosed cop in on it so he would quit poking around.

"And you didn't stop there, did you?"

I chew the inside of my cheek. He leans back and pulls another photo out of the folder. He slaps it onto the table. I turn away. It's Drake's body, lying on a metal slab under cold fluorescent lights.

"Christiansen liked you. You reminded him of his younger sister. At one point he had a crisis of conscience, almost gave up everything and told you." My throat tightens. It was the night I found Shonda—in the car when he told me to stay away from Jordan.

"But then I reminded him of what we were really after." Weathers tosses more photos at me. Jordan at different ages.

"Jordan Edelweiss. Twenty-two. Originally from Miami,

Florida. Pathological liar. Lieutenant of this man." My breath catches as I see the man from the house staring up at me.

"Calls himself the Koi. Started off working with the Yakuza, but then decided to go freelance. He's a nasty son of a bitch. Specializes in little girls. Doesn't leave witnesses." A drop of water splatters on the table. In my numbness, I glance up at the ceiling. Then I realize it dripped off my face.

"I was *this* close to getting him. Years of work all came down to tonight. Then you came along. You self-centered little girl." His tone wakes me up like a slap in the face.

"I didn't do anything!" I cry out.

He stands up and paces along the length of the conference table. "There's only one road to that house. Only one road to get SWAT in. Only one road to get Christiansen out."

"Oh my God." It hits me like the building has collapsed. *Finn's car.*

He perches on the table and hovers over me. "That's right, sweetheart. You did that. I had to send in the helicopter. By the time I got my people on the ground, the Koi was already in Canadian waters. Everything that happened tonight is your fault." He has one more photo in his hand. I know what it is. I won't look. He slaps it down on the table. I turn away. He grips the side of my head and forces it forward. "You're going to look at it, because you did this."

The sob sitting at the back of my throat for hours explodes. Grace's innocent blue eyes stare at nothing. Her pink lips are parted. Her skin is gray.

Weathers leaves me alone to beg the forgiveness of her ghost.

Ten minutes later, he comes back, neatly gathers the photos, and places them in the folder. A crisp sheet of paper with bold black writing is set in front of me. He places a pen next to my right hand.

"This is what happens now. You will sign this statement. You will be sent to a secure location of my choice. You will be afforded basic protection. You will stay there until Jordan or the Koi are apprehended. Then you will testify. In exchange for your testimony, you will receive a reduced prison sentence. If you're a good girl, you'll be out by the time you're fifty."

I jump. Adrenaline replaces the shock that had overtaken me. The fuzziness in my head clears. "Prison? I didn't do anything. It was a mistake, an accident. You can't send me to prison for that. And I want a lawyer and my mom. I'm a minor. I can't be here alone."

He sighs. "This is the easy way, Kayla. You want the hard way? Fine. I release you. I send you out that door into a room with twenty FBI agents who have been told you killed one of their brothers. Assuming you make it out of the building, do you know what happens next? The Koi has people everywhere. They will figure out Jordan left you alive. A witness. They will hunt you down and kill you. And not just you. Your family. Your friends. Anyone you have ever cared about."

"He barely saw me. He doesn't know who I am. If Jordan wanted to kill me, he would have. I'll dye my hair. They won't be able to recognize me."

He grabs the zipper of my jumpsuit and yanks. I flinch as it splays open, exposing the top of my breasts. "They won't have to recognize you. You're marked. Jordan recruited young men all over the country to be part of his network. Any of them who sees that will know." He turns away. I forgot about the carp.

None of this would be happening if I were Paige. If I had an army of fancy lawyers and a family to search for me if I disappeared. Weathers wouldn't treat Paige like this.

He'd never set her up in the first place.

Marie and her little bear flash through my mind. I have to protect them. I reach for the pen.

In the middle of a chunky block of text, a line catches my eye.

AFTER MY CAR BROKE DOWN, I WALKED TO THE HOUSE AND SAW JORDAN ARRIVE WITH THE LITTLE GIRL.

"Wait," I say.

Weathers throws up his hands in exasperation. "What? What is it now, Kayla."

I flinch at his attack, but I persevere. "The girl didn't arrive that night. She'd been there for months. And Jordan didn't bring her. Drake did."

And then I see it: the slightest bounce of his eyebrow. A chink in his armor. I've got him.

CHAPTER 35
BETSY

The man never looks at Angie and Lawrence. His eyes rove around the reception, examining each individual face. I dash into the gym before he sees mine.

Someone's turned on the lights. I make my way to the girls' locker room at a brisk pace. Anyone watching would think I needed to go to the bathroom and not that I'm running away.

I go into the middle stall and sit down fully dressed on the toilet seat. I need a plan. A plan that won't get anyone innocent killed.

I have the gun. But how can I use it against him? Have *his* blood on my hands?

Music starts up outside. The speeches are over. Lawrence and Angie will now be twirling around the wooden squares laid down over the cement to create a dance floor.

I stand up. Time for me to face the music. I care about those people. I'm going to take care of my business.

I stride out of the gym. My plan is simple. I'm going to

walk over to him and give myself up. That's it. Then we can slip away. No one will ever know. I will just be gone. Their lives will go on without me.

It's happened before.

I step onto the cement. A mass of people sway back and forth on the crowded dance floor. I don't see him. My heart lifts for a second. Maybe my change of appearance fooled him. Maybe I am as pale, thin, and sickly looking as I think.

Someone grabs my shoulder from behind. I whirl around, fists up and ready to fight.

Adrian raises his hands. "Whoa." I drop my fists. I don't want to make a scene. "Dance with me," he says. "We need to talk." When I don't move, he takes my hand and leads me through the other dancers to the middle of the floor. He drops his hand to my waist, straightens his back, and raises his other arm out to the side, like we're about to compete in professional ballroom dancing.

"My mom made me take lessons," he says by way of explanation. It would be kind of cute, except he's a psychopath and I'm about to give myself over to the devil.

I place a hand in Adrian's and rest the other on his shoulder. My yellow purse bounces between us.

"Since you seem determined to always be around whether you're wanted or not, maybe we can come up with a compromise," Adrian whispers into my ear. "A deal."

I jerk back. "No deals," I say. I'm never making a deal again. Adrian's hands are tight on me. I'm blocked in by dancers. Is this their plan? To keep me trapped between them so I can't run?

"Whatever," he says. "But I still wanted to tell you that what you did at the church was nice."

"What?"

"What you did for Lawrence and Angie by taking Debbie away. That was nice." Adrian's deep brown eyes search my face, as if he's seeing it for the first time. Something is happening inside his head, changing. Like maybe he's having second thoughts. Like maybe I have a chance to get away.

The couple next to us shuffles to the side, creating a break in the bodies. There he is—the man with the sling—kneeling in front of Rosie. She smiles and coyly looks down at her feet. Then she does something that makes my heart stop. She reaches into her second basket and hands him a rose.

CHAPTER 36
KAYLA

"Just sign the damn statement!" Weathers yells. The door opens a crack. Football Player sticks his head in. Weathers flaps a hand to shoo him away.

"Who was she?" I ask in a calm, steady tone. Every movement he makes shows me he's losing control. "Who was Grace, really?"

"Sign the statement!"

"Who was she?"

"She was some kid. I needed a kid to get the Koi to show." He realizes what he's said. His eyes widen.

I push the statement away. "She was bait. You used a little girl as bait." The smugness in my voice scares me. "I can prove she was there before last night. I have a photo."

He charges to the door and whispers something to Football Player.

"It's not at my house. You can toss all of Bluebird Estates and you won't find it." He sends Football Player off anyway.

Mom is going to get the shock of her life when the FBI show up, but I can't think about that now. I have the power in the room. And, as much as it sickens me, I'm going to use it.

"I want to go into witness protection."

"Not happening," he snaps.

"Where'd you get her from? Did you pick her up off the street? Offer some junkie a hundred bucks for her?" His face turns red. I'm afraid he's going to lunge at me. "Witness protection for me and my mom." I look straight ahead and lean back in my chair.

When Weathers comes back, he seems even smaller than before. His suit is wrinkled, and his face scowling. He's followed in by a tall, lanky man in jeans and cowboy boots who's munching on a bag of potato chips. Pieces get stuck in the thick brown comb of his mustache.

He holds the bag out to me. My mind flashes back to the soggy cupcakes ground into Jordan's carpet. I shake my head. I'll never be able to eat again.

Weathers sits down. "New name, new town, someone to keep an eye on you. Unofficial. Under the table."

"Witness protection. The whole thing." My voice is weak, less confident than before.

"No such luck, sweetheart. I told you, it's not going to happen. It doesn't matter what you do to me. It still won't be approved. They don't protect cop killers."

"But I didn't—"

"This is it, Kayla. The best you're going to get. You play

by the rules, you testify against Jordan, and I'll cut you lose. Take it or leave it."

I don't have the strength to argue anymore. I nod.

Weathers points to the cowboy. "This here's my eyes and ears. He's going to give me status reports. Tell me what you're up to. Make sure you're upholding your part of the bargain."

Cowboy crunches another potato chip. "I was a US Marshal in the Witness Security Program for twenty years."

"Was?" I ask.

"Don't worry," Cowboy says. "I'll take real good care of you."

I look at Weathers. He grins.

There's a knock on the conference room door. "Um, come in?" I say. The door opens and reveals a woman holding a box of hair dye. She's sausaged into a maroon skirt with a white blouse that ties in a giant bow in front. She doesn't look anything like an FBI agent. She looks like someone's secretary. A secretary who is several years past retirement age.

She holds up a pair of orange-handled office scissors. "Come with me, please." She takes me through a maze of cubicles. No one's in them. Weathers has cleared the building so I can make my escape. In the hallway in front of the women's restroom, the elevator dings. When the doors open, Mom leaps out.

"Kayla!" She smothers me in a hug. I don't say anything. I don't know what they've told her. Football Player follows her out. He holds two duffel bags in one hand.

"This way, please." He reaches out for Mom's shoulder

and leads her away, as if she's a baby bird cradled in his giant hands.

In the white-tiled restroom, the secretary efficiently hacks away at my hair. Her face is set like the most professional hairdresser, but her shaking hands betray her. Chunks of my hair fall into the sink.

She rinses the last of the dye out of my hair, and I flip my head up, sending droplets of water flying around the bathroom. I look like a five-year-old who has been playing beauty shop. In the mirror, the secretary's stern countenance breaks into worry.

"I used to trim my boys' hair when they were little."

"It's great," I say, and wonder why I feel the need to reassure her. A few hours in this place and they have me convinced I am guilty, a criminal—a murderer. "I look totally different." Which is true. The black mop on my head washes out my skin, making me sickly pale. The crooked bangs fall into my eyes, covering them if I tilt my head down.

She shuffles into the hallway, leaving the mess in the restroom for some underpaid, hardworking janitor to deal with later.

"Turn this way," she says. When I do, a flash goes off in my face. She hustles me back into the conference room.

One of the duffel bags sits on the table. Football Player has packed for me. Inside are tennis shoes; a pair of jeans; worn, utilitarian underwear; an old, long-sleeved shirt from Goodwill; Finn's sweatshirt; and the teddy bear. That's it. My entire life reduced to one carry-on.

I throw the jumpsuit off and get dressed. The jeans were in the back of my closet for a reason. I have to lie on the floor to zip them up all the way, and the shirt doesn't do much to hide my muffin top.

I wait again for what feels like hours. My only contact with the outside is when Football Player drops a cup of coffee and a doughnut in front of me. The coffee's black. The doughnut smells like sugar and grease. I push them away.

When Weathers comes back, he's rested and refreshed, like he's ready to take on the world.

"Good morning, sweetheart," he chirps. "Don't you look lovely." The glint in his eye and the curl of his lip tells me I'm in trouble. He's had time to think, ponder what to do with me. I shrink back in my chair and regret my earlier bravado.

"Where's my mom?" I ask in a small, little-girl voice.

"She'll be joining us in a second. But first, you and I have got to go over the rules." He smirks. Any power I had before evaporates. He clunks a black cell phone down on the table in front of me. It's big, a heavy chunk of metal and plastic. The light on the top flashes.

He points to it and chuckles. I blink hard to trap my fear in the back of my mind.

"From time to time, I'm gonna call this baby and leave you a message. Some words of encouragement to make sure you stay on track. As soon as that message light blinks, your timer starts."

Weathers taps the phone. "Twenty-four hours," he announces. "You will have twenty-four hours and not a second more to call me back and tell me you got the message. If not . . ." He drags a finger across his throat. "You'll pay with your life."

"What?"

"The Koi would love to know that you're alive. I know a guy who knows a guy. One word from me, and in less than a day, the Koi's henchmen will pay you and your mother a visit. You don't want that, do you?"

"You can't. If I'm dead, you'll have no one to testify."

Weathers shrugs. "Then I'll just have to put him away for ordering the murder of a teenage girl. It makes no difference to me as long as he's in prison. I'll find another young pretty thing to get me Jordan."

I shrink down farther into my chair. I don't think he's bluffing. He'll really do it.

"Do we have an understanding?"

"Yes," I whisper.

He claps his hands. "Great. We're all set, then. You be a good girl, and life will be fine—peachy, even. If you're a naughty girl . . ." He raises his eyebrows at me to elicit a response.

"I'm dead."

"I'll have my eye on you. Every second of every day."

"My mom can't know about this," I blurt out. "She's, uh, fragile. She needs to think we really are in witness protection and starting over."

He waves a dismissive hand at me. "We're clear on my rules. I don't care what you tell your mother."

I put the black phone in my bag.

Football Player brings Mom in. Her hair has been dyed a natural red color, blow-dried, and styled. Confusion is all over her face, but pride leaks out in her gait. She likes the way she looks.

She gives me another hug. Then she picks up a piece of my lank, dark hair. She lets it drop. "Thank goodness you're okay." She wipes a tear from the corner of her eye. "I can't lose you again."

I pat her hand to reassure her like always, but this time she doesn't search my face for forgiveness. "I knew something had happened. I could feel it." She stands up straight. "I went outside to look for you. The police were in the woods setting up crime tape. I was so afraid it was you." She wipes away another tear. "Then the FBI came to the apartment. I didn't know what to do. But I wasn't going to let anyone take you from me again. I told them I would do anything, anything, as long as you were okay."

"What did they tell you?" I glance at Weathers skulking in the corner. I haven't had time to think through a lie.

"Not much. Just that something happened, but you were okay. After I saw you, they said I had to get my hair done before I could see you again. I didn't understand. But I will do anything not to lose you, Kayla, I mean it." For the first time, I believe her.

"Mom, something bad did happen. I saw something I shouldn't have. We're in danger."

She gasps. I have to play this cool. She may have had an epiphany, but she can still be sent over the edge.

"We're going into witness protection. We're moving to a new town. We'll be new people. Everything here is going away."

She slumps down in the chair across the table. I expect her to barrage me with questions. Her usually tense, moving body goes perfectly still. "Really?" she asks. "We get to start over somewhere else?" I nod. Her face relaxes in a way I've never seen before. Relief.

Cowboy comes in with two sodas and a thick folder. "Are you ready to get started?"

"Mom, he's a US Marshal. He's going to take care of us and make sure we stay safe." Lying gets easier and easier.

Cowboy sets a soda in front of Mom. "Thought you might be thirsty." A smile lights up his whole face. Mom blushes.

He thunks the other soda down. No smile for me.

"Okay, ladies. We need to go over some things. No phone calls, no emails, and no letters to Clairmont. No Facebook, no Twitter, no whatever else there is out there at all. No contact with anyone from here. Ever. From this moment forward, you cease to exist."

"But I have to say goodbye, tell everyone I'm okay," I protest.

"Nope," Cowboy says.

"But Marie . . ." Weathers, still lurking in the corner, lifts his head. I realize my mistake.

"Who's Marie?"

"No one. My friend on the dance team." I glance at Mom in warning. She doesn't hear me. She's too busy looking doe-eyed at Cowboy.

Weathers's weaselly face smiles. "Don't worry. It's all taken care of."

"Back to the rules," Cowboy says. He opens the folder and tosses a stack of paper-clipped documents to each of us. "These are your new lives. Where you were born, where you went to school. Work history. Memorize them."

I take my packet. On top is a driver's license.

"We're going south?" Mom asks, as if Cowboy wasn't a dead giveaway. The picture on my license is horrible. Wet hair and a surprised look. They made me sixteen again. Maybe to rub it in, or maybe out of some kindness to let me have a second chance at living the year over. Then I see the name.

I twist around to Weathers. "No. You can't call me that. It's an old lady's name."

Cowboy taps the folder on my head. "Hey. That was my mother's name."

"You might as well call me Tangerine or something," I mutter.

"Kayla," Mom snaps at me under her breath. Nope. Not Kayla anymore.

Football Player drives us to the airport like a hired chauffeur. Mom, holding two plane tickets, looks startled, unsettled. She turns to me, and her face changes. Determination. She places an arm over my shoulder.

"I can do this," she says. "I'll get a job. I'll make pancakes for breakfast. I'll pack your lunch for school and help you with your homework. I'll be the mom you deserve. That you've always deserved."

I nod. I believe she'll try. I don't know if she'll succeed.

"It'll be different this time. I promise."

The monster of a cell phone is in my bag. I already feel it flashing, laughing at me. Everything is already different, but not in a good way. Mom thinks we're going to hop off the plane and the whole past will be washed away.

No such luck, Mom.

———

"Let's go," Mom says.

The airport doors whoosh closed behind us as we step into the chilled, new-carpet-smelling air. It's late. Most of the travelers have long ago reached their destinations. We walk right up to the counter.

I've never been on a plane before. I have no idea what I'm supposed to do. I hesitate behind Mom. She chats, makes a joke. The woman at the counter smiles politely and hands her back our IDs and boarding passes, like we're two normal people going on a normal trip to a normal place.

Security scrutinizes our driver's licenses more carefully. With one gloved hand he holds up the rectangles of plastic. He could call us out. Yell for backup. Haul us away. Send me to prison.

"Thank you," he says curtly, and hands Mom all the documents. "Next."

My feet shuffle forward. Overwhelming exhaustion falls over me like a heavy down comforter. Twenty-four hours ago I was happy, in love. Now I'm a different person, standing in a strict line on black-marked tile while a stern woman demands I take off my shoes.

I can't do it. Bending over is too hard. I might collapse and never come up again. I feel Mom's hands on my feet, untying and lifting off my shoes. She makes an excuse for me. I'm impressed. She's good at lying.

With my shoes still untied and flopping against the floor, we walk down an endless corridor. Mom takes my duffel bag and sits me in a chair.

I close my eyes, but I can't sleep. Jordan, Drake, and Grace loop over and over again in my head. I feel blood on my hands. I wipe them back and forth across my too-tight jeans.

Mom's startled gasp snaps my eyes open. She's staring at a TV above our heads. A reporter with shellacked hair and unnaturally tan skin stands in front of Clairmont High.

". . . was found early this morning in the woods near her home. She was a student here, and as you can see"—the camera pans to where a makeshift memorial of candles, cards, and flowers has formed—"friends have been coming by all day."

The scene jumps to earlier in the evening. I grip the wooden armrest and cry out. Marie is on the TV, her mascara running. She hugs Paige while Carol Alexander hovers. And someone else is there, laying a carnation on the pile. Even through my horror, a piece of my heart warms. Elton. He turns toward the camera. His eyes go wide before he quickly disappears from the shot.

It cuts back to the reporter. "Police haven't released many details about the cause of death, but we know the victim's name is Kayla Asher. Yesterday was her seventeenth birthday."

I can't watch anymore. I can't look at Mom or the other people gathered around the gate. I can't breathe.

I'm Girl Number Four.

CHAPTER 37

BETSY

I shove Adrian away and knock into the couple dancing behind us. I race off the dance floor. I have to get Rosie. Keep her safe. When I'm about twenty feet from her, I yell, "Hey, Rosie," in a chipper voice. I squat down and throw my arms open. "Can I have a hug?"

Rosie charges into my open arms. Over her shoulder, the man does a double take. Then I see it on his face. He's found me.

If I take Rosie to Angie or Mrs. Morales, she'll wander off as soon as their backs are turned. There are too many people here. It could be hours before anyone realizes she's missing. All he needs is seconds to make that happen. We can't stay here.

Rosie lets go and showers me with rose petals. I take her by the hand. "Do you want to play a game?" She nods enthusiastically. "Okay," I say. "Let's go."

I pull her through the dance floor and out the other side. Rosie laughs and stumbles to keep up. We run around the gym and into the parking lot.

I crouch down behind the front tires of a truck and take Toxic Pink out of my purse. "Do you remember that day in the park when you hid in a place that was so good I couldn't find you?" Rosie's lips roll under, like she's about to get scolded.

"No," I say to reassure her, "that was a great trick. Do you think you can do it again? Can you hide in a place where no one will find you, no matter how hard they look?"

She nods. I hold Toxic Pink up and select the first number in the contacts. "This is part of the game. When you get to your hiding spot, I want you to hit this button right here and say the magic code word. Okay? The word is *tangerine.*"

She takes the phone. "What's the magic word?" I ask.

"Tangerine!" she shrieks.

"Shhh . . . This is a quiet version of hide-and-seek. You have to tiptoe and not make any noise. Ready? Go."

She giggles and runs over exaggeratedly on her toes. When she glances back at me, I give her a thumbs-up.

I watch her disappear into the darkness. She'll be safe. Someone will come and get her. They'll protect her. This time my conscience will be clear.

That was it. The last thing I had to do. I stand up.

"Is it really you?" a voice says behind me. A voice that flows like honey. A voice that's soft and wispy like clouds. A voice that still makes my heart flutter.

I turn around and face Jordan. Under the yellow lights of the parking lot, his dyed hair looks black. His eyes are shadows. New lines have carved their way into the skin around his mouth, but the smile is unmistakably his.

"Kayla?" His composure breaks.

"Yes," I say in that old voice. Because, truth is, I'm tired of lying.

Jordan steps forward. He wipes his hand over his face. "I've spent the last year looking for you."

I move around the truck, keeping the bed in between us. "How did you find me?"

He reaches into his pocket and pulls out a small rectangular card. "When I heard about the fire, I thought you might come back. Your mom sent flowers to the funeral of that guy Finn who died. It was nice of her. They were the only ones."

He responds to my horror and stops moving forward. He raises his hands. "She didn't put her name on them. She sent them anonymously. But the clerk at the florist in Clairmont was a sad, lonely woman. It didn't take much of this"—he points to his teeth-baring smile—"to get her to tell me they came from some spot on the map in Texas."

This version of Jordan is different. He's not calm and in control. He's not able to stand still. A crazed look floats around his wide-open eyes.

"What do you want, Jordan? If you're here to finish me off"—I open my arms and expose my chest—"just do it."

"No." He slams his hand down on the truck. "You don't understand, Kayla. You don't understand at all. I want to talk. I want to explain."

"Fine, let's talk." It will give Rosie more time to get away.

"I was six. Six. Living on the streets of Miami, hustling for money while my mom was in a motel with some man, fucked-up out of her mind. At night, I had no choice but to go back to her. I would hide in a closet or a bathroom, hoping the man didn't know I was there. Praying he wouldn't beat me or touch me or . . ." He swallows hard and shakes his head to get rid of the memory.

"I was good at getting money out of people. Before they knew what happened, I had a five or a ten in my hand. And you know the funny part?" He chuckles. "No one ever called the cops or social services. I was six, wandering around by myself, and no one did a thing. One day, I tried to scam the Koi's lieutenant. He gave me some money. I saw him again the next day, and the day after that. He watched me for a week. Then he told me he wanted to give me a job. A job and a house to sleep in and all the food I could eat.

"I went with him. I didn't go find my mother and tell her. I just left. And you know what? For years I looked at those pictures of missing kids, and never once, not one single time, did my face ever show up."

My stomach flips. Hearing his voice, seeing the pain in his eyes. I feel a pang of sympathy. It makes me sick. He's still a monster.

"The Koi did everything they said he would. I had my own room, three meals a day. They taught me to read and write. They were my family. All I had to do was point out kids like me. Kids with nothing and nowhere to go."

"So the Koi is some kind of saint? Do you know what happened to those other kids?" I demand.

His agitation grows. He shakes his head forcefully. "You still don't understand, Kayla. Nothing happened to those kids that wasn't going to happen to them anyway. You don't think they would have been hooked on drugs or raped on the street? At least we were offering them a chance to have a bed, food, maybe someone who would be nice to them."

That sick pride flashes in his eyes. It almost brings me down to my knees. This perverse argument makes sense in his brainwashed head.

"But that's the past, Kayla." He pulls his arm out of the sling. His hand is wrapped in a bloody bandage.

"I'm out. I took a butcher knife, and I did it. I gave the Koi my pinkie." He flaps his bloody hand around. "I did it for you."

Another wave of nausea washes over me. The car next to the truck is parked at a thoughtless angle. I back up until I'm trapped in the V that's formed by them. I won't be able to push through it.

"We can go now," Jordan says. "We can be together."

His eyes latch on to my face. They pull me in. For a second, I remember. I remember what it was like being with him. Sitting in the Jeep so close together. Feeling warm and whole, like I could be something to someone.

If I go with him, maybe it will keep me alive. I will find a way to get word to Mom that I'm okay. She can keep her life here. No one has to die.

"Okay," I say to Jordan, and step out from behind the truck. "Let's go."

The clack of dress shoes comes from the sidewalk behind me. "No," I whisper. I spin around. "No!" I yell. But he's too close.

I should have known the Koi would never let me go. Would never let Jordan walk away. There's always a backup plan. Adrian is his.

CHAPTER 38

"Betsy, what are you doing out here? Where's Rosie?" Adrian steps between me and Jordan. Will he kill us both here in the parking lot? Or are there others lurking in the shadows?

"Who are you?" Jordan asks calmly.

Adrian glances at the bloody bandage on Jordan's left hand. "Betsy, what's going on?"

Jordan steps forward. Placing himself between Adrian and me. "Her name's Kayla. Who the fuck are you?"

I touch Jordan's shoulder. "Let's just go, okay? Before the others come for us."

Jordan doesn't look at me. "What others?" he asks. "Who is this, Kayla?"

"He works for the Koi," I say, but as soon as the words leave my mouth, I'm not sure. I want to take them back, but it's too late.

Jordan reaches behind him and pulls a gun from his waistband. His hand doesn't shake. The scary Jordan is back. The Jordan who will pull the trigger.

"Betsy?" Adrian cries. His hands go up to show they're empty.

I don't know what I'm doing. My feet move before my brain can catch up. I step between the gun and Adrian. I have a nagging feeling this is wrong. That I'm wrong. "Let's just go, Jordan. No one will know you were here. Adrian won't tell anyone."

"No, Kayla. No witnesses. Move out of the way."

I turn back to Adrian. His face leaks fear. It could be an act. He could be as good a liar as Jordan. This could be a game to him.

I stare him down and wait for him to do something. Something to show me who he really is. To call for backup or pull out his own gun and point it at my heart.

He doesn't. His eyes stay locked on Jordan's gun. He's trembling.

I feel Jordan getting impatient behind me.

If I step to the side and let Jordan shoot Adrian, it could save my life.

If I step to the side and let Jordan shoot Adrian, it could be innocent blood on my hands. Again.

It's my choice.

The longer we stay here in the parking lot, the more of a chance there is that a wedding guest will wander by. Wander by and witness Jordan and his gun.

"Kayla," Jordan says.

"Betsy," Adrian implores.

My head whips back and forth between them. I'm dizzy, like the weight of the decision will make me fall over. But I have to choose.

There's only one person I know for sure is guilty. Only one stone-cold person who casually sold a little girl and watched her die. Only one person who haunts my nightmares.

I make my decision.

I reach into my purse and wrap my fingers around the gun. I flick the safety off, swing around, and aim. I close my eyes.

I pull the trigger.

The gun explodes and throws me back. My ears ring. My fingers tingle.

I squeeze my eyes closed tighter. I can't look. Either Jordan is dead or he, or Adrian, is going to kill me now.

I flinch at the sound of screeching brakes and heavy-booted feet. Moans of agony. Thumping. Peeling tires.

Quiet.

"Betsy?" Warm hands wrap around mine. I open my eyes. I still have my arms out—gun pointed. Teddy takes it from me.

"Is he dead?" My whole body shakes. My heart and lungs won't work together. I gasp for air.

Teddy shakes his head. "That was one hell of a shot. You hit him in the right arm. He'll be okay."

I look Teddy straight in the eye. "I was aiming for the carp."

Teddy glares into the darkness. "The FBI has him now." His face twists in disgust. "They had a van waiting." He turns back to me and weighs the gun in his hand. "I don't even want to know where you got this." He pops the remaining bullets out.

Music from the party wafts over us. Thank goodness it's loud. Almost blaring. Teddy looks in its direction. "We need to get you back there. Someone may have heard the shot." He takes a step forward but then stops. Hard breathing makes us both turn around.

Adrian is pale and vacant-eyed, like he's going into shock. Teddy moves to help him, but I put my arm out to hold him back. I didn't let Jordan shoot him, but I'm still not fully convinced.

I get right in his face. "Are you one of them?"

"What? One of who?" His breathing is ragged. If this is for real, he's going to pass out soon.

"Your carp." I motion toward his pocket. "Why do you have it?"

"I got it in Seattle." Gasping sucks of air. "It was the first big city I had ever been to. I got it to remind me there's more to the world than San Justo." I examine every inch of this face. "They were for sale everywhere," he whimpers.

I pull the neck of my dress down until my carp shines under the parking lot lights. His eyes widen in surprise. You can't fake that. He didn't know what it was. He never knew anything about me. He's telling the truth.

I slap my hand over my mouth as my eyes fill with tears. "Oh my God, Adrian, I am so sorry. The carp is their symbol. When I saw yours, I thought . . ."

He doesn't look away from where my tattoo lies under my dress. "Couldn't you have gotten a lucky cat figurine in Seattle?" I joke, and let out a forced, tear-smeared laugh. One that tries to cover up what almost happened. That I suspected Adrian this whole time. That I've been horrible to him. That I almost let him die.

Adrian's fear turns into red-hot anger pointed right at me. "Who was that guy, Betsy, or whatever your name is? Who did you think I was?"

I shrink back. After what he's seen, there's no point in lying to him. "He's a human trafficker and murderer."

"And you thought I was working with him?" He points to my now-empty yellow purse. "You've been carrying a gun? What were you going to do? Shoot me?"

"I didn't want to!" Tears stream freely down my face. "I wouldn't have done it."

That's a lie, and he knows it.

His voice goes a deadly quiet. "Where'd you get the gun?"

I shake my head. I won't tell him.

"You made Tomás do it, didn't you? That was what he asked me to pick up for him. What Happy couldn't find out about."

I slap my hand over my mouth. The Walmart bag. Because Adrian is a good, loyal friend, he bought the gun that I almost killed him with.

I reach for him. "I'm so sorry. These things happened to me. . . ."

He jumps back to avoid my hand. "No."

That's it. Probably the last word he will ever speak to me. He turns and leaves me standing in my frumpy dress under the dusty parking-lot lights.

Teddy jogs after him. "Son, we need to have a talk."

A couple of guests approach them with worried looks on their faces. Teddy says something that makes them roll their eyes, shake their heads, and turn back to the party.

As soon as they're all out of sight, I collapse to the asphalt. My brain can't sort out everything that's happened.

Everyone is alive. Even Jordan. A mixture of intense feelings swirls and twists through me. I can't work out what they all are—relief, regret, love, hate. One thing I know for sure is I have no idea who I am right now.

Little feet in white patent-leather shoes click to a stop in front of me. "You didn't come find me," Rosie whines.

I wipe my eyes, sit up, and try to smile. "That's because you did a great job hiding. A *great* job. I'm proud of you."

She turns her head and purses her lips. "Who's Kayla?"

My heart that had almost resumed a normal beat pounds again. If she saw any of what happened, I will never forgive myself. "Where did you hear that name?" I ask, trying to keep my voice steady.

She holds Toxic Pink under my nose. "He wants to talk to Kayla." She leans in close. "He's kind of mean."

I take the phone. "It's probably a wrong number." Despite it all, Rosie still has her two flower baskets. I point to them. "I bet if you go find my mom, she'll refill those for you."

Rosie can't resist renewing her flower girl duties. She bounces on her toes and skips off back to the party.

I place the phone to my ear. "Hello?" I whisper.

"I knew you would come in handy one day. Knew it the first time I saw you. Didn't expect you to be as much trouble as you turned out to be, but what can you do?"

Hearing Weathers's whiny little voice and imagining his weasely face sets my teeth on edge and produces enough anger and adrenaline to propel me to my feet.

"You knew he was coming for me, and you didn't try to stop him. You could have arrested him. Someone almost got killed." Hot tears splash down my face.

Weathers sighs. "It's not that easy. Do you know what would've happened if I'd arrested Jordan? He would have hired a fancy lawyer and made bail. Then he would have disappeared forever. You'd never be safe.

"I needed him to cooperate. To *choose* to turn on the Koi. And for that I needed you."

"Me? Why?"

"Now he knows that I have you. I'll tell him the same thing I told you: I'd happily put the Koi away for ordering the murder of a teenage girl. Your life will depend on his cooperation."

"No!" I cry out. I won't let him use me like this again.

Weathers laughs. "It's a bluff, Kayla. One that will work. Jordan is oddly sentimental about you. He'll be spilling his guts before we even get him in an interrogation room. It's over. You're free."

"But what about the Koi?"

"I've been following Jordan since that funeral in Clairmont. I'm a hundred percent confident that the Koi thinks you're dead. Keep that tattoo covered and no one will ever know."

My head spins. After all that has happened, Jordan would give up everything for me?

"What's going to happen to him?" It's not anger in my voice now, it's something else. Something soft. Something that makes me sick to my stomach.

Weathers hears it too. He clicks his tongue. "Oh, Kayla. Don't tell me you're getting sentimental, too," he mocks. "Jordan will be tried and convicted. He'll cut a deal to avoid the death penalty. The Koi will go deep underground, now that we have his lieutenant. We'll hold Jordan in a supermax until I find another way to ferret the Koi out."

So many mixed-up emotions run through me that I don't know what to say.

"Jordan will sign whatever statement I tell him to. You and your photos are not my problem anymore, Kayla," he says with a definite finality.

"My name is Betsy." I hang up.

"Betsy?" Mom calls from behind me. "What are you doing out here?"

I take a breath to compose myself and rub the tears out of my eyes.

I turn around. "I just needed to get away from people for a while."

Concern crosses her face when she gets a good look at me, but then it resolves into satisfied exhaustion.

"It will be over soon." She smiles. "It has to be. I'm almost out of flowers for Rosie."

CHAPTER 39

Teddy stands in the living room holding a bottle of sparkling cider and looking uncomfortable. This is his fake retirement party.

Mom smiles with pure happiness when she sees him. This party is real for her. It's a party for us too. For Mom's sake, Teddy sat us down the day after the wedding and gave us the formal news that the threat had been neutralized. We no longer needed protection and were free to do as we pleased with our lives.

He cringed when he said that last part, as if he expected Mom to pack up the car and take us back to Clairmont. She didn't. She threw her arms around his neck and kissed him.

Then Teddy dropped another bomb. He was "retiring" from the US Marshals Service. He looked at me meaningfully when he said it. I guessed that meant he fulfilled whatever his deal was with Weathers, and he too had been released and left by the side of the road.

Adrian won't speak to me, but otherwise, things are good. Peaceful. Normal. Still, there's a buzzing in the back of my brain. It's been there since the wedding, humming in the background like a generator in my head, distracting me from class, making me absentminded and forgetful.

By the beginning of May, the buzzing consumes my every waking moment. I have to do something.

I text Happy that I'm sick and can't see her after school. I go straight home. The house is quiet. Mom will be at the flower shop for another couple of hours.

Teddy got rid of the black monster. So I hold the beat-up stuffed bear in my lap and dial the number from the call Toxic Pink received the night Jordan was taken away.

As soon as he picks up, I start talking. "Who was Grace, really?" My question is greeted with silence.

"Who was she?" I demand.

Silence.

"The Koi's still out there. He's still hurting children."

A long, deep sigh.

School will be over in two weeks. The sweltering San Justo summer stretches out in front of us. Mom's good work at Angie's wedding has spread all over town. She's in high demand. Her boss agreed they needed extra help, so soon, I will be joining the ranks of part-time florist-in-training. It will be nice. Mom and I are still getting to know each other and making up for all those years we missed.

I tie the trash bag in the kitchen. Buried at the bottom in a million pieces, under coffee grounds and apple cores, is the letter I had written to Marie, the one I didn't send because Tomás showed up with my shoe. The ink on the address was too smeared to read. And anyway, it has to be over. I'm letting Marie go.

I convinced Teddy to take Mom out on a real date to a real restaurant in El Paso. He came to pick her up an hour ago. He was wearing a suit coat and holding a bunch of grocery store flowers. He didn't get the irony, and Mom was polite and gracious as she fluffed them in a vase and filled it with water. I don't expect them back anytime soon.

Happy and Tomás are visiting Happy's dad. He adores little Manny. He's even talked about buying a bigger house so they can all live together. Happy said her stepmother wrinkles her nose every time he mentions it.

I'm alone tonight. No one is going to randomly show up at the front door. It's just me and my thoughts.

Even though it's too warm for it, I'm wearing Finn's sweatshirt. It feels soft and comforting against my skin. It makes me think of some of the nice but blurry memories I have of being little, when I was too young to know what was going on around me.

I lift the trash bag out and walk it to the side of the house. The trumpet vines on the neighbor's fence are in their full glory, opening their big orange blooms to invite marauding bees and hummingbirds.

I lift the giant lid of the black trash can, and it thumps against the wall.

"You're a lot of trouble, little girl." A voice echoes off the stucco wall of the house.

I drop the bag onto the rocks and turn around.

The Koi has his shirtsleeves rolled up. Sweat beads on his forehead. An unlit cigarette rests between his lips.

My heart pounds like the bass in Tomás's truck. "So I've been told," I say.

He laughs and lifts a lighter to the cigarette. He blows a stream of smoke over me and runs his eyes up my body. He stops over my heart, shakes his head, and takes another drag, as if he can't believe Jordan would be so stupid as to want *me* in their nasty club.

"Her name was Grace," I say in a solid, clear voice. If I'm going down, I'm going to make him listen to me first.

He's unmoved. His face stares blankly at mine. "The girl. Her name was Grace. She was six years old." *And no one ever reported her missing.*

"That's of no consequence," he says. "Yes, I lost out on an investment, but she was in the way. Jordan should have known better than to be fooled by a cop."

"You didn't have to do it."

He laughs. "I didn't have to kill them, you mean? Oh, little girl, you are so young. I'm a businessman. I had to kill them. They were a liability."

His hand doesn't move fast. It's almost as if he wants me to run away, like chasing me would make it all the sweeter. I don't run. I stand tall in front of him.

The gun points at my heart. At the carp. It has a silencer on the end like in the movies. "I don't have liabilities."

Pain spreads across my chest, almost before I hear the sound. It's not loud. Just a quick *pop-pop*. As I fall backward, bees scatter from the trumpet vines and lift off into the clear, blue, evening sky. My head hits the ground. Pain shoots up my neck.

The sky goes black.

CHAPTER 40

I crack one eye open. Everything aches. My chest, my head. My leg is asleep. I try to breathe. Inflating my lungs makes my whole upper body scream.

"Hurts like a mother, doesn't it?"

I raise an eyebrow—just about the only motion that doesn't hurt—at the figure leaning over me. I snort.

He laughs. "What? You've met me, right? You think no one has ever taken a shot at me?" Weathers pulls aside the neck of his shirt to expose the strap of a bulletproof vest. "Never leave home without it."

I tentatively rub my head. "That is not my fault." Weathers points. "My job was to keep you from getting killed. You hitting your head on the way down is not my fault."

"Did you get him?" I rasp.

Weathers looks like a little kid who has been handed the keys to a magic candy shop. "Yep. Him, his men, his confession to killing Christiansen and the girl. We simultaneously raided his known associates. We've taken down the whole ring."

"So it's over for real this time?"

He pats my hand awkwardly, like someone who isn't used to much human contact. "It's over."

"Where's my stuff?"

He rolls his eyes but retrieves a large manila envelope from a briefcase in the corner.

"Social security cards and driver's licenses for you and your mother. Totally legit and clean."

I undo the clasp and peel it open. On top are transcripts. My real transcripts from Clairmont, but printed on the letterhead of a high school in Williston, North Dakota.

There's something under the transcripts. A smaller white envelope. I rip it open and pull out a newspaper clipping with a sticky note on top that says "This is the guy."

I look to Weathers for an explanation. "That big-nosed cop demanded I give that to you. I asked him for one small favor in faking your death, and now he thinks he can get me to do whatever he wants."

I pull off the note. Underneath the headline "Clairmont Killer Caught" is a mug shot. Of a man. Elton. "Oh my God," I whisper. He snuck up behind all those girls and used his cane to beat them to death. He killed two more after I left. Four girls dead. I rub my hand over my leg. I *touched* that cane.

Under the mug shot is another picture. An altar in the back of his station wagon. In the carefully displayed collection are a Northside sweatshirt, a stuffed bunny, a tiny diamond nose stud, and a name tag that says KAYLA.

I'm going to be sick.

Weathers leans in to look over my shoulder. "Yep," he says.

"That's totally a serial killer. How many bodies had to pile up before Big Nose figured it out?" He's getting cocky again. But I don't have to take a swing at him. Teddy does it for me.

He comes barreling into the hospital room with his fist already in motion. "You son of a bitch!" His hand smashes into Weathers's face, sending him down to the shiny floor. "You used a kid again! She got shot. What the hell were you thinking?" He's ready to swing again. Weathers glares up at me.

"Stop," I say. Teddy doesn't hear. Weathers's head slams into the linoleum from the force of Teddy's fist.

I sigh. "Teddy, stop," I say loud enough to send a shock wave of pain through my upper body. But he doesn't snap out of it until Football Player runs into the room and pulls him off Weathers.

Weathers touches his bleeding lip. "Tell him," he snarls at me.

I try to sit up, but the pain forces me down again. "It was my idea," I say to the ceiling. "We had to get the Koi to come out into the open. Weathers broadcasted a message that I was still alive. We knew the Koi wouldn't be able to resist coming after me."

I had to finish it. Weathers was going to get even more people killed hunting down the Koi. This wasn't about my life or safety. It was about all those future children. The future Jordans. The future Kaylas.

"You can't make that decision, Betsy. You're a child." Teddy turns to Weathers. "Children are supposed to be protected." Football Player steps forward and places a hand on Teddy's chest to hold him back.

"Betsy is a child," I say. Teddy's attention focuses on me. "Kayla turned eighteen weeks ago."

"But . . . ," Teddy says.

"Until now"—I hold up the envelope—"I was still legally Kayla. It was my choice. My decision."

Teddy deflates. Football Player glances out into the hallway. "We need to go."

Weathers stands up and produces a handkerchief from the pocket of his suit coat. He dabs his lip. "Just so you know, I had a nice home picked out for the little girl. An agent and his wife in Los Angeles. She would have had everything. She would have been loved."

It's too much for Teddy. He grabs Weathers by the lapels and slams him into the wall. "I'm going to be watching you," he growls. "I've got the pictures that prove you were responsible for that girl's death." He's bluffing. The pictures are still in Marie's wall, but Weathers doesn't know that. "If you ever go near a kid again, I'm sending those pictures out to the media, the FBI, and the Justice Department." He smiles. "Maybe you and the Koi can be cellmates."

Weathers blanches. Teddy lets go. Football Player, who's been standing back watching, takes Weathers by the arm and steadies him on his feet. He nods respectfully at Teddy.

They leave as loud, determined footsteps echo in the hallway outside.

"I told her you tripped taking out the trash and hit your head. A neighbor saw you and called 911," Teddy says, and hides my envelopes behind his back.

Mom peeks around the doorway. When she sees Teddy,

she looks relieved. "I had the hardest time finding you. After I talked to the doctor, the nurse took me to the wrong room."

Her relief goes away when she sees me. "Betsy! What happened?"

I shrug and instantly regret it when the pain flares up so much I see stars. "I guess I'm a klutz."

She doesn't believe me. "You broke two ribs and got a concussion taking out the trash?"

"I'm a superklutz?"

She backs off. "I'm just glad that you're okay. The doctor said you need to take it easy for a few weeks, but soon, you'll be good as new."

"How was your date?" I ask to take her focus off me.

Teddy blushes and looks down at his feet. Mom can't help but smile. That tells me everything I need to know.

"I'm glad," I say. Teddy isn't touchy-feely, but I reach out for his hand. "I've kind of gotten used to you."

Manny has learned how to smile. He gives me a big gummy one when I walk through the front door of the mobile home. Happy deposits him in my arms and makes my still-sore ribs twinge. She flops down on the couch. "I don't know if I'm more bored or more tired," she says, and flips off the TV. "I actually wish I was at school." She didn't go back after the baby was born. In the fall, she'll transfer to a school in El Paso where she can take Manny and they'll help her graduate. I'll miss her.

Happy points to my head. "I like your hair." It's still dark and short, but it's professionally cut. Mom and I went shopping and bought new clothes, too. I still have to wear shirts that go up to my neck, but we found a bunch of cute things. Today, I have on a pink top and a black skirt. Tomorrow, I might wear holey jeans and a T-shirt. I'm still trying to figure out who Betsy is.

A polite knock on the door rouses Happy from the couch. She looks at me with concern. No one ever knocks. They just walk in.

Happy opens the door. Out of reflex, I turn my body to shield the baby against whoever might be out there.

"Um, it's for you," she says. She scoops Manny up. "We're going to take a nap." She disappears into the bedroom.

I hesitantly make my way to the door. Adrian stands on the other side of it. "What are you doing? Why aren't you coming in?" I ask.

His body practically vibrates with nerves. "Maybe you should come out." He glances over my shoulder to the hallway where Happy hovers, smiling at us. When I turn, she dashes back into the bedroom.

I step out and the rickety door slams behind me. Adrian's gaze moves from my face down to the spot over my heart where my hidden tattoo lies.

He lifts his eyes. "Teddy told me what happened to you. What happened before and"—he points to my ribs—"what you did that got you hurt."

"I'm sorry," I say too fast, like if it doesn't come out now, it never will. "I'm sorry about everything."

"Stop," he says. "I'm not here for an apology. I don't accept it. Not now, maybe not ever."

"Okay," I whisper. "I deserve that." Still, part of my newly mended heart breaks.

"I'm here to tell you that I get it. If something happened to Rosie, I wouldn't rest until the bastard was dead." He digs his toes into the earth. "I got rid of my carp. Happy's is gone too. I told her that it was covered in lead paint and would make the baby sick."

He doesn't say anything else. He's silent for so long that I'm afraid he's done. That he's going to march away and never speak to me again.

"Can we start over?" I plead. "You don't have to like me, but give me a chance to prove I'm different. That the girl from before is gone now."

He's hesitant, but he nods. I stick out my hand. "Hi, I'm Betsy Hopewood."

Adrian's brown eyes flash, like maybe he's suppressing a smile. He takes my hand. "Nice to meet you, Betsy."

Over his shoulder, I catch a reflection in the window of the mobile home. I see a girl staring back at me. A girl who's been scarred and battered and hurt. A girl who will have to relearn how to trust and love. A girl who will get up and try again.

I see Betsy.

I see me.

ACKNOWLEDGMENTS

You would not be holding this book if it weren't for Stacey Trombley, Brenda Drake, and Pitch Wars. Stacey, thank you for picking me and for putting your time and thoughtfulness into this story. Brenda, you have made so many dreams come true. I am in your debt.

Thank you to my kick-ass agent, Rachel Brooks, for her enthusiasm and guidance.

A huge thank you goes to my editor, Krista Vitola, for believing in this book from the start and for loving M&M's as much as I do.

To everyone at Delacorte Press who worked to make this book a reality, words cannot express my gratitude.

I am also eternally grateful to Bonnie Bryant for reading everything I foist upon her and for being my biggest cheerleader. And to Kelly Darnell who was an early beta reader.

Thank you to Bonnie Hearn Hill for believing so strongly in me when I first began walking down this path. And to

Sudipta Bardhan-Quallen for all the aha moments and for being a role model for writers everywhere.

I would have never made it without the support and friendship of the 2017 Debuts. Thanks, guys. Here's to many more books.

To the Pitch Wars class of 2015: We fought a battle together. I wish you all great success.

ABOUT THE AUTHOR

Amanda Searcy has a BA from New Mexico State University and an MA in human rights from the University of Essex in England. She works in collection development for a public library system and loves chocolate, cats, and curling up with a good book. She lives in New Mexico. Visit her online at amandasearcybooks.com and follow @aesearcy on Twitter.